THE MIDNIGHT SHIFT

밤에 찾아오는 구원자

AF729136

CHEON SEON-RAN

BLOOMSBURY ARCHER
LONDON • OXFORD • NEW YORK • NEW DELHI • SYDNEY

BLOOMSBURY ARCHER
Bloomsbury Publishing Plc
50 Bedford Square, London, WC1B 3DP, UK
Bloomsbury Publishing Ireland Limited,
29 Earlsfort Terrace, Dublin 2, D02 AY28, Ireland

BLOOMSBURY, BLOOMSBURY ARCHER and the Archer logo
are trademarks of Bloomsbury Publishing Plc

First published in Great Britain 2025
This edition first published in Great Britain 2026

밤에 찾아오는 구원자
THE MIDNIGHT SHIFT

Copyright © 2021 by 천선란 (Cheon Seon-Ran)
English language translation © Gene Png, 2025
All rights reserved.
Original Korean edition published by Safehouse Inc.
English translation rights arranged with Bloomsbury Publishing Plc through
BC Agency, Seoul and Mulcahy Sweeney Associates Ltd, London

Cheon Seon-Ran is identified as the author of this work in accordance
with the Copyright, Designs and Patents Act 1988.

This book is published with the support of the Literature Translation Institute
of Korea (LTI Korea).

This is a work of fiction. Names and characters are the product of the author's
imagination and any resemblance to actual persons, living or dead, is entirely coincidental

All rights reserved. No part of this publication may be: i) reproduced or transmitted in any form, electronic or mechanical, including photocopying, recording or by means of any information storage or retrieval system without prior permission in writing from the publishers; or ii) used or reproduced in any way for the training, development or operation of artificial intelligence (AI) technologies, including generative AI technologies. The rights holders expressly reserve this publication from the text and data mining exception as per Article 4(3) of the Digital Single Market Directive (EU) 2019/790

A catalogue record for this book is available from the British Library

Library of Congress Cataloguing-in-Publication data has been applied for

ISBN: TPB: 978-1-5266-7982-6; ANZ EDITION: 978-1-5266-7983-3; PB: 978-1-5266-7984-0;
EBOOK: 978-1-5266-7981-9; EPDF: 978-1-5266-7978-9

2 4 6 8 10 9 7 5 3 1

Typeset by Integra Software Services Pvt. Ltd.
Printed and bound in Great Britain by Clays Ltd, Elcograf S.p.A.

MIX
Paper | Supporting
responsible forestry
FSC® C018072
FSC www.fsc.org

To find out more about our authors and books visit www.bloomsbury.com
and sign up for our newsletters
For product safety related questions contact productsafety@bloomsbury.com

SUYEON

'A vampire did it.'

The only way to make sense of this woman's bullshit was to go back in time.

*

Suyeon pulled over at the curb. She got out of the car, leaving behind Chantae, who was rummaging through the glove box for a plastic bag. A police officer greeted her from afar. She cut through the small crowd and made her way up to the corpse lying underneath a white sheet. Nearby, a lone apricot tree flaunted its late pink blooms, oblivious to circumstance.

'The victim was seventy-four. First discovered by a nurse on her way to work this morning.'

'A jumper?'

'Yes, from the sixth floor. He was a patient at the hospital.'

‘Was there a note?’

‘Yes. One was found on this occasion, too, Detective.’

The officer handed over the suicide note. The victim had bid his final farewell to his family in a few sparse lines.

‘Seems like everyone’s dying to see this “hill of flowers”,’ muttered Suyeon.

Her eyes latched onto the words: hill of flowers. The same phrase had been written in the last suicide note they’d found, and it was at the same hospital, too – Cheolma Rehabilitation Hospital.

Suyeon took a photo of the note with her phone before handing it back to the officer. She knelt down, put on her glasses and lifted the sheet. A face mangled against the tarmac. The stick-thin corpse was blanched of all colour and its hair follicles jutted upward. Rigor mortis had set in already, it seemed. As Suyeon gave the body a final once-over, she noticed that one hand was tightly balled into a fist. With a handkerchief covering her fingers, she pried open the man’s stiff hand. Inside was a crumpled ball of orange paper that Suyeon assumed had once been carefully folded into some type of flower.

‘Has that camera been fixed yet?’ Suyeon pointed to the security camera attached to the telephone pole.

The officer shook her head. Most of the CCTV cameras in the vicinity either weren’t working or were just dummies. And although there was one installed on each floor of the hospital, they all faced the lifts and emergency stairs, so there was no way of knowing what was happening in the foyer. Suyeon looked up at the sixth floor. There was a silhouette in the window, but as soon as she noticed it, the figure turned back around and vanished.

Chantae crossed the police line with the handles of a plastic bag hooked onto his ears.

'Nothing more to see here,' announced Suyeon, waving her superior away. They'd seen all of this before in the previous three cases outside the hospital. And besides, her squeamish colleague had never managed more than one proper look at a dead body.

'Another one?' asked Chantae.

'Yes. Another one.'

Chantae scowled at the sun and removed the make-shift mask from his ears before walking away from the scene. But Suyeon's feet wouldn't budge. Even though it was just 'another one.' Even when, as she said, there was nothing more to see. This made four.

The scene had piqued the interest of a few patients who were out on their morning strolls. A familiar voice interrupted their hushed chatter. Suyeon turned towards the nasal shout and saw two police officers holding back a stout elderly woman scrambling to break past the police line. It was Granny Eunshim. Like the other patients, she was dressed in her hospital gown. She wore a floral vest over it. The towel Suyeon had bought her was draped around her neck. The old lady thrust a finger at Suyeon, gripping a small yoghurt drink and a white straw in her other hand.

'I'm her grandmother!' she yelled. Suyeon approached her with a smile. The police officers released the old woman and with a firm yet gentle hand, Suyeon led her away from the crowd and towards the hospital entrance.

Suyeon hadn't expected to see Granny Eunshim this early in the morning. She always forgot what early risers these old folk were. Suyeon bent over slightly to meet the old woman's eyes. Granny Eunshim stroked Suyeon's face with her small hands. The straw and the yoghurt lid scraped Suyeon's face, but she didn't mind it at all.

'My, your cheeks look hollow. Why didn't you call before coming?'

Granny Eunshim's memory was lapsing and she often forgot about previous incidents. At times she would also confuse Suyeon for her doctor or, every so often, the postal worker.

'I'm not here to visit today, halmoni.'

'What brings you here then? Did something happen?'

'Nothing you have to worry about. Why are you up so early?'

'Uh… Eungyeong unni… She appeared in my dream. I wondered why, but then realised it's her birthday today. I'm on my way to the market so I can make her some seaweed soup later.'

Granny Eunshim really did think that Suyeon's colleague Eungyeong sunbae was older than she herself was, and that was why she called her 'unni'. She thought Eungyeong was a girl from her neighbourhood who had looked after her like a sister when she was young. The halmoni used to say how much Eungyeong resembled the girl, until she eventually started to believe they were the same person. Suyeon had tried to correct her, but Eungyeong stopped her. In fact, Eungyeong would chime in and point out how they did have similar names, just like sisters.

'You really should make time to come to dinner! Eungyeong unni always looks out for you, yet you barely show your face these days,' Granny Eunshim scolded.

Suyeon nodded repeatedly, *Yes, yes*. Only then did Granny Eunshim put the yoghurt drink in Suyeon's hands.

'And stop putting your face through so much! Or you'll be left on the shelf!'

Suyeon would have liked to reply that marriage was the last thing on her mind, but that would only mean angering Granny Eunshim and getting an earful. And so instead she smiled and put the drink into her pocket without a word. Straightening up, Suyeon announced it was time to leave, and told Granny Eunshim to hurry back inside, but the old woman only muttered a feeble 'OK' before rooting herself to the entrance. Seeing that Granny Eunshim was going to wait until she was completely out of sight, Suyeon hurried off. As she turned back and waved her inside, Granny Eunshim hollered even louder, 'Look in front of you when you're going somewhere! You'll trip!'

***

Chantae believed that the reason Suyeon couldn't let the Cheolma suicides rest was Granny Eunshim. Was it really because the hospital – where Suyeon paid a visit every week without fail – was where Granny Eunshim was put up? Would she have extended the same consideration to the victims and their families if she didn't know anyone in the place they'd died? If the place hadn't held any memories for her? She had mulled over this, but couldn't find an answer. All she could do was accept the fact that something was eating her up.

Chantae, however, saw things differently. To him, the suicide notes spoke for themselves. *They wanted to join the flowers of heaven, end this suffering, etc.*

She shook her head again to clear it. Perhaps, like he said, suicide was simply catching on like a trend in this sad place. Cheolma Rehabilitation Hospital was a long-term care facility located in an old part of Incheon that had been designated for redevelopment. Since the redevelopment project was announced a year ago, all the businesses and facilities had either shut down or been relocated, leaving the hospital's surroundings deserted. Of course, there had been plans to move the hospital as well. It had been set to be relocated to a nearby district, but the plans were cancelled on the pretext that it wasn't ideal for patients to be moved to an unfamiliar place, especially since most of Cheolma's patients suffered from dementia. But the biggest obstacle had been the difficulty of obtaining permission from family members who had gone off the radar.

Whatever the reason, the hospital remained right where it was. By next year, the remaining shops would all be gone. Suyeon recalled what Chantae had said after they had just returned from inspecting the hospital's third suicide: *In a place like this, it's only a matter of time before people start killing themselves. And you know why they do? Because that's their only way out. Look, kid. Unless someone comes to get them out of here, they're all going to rot in this hospital.*

Suyeon didn't disagree, but there was something odd about the case that she couldn't wrap her head around. If the deaths were all part of a pattern, no matter how depressing, she wanted to know what it meant.

Suyeon took out the yoghurt drink and pierced the lid with the straw. Chantae frowned in disapproval as he plopped a pickled radish onto his plate.

'You're drinking *that*? What are you? A baby?'

Suyeon looked around. They had stopped by the old restaurant near the station for lunch. Save for two groups of balding ajeossis and the familiar restaurant server, the place was empty. On the wall beside them was a faded menu listing old-fashioned dishes – blood sausage soup, hangover soup, ugeoji soup and steamed pork. Suyeon took a big sip out of her tiny bottle, drawing a chuckle of defeat from Chantae.

'Don't look at me like I'm the weird one,' said Suyeon, setting down her drink. 'For someone who can't even look at a corpse, you seem to crave meat every time we're done at a crime scene.'

'Gotta refuel after a long day of using my brain, you know?'

What brain? Suyeon almost said, but swallowed the words along with another sip of yoghurt. The server rolled the cart to their table and placed a bowl of sundae soup in front of Chantae who stirred in a big dollop of yangnyeom sauce.

She sighed. 'You *really* don't think it's strange that this "coincidence" has happened four times in a month?'

Chantae stared at Suyeon, his mouth stuffed with food. Taking her chance, Suyeon continued: 'I don't doubt that they were influenced by previous suicides, but to this extent? *Think*, sunbae. All four victims left behind suicide notes. Doesn't something about that feel staged?'

'No, it feels like they were *influenced*,' Chantae said as he stirred his soup. From his listless tone, Suyeon knew that what he meant was, *Why are you making things difficult?*

'Staged?' Chantae continued. 'They're stuck in a hospital, their minds failing, in a dying neighbourhood and people around them are killing themselves. Seems pretty clear-cut to me. Tell me, what was written in those notes? "I'm escaping this godforsaken place" or something, right? You have pictures on your phone, don't you? Pull them up, let's have a look.'

She didn't have to. She knew the notes almost by heart and he was right. Chantae told Suyeon to save her energy for the paperwork instead, and she gave an impassive nod. As she reached for a piece of radish, she decided, *All right, no more overthinking.*

But the resolution lasted barely a day. As she was writing up the report back at the office, Suyeon went back and looked at the photographs from the previous case. The third suicide had happened a week ago. The victim was a 68-year-old male and, just like today's case, he had jumped from the sixth floor of the building. He had also suffered from dementia and left a suicide note. Suyeon placed both the third and fourth victim's photographs side by side and looked at them for a long while before pulling up a new picture. A bar fight in Bucheon had broken out last month, in which someone had smashed a plate on a man's head. The victim had died after losing a significant amount of blood. Suyeon's eyes slid from one photo to the next. She'd puzzled over why the two hospital deaths had looked strange, but she saw it now:

There's hardly any blood.

After a short pause, Suyeon picked up her desk phone.

Her call was answered by a weary Jiseon. Jiseon worked in forensics. The two had first met when Suyeon was a junior police officer. Jiseon had watched Suyeon obsess over the smallest leads for years before pointing out the obvious: that she had the makings of a detective. Observation is one thing, but having faith in people is rare in a police station. As a result, Jiseon became the person Suyeon would turn to whenever she hit an investigation roadblock. In her first few years in the field, Suyeon would feel bad for 'using' Jiseon, and furnish the conversation by asking after her life and making mindless small talk. But nowadays they knew one another better than that and Jiseon told her to skip the pleasantries and cut to the chase. *Saves us time and keeps things simple.* Clutching the phone, Suyeon got straight to the point.

'We've had two cases of suicide by jumping, but there was barely any blood at the scene or on the victims' bodies. None from their noses or ears. Remember the guy from last month who had his skull cracked open? Less blood than that.'

The third victim's skull had smashed against the tarmac, and the fourth victim's right cheekbone was shattered. But aside from the visible bloodstains on their wounds, there were no signs of blood loss. In other words, their deaths were too pristine. How was she only realising this now? The corpses in the first two photographs were as still as embalmed bodies, ready for their funerals.

'Floor type?'

'Tarmac.'

'How long before the bodies were found?'

'Five and four hours.'

'Which floor did they jump from?'

'Sixth.'

It was a while before Jiseon spoke again.

'In such cases there's sure to be severe blood loss. Once a head cracks open, it's a bloody mess. If you didn't see blood, there's a possibility that it had seeped into the ground. Or you could've missed it, since it's hard to see blood against dark surfaces.' Suyeon heard a pause at the other end of the line. 'Where did this happen by the way? We haven't received any bodies recently.'

'In a rehabilitation hospital in Incheon, somewhere in Cheolma, where the redevelopment is about to start. Four suicides in a month.'

'Four?' Jiseon repeated in a startled voice. No matter the cause of death, it was deeply unusual that an autopsy hadn't been requested, given that four people had died in the same location.

'It seems none of the family members wanted to bother with an autopsy. Probably because the suicide notes were enough for them.'

Jiseon told Suyeon to keep her in the loop, before hanging up. It was getting late and the office was already empty, but Suyeon got up and grabbed her vest. She had to take another look at the ground before the fickle spring weather washed all the evidence away.

Suyeon arrived in the vicinity of the hospital at eleven. Aside from her own car, the road on the way there had been empty. She drove through the gates of the hospital into the dark car park before pulling to an abrupt stop – another visitor had beaten her there. Until the headlights illuminated the figure, Suyeon assumed it was an animal. A wild boar from the nearby mountain or a wandering dog, she figured, because only that would explain why it was on all fours with its nose buried in the ground.

But it was a person. Crouching on the ground was a woman wearing a long, black leather coat. Suyeon parked her car in the middle of the road and stepped out. The woman's face crumpled at the blinding lights as she stood up. Her silver hair suggested advanced age. Suyeon would've assumed that she was in her mid-thirties, otherwise. She had a young face, which reminded Suyeon of Eungyeong sunbae. Perhaps it was the paleness of her skin, the confidence in her eyes.

As she approached the woman, Suyeon tried coming up with possible explanations for why someone would plaster her face to the spot where someone had died, but she drew a blank. In fact, this was her only conclusion:

More shit to deal with.

'You there!' Suyeon shouted as she crossed the police line. 'What do you think you're doing?' She was ready to take hold of her, but the woman got up and brushed past her brazenly, curiosity apparently satisfied. The stranger stepped over the police tape in an elegant manner then turned to address Suyeon in a low, steady voice.

'Strange. The ground was clean, so we can assume that the blood left on the victims was all there was. Added to which, the victims couldn't have thrown themselves this far. But you're already thinking the same thing, aren't you, Detective?'

Suyeon was taken aback by the question. The fact that she hadn't considered where the victims' bodies had landed prevented her from speaking.

Without waiting for an answer, the woman asked again, 'I mean, surely you came to confirm that for yourself?'

Suyeon recovered enough to clear her throat and stammer, 'Who are you? A detective?'

'Something like that.'

Suyeon thought back to the afternoon. Had this woman been at the crime scene earlier? The answer was no, not as far as she remembered. There hadn't been that many people at the scene in the first place. Even if there had been, surely she wouldn't have missed such a conspicuous character. Not to mention the woman's ghoulish complexion.

Her hands in her pockets, the woman ambled along the police line and stared up at the sixth floor.

'They were thrown. Picked up after they were already dead, or as good as dead, and hurled. Hard.' As the woman spoke, Suyeon followed the woman with her eyes, keeping her guard up. 'That way, the bodies would avoid getting caught on a tree or anything nearby. Landing on the tarmac, no one would question why they didn't have any bleeding wounds. And they didn't, did they?'

Suyeon's mind was racing. Given that she knew so much about the blood, it was fair to assume the woman had seen the scene before Suyeon had, perhaps even before the police first showed up. If she'd arrived after Suyeon had left, on the other hand, it meant that she had been authorised to inspect the body.

'I'll ask you one last time. If you're with the police, which bureau do you work for?' Suyeon asked.

The woman stopped walking and turned around. A smirk crossed her face. 'My name's Violette. I put away bad guys too.'

The crease between Suyeon's brows deepened – half because she'd caught yet another glimpse of Eungyeong sunbae, and half because the woman had a name that didn't match her Korean features.

'The culprit you're looking for is not an entity that you can catch, Detective,' said Violette. 'I can assure you they're not under your jurisdiction, so it's probably best if you drop the case now.'

Suyeon stopped short at the word 'culprit'.

Sensing this, Violette continued, 'You think there's a culprit too, don't you? But there's no way somebody could've thrown themselves this far. Unless the culprit's what I think it is.'

Suyeon quirked a brow. 'And who's this culprit you have in mind?'

As midnight drew close, a heavy silence blanketed the night, thickening the air. A veneer of moisture clung to Suyeon's skin. Above the two of them, a broken street light blinked fitfully. Suyeon waited for Violette to speak. She'd had her doubts about this case, and she was learning she wasn't the only one. But instead of the answer she was waiting for, Violette burst into a lacklustre laugh. Suyeon bristled.

'Sorry, it's just kinda funny to me that I'm talking to a detective,' said Violette.

'Mind sharing what's so funny about that?'

'Oh, you know, the fact that you'll never believe me. No matter what I say, you're the last person who will. In fact, you'll probably say it's all bullshit. And why should I put myself through all that?'

'I don't know why you'd jump to that conclusion. I'm not like that.'

Violette was clearly intrigued by the young detective's bluntness, but studied her with an impassive look.

After a long pause, she obliged. 'OK. A vampire did it.'

Suyeon was forced to eat her own words.

This *was* bullshit.

'Our culprit's not human, but a vampire,' said Violette.

Suyeon scoffed. The tension that had seized her body finally loosened. This was absurd. Absolute bullshit. And it angered her. To think that she'd given this woman her time.

Suyeon dipped out of the police line, but not before giving Violette a sharp warning.

'A crime scene isn't somewhere you can enter as you please. If I catch you snooping around again, I'm afraid I'll have to take action.'

In her line of work, she'd met all sorts of people who'd shown her just how cruel the human race could be, and amongst them were the likes of Violette. Those who saw someone's death as nothing more than an object to satiate their morbid boredom. Who was worse – them or the actual culprit? To Suyeon, they were equally cruel. She didn't need people to go so far as to show empathy for the dead. But showing courtesy was the least the living could do.

But really, a fucking vampire?

Suyeon bit her lip. It was only a fraction of a second, but the knowing look in the woman's eyes – the same one that Eungyeong sunbae wore every time her guess turned out to be true – made anger rise up her throat. Suyeon turned to leave.

'If you find another victim within the next few days...' Violette's words caught Suyeon's attention. She whipped her head around to find Violette standing in the same spot as before. 'Look for two holes near their nape or collarbones. They're vampire bite marks – you won't miss it. It wouldn't hurt to check for those on the previous victims too.'

With those final words, Violette strutted off. As Suyeon watched her disappear into the darkness, she tried to shake off her rage. *Calm down. It's not like you'll ever see that woman again.*

That was what she thought, until the fifth victim.

Suyeon waited until Violette's silhouette was out of sight before turning to leave. From the sky came the first drops of rain – thick and dense.

NANJU

A week ago, Nanju's peace began to collapse.

The cracks hadn't made a sound, and therefore, there was no way of telling when the first one appeared. But the most pressing issue now was the fact that they'd grown too large to be ignored. That anxiety had seeped through the fissures, filling up her insides. Throughout the day, her heart would beat too fast for comfort, and she flinched at the smallest noise. When she closed her eyes, worry seized her body, making it impossible to fall asleep. She found even the slightest moment of darkness unbearable. Her consciousness turned cloudy as her days and nights, dreams and reality, bled into one another. To prod herself awake, she replaced proper meals with coffee and energy drinks, ruining her stomach as a result. Although her condition was further exacerbated by gulping down medicine on an empty stomach, Nanju held fast to her rule of not drawing the blackout curtains, even at high noon.

Today was no different. Lying on her bed, right next to the window, Nanju observed the rays of the spring sun before shutting her eyes. It would be a while until she could fall asleep. She fidgeted at every sound, and each time she did, she curled up even tighter, as if the sunlight was urging her to protect herself. It was *exactly* a week after the cracks began; a week of watching her life crumble before her, as if she were an idle bystander.

When she stirred from her light sleep, prying open her eyes, the day was almost gone. The sunset glowed purple against the dusky sky. Rubbing her stiff neck, Nanju sat up. After switching on the table lamp, she placed her feet on the cold floor and switched on the only ceiling light that illuminated her one-room apartment. Only three hours until her shift began.

Nanju preferred eating at the convenience store or one of the restaurants near the hospital. It was her way of keeping away from the apartment. Most of the long-neglected food in the fridge had lost their original shape. Even the tomatoes that she'd thought looked fine were mushy at the bottom. Crinkling her nose, Nanju dumped everything from the fridge into the sink. A curse escaped her when the sour stench of mouldy pickled gochujang assaulted her nose. Annoyance breaking through the tiredness at last, she slammed the banchan container into the sink. The empty box clanged in protest. Gripping the edge of the counter, Nanju took a deep breath. *Everything's OK. You're just imagining things*, she told herself, but her conviction lasted no more than five minutes.

That detective. Did she see me?

She was sure they'd made eye contact. The detective had turned her head towards Nanju, who had been staring. But then again, Nanju had been on the sixth floor and the window was coated with a sheet of vinyl on which the hospital name was printed. Although some of the printing had cracked or fallen off, getting a clear look into the hospital from outside would have been near impossible. However, despite not getting a good look at the person's face, a detective might be attentive to the fact someone had been standing there at all. Surely that in itself was enough to arouse suspicion.

Once she arrived at that conclusion, frustration fizzled out and her peace of mind returned. She picked up the banchan container, tossed it whole into the bin and started clearing the food waste from the sink. While her hands were busy, she maintained a calm face, all while knowing it wouldn't last.

With two hours still left until her next shift, Nanju got ready to leave. She crammed her car keys and wallet into her purse. Once she had put on her shoes and opened the front door, her mobile phone rang, as if it had been waiting its turn. She didn't have the number saved, but she knew exactly who it was. She waited for it to stop ringing, but her caller was relentless. She had to answer.

She knew that if she didn't, they might bring trouble to the hospital.

As soon as Nanju answered the phone, the person on the other end sneered, 'What's due is due. How about we stop dragging shit out?'

'I need more time.'

'I'd say we've given you enough, haven't we?'

The caller's question wasn't directed at Nanju, but someone standing next to him. 'Yes, boss,' another voice said gruffly. The second voice wasn't wrong, but he wasn't right either. The original debt had been paid off some time ago. But the interest posed a different problem. Far surpassing the first amount, it had now snowballed into a sum that Nanju couldn't bear. Time and time again, she had tried to protest the unfairness of it, but her argument was always countered by documents bearing two red stamps – proof of her parents' accord.

Her parents were the ones who had turned to the money lenders, desperate for money to pay for her father's cancer treatments. Sensing that something was off, yet too afraid to face diagnosis, Nanju's father had put off going to the hospital until it was too late. This last part, Nanju could never understand – if he had been so adamant on ignoring his illness, why didn't he just wait to die? Instead of crawling to the hospital, begging to be saved when it was already too late.

Since the cancer in his stomach had progressed past the treatable stage, his doctor said they had no choice but to try every method in the book to keep him alive. He might have had a fighting chance had he gone to the hospital earlier, but no miracle could restore to life a body that was shrivelled black like a piece of rotten tree bark.

Nanju's parents' retirement fund was sucked dry in an instant. They tried everything to find the most effective treatment, but the cancer showed no signs of shrinking. Once a week, Nanju visited the hospital, bringing along whatever her father needed. She hadn't forgotten the negligence she suffered in her childhood, and thus felt she was going above and beyond by doing more than just showing her face. She didn't think to offer financial help as well, because her unscrupulous parents were thick-skinned enough to ask for favours whenever they needed it.

But she was wrong. The word 'money' was never once mentioned to her. Once it became difficult to borrow from banks, her parents turned to money lenders, putting down her name as their guarantor. Nanju only learnt the truth after her father's death, when the interest her family had accrued had already far exceeded the principal. That was no more than four months ago.

The money lenders had waited for the interest to pile up before they contacted Nanju. They knew she was working as a nurse. Nanju scrambled to find a compromise or loophole, but everything was meaningless in the face of the exhaustive contract. One specific clause prevented her from forgoing her inheritance rights, and on the off-chance she found herself no longer legally bound to pay off the family debt, it seemed they would find a way to breathe down her neck outside of the law. At the rate things were going, that debt would continue to grow, and she would spend her whole life trying to pay it back.

She wasn't entirely out of options. Four months ago, she'd been offered a way out. But it was one that accumulated in blood instead of numbers.

The man on the phone demanded that Nanju deposit the money by the end of the day. Having neither the intention nor capacity to fulfil such a request, Nanju simply said OK and hung up.

What should I do? Darkness's familiar hand stretched out towards her. At that moment, she recalled the sight of the detective looking up at the hospital building. That woman wouldn't be able to help her in any way – she knew this. Yet why was her face floating in her mind like some kind of saviour?

Nanju stood in a daze for a while, before hurrying out of the gloom of her apartment.

VIOLETTE

January 1983

Two days had passed since New Year's Eve, and still the calendar on the noticeboard read 1982. The broken lightbulb above it, too, remained to be changed. On one side of the narrow corridor were the toilets. The wooden door had an open arch in the middle, rendering the entrance more decorative than functional, since every fart and every conversation spoken before the mirror wafted out freely. Little more than a metre away from the toilets was Violette's spot – a row of five velvet seats which she'd made her private reading corner.

In the summer, the sun poured through the nearby window, cooking the seats; and in the winter, the cold froze them. But no matter the time of year, the corner was invariably dark, damp and glazed with the scent of tobacco. Though the seats had been placed there for the cinemagoers' comfort and convenience, people would rather stand and wait elsewhere for their film to start.

And so Violette never rushed, knowing she could count on those seats to be empty. That morning was no different. After fighting the urge to stay wrapped in the warmth of her duvet, Violette trudged to the bathroom, pulled back her frizzy hair and stuck her toothbrush in her mouth. On the fridge was a note that read: *Resto ce soir – on rentrera tard!* She opened it to find milk, cereal, sandwiches and juice, always left in the same spot by her parents. After rinsing her mouth, Violette took a perfectly wrapped sandwich from the fridge and chucked it into her bag, where her books and some loose stationery were messily tangled up.

Winter was always known to show no mercy, but the snow this year was particularly harsh. Once the temperature fell below zero, the weather had showed no sign of letting up. Almost every family in town shared the same headache of dealing with burst pipes. Icy roads made it impossible to receive help right away, with some repair companies taking days to arrive, forcing people to resort to fend for themselves – pouring hot water over their pipes or using hammers to crack the ice. Once Christmas was over, some people even stripped the fairy lights from their trees and wrapped them around their pipes to keep them warm. Everyone had their own way of surviving the freeze. Violette's father, Maurice, relied on his trusty hammer. He banged on the pipes, keeping a steady tempo as if to prove he'd really played drums back in the day. Whenever her father's incessant clanging woke her up at dawn, Violette would burrow deeper into her thick duvet. On those days, she'd get up later than usual, making up for lost sleep.

From the living room, there now flowed heated reports of the upcoming municipal elections. By now, Violette could predict what the news anchor was going to say next: something about not underestimating the National Front's ability to turn the tides, followed by a depressing update on how the economy was at a standstill.

Violette's father wasn't the type to leave the TV on by mistake. Even if he'd forgotten, it wouldn't have gone unnoticed by her mother, Claire. Violette figured they'd left it on to wake her up and make the house feel less empty. Last holiday, her parents had stayed at home until it was time to open the family restaurant for dinner service. Violette rarely had the house to herself. But this holiday, things were different. Violette had noticed fewer Christmas presents under the tree, and her parents, who were strict about spending quality time together, had spent their precious New Year's Eve at the restaurant. Maurice complained way too often about how everyone was being put out of a job, and eventually decided to pull forward the restaurant's daily opening time. To a sixteen-year-old who slept in during her holidays, it felt like her parents were always gone before the sun came up.

Violette switched off the TV before leaving. When she took her first step out of the house, she felt the soft crunch of snow beneath her boots. A blanket of white was spread out before her. It must've only just started snowing, since only a few of her neighbours had cleared the snow covering their doorsteps. She glanced at the shovel beside her. Snowflakes drifted lazily to the ground. Although it seemed unlikely that the weather would worsen, it would only be a few hours until the snow on the ground collected into a heap. If the sun decided to shine a bit harder later in the day, the snow would melt and freeze, turning the ground into solid ice.

Last year, her father had slipped on ice and hurt his tailbone. It had been quite funny watching him waddle around the house, but Violette hadn't forgotten how her heart had plunged into the pit of her belly when the accident happened. She slipped off her backpack, tossed it behind the door and grabbed the shovel. Without gloves on, her hands soon turned red, but she didn't mind. She drove the shovel deep into the ground and heaved until she was satisfied with the clean grey strip before her.

Exhausted from the unplanned workout, Violette collapsed on the sofa. Before she knew it, she was opening her eyes to the sun's orange glow streaming in. Morning had passed. Her heavy lids begged her to go back to sleep, but she couldn't stand the thought of wasting a whole day. Besides, at this time of year the cinema was sure to be empty. Violette peeled herself off the sofa. Her parents weren't coming home until after midnight, so either way, she'd be by herself until then. As she picked up her backpack from the floor, a tinge of guilt needled her.

'How was the library?' When Claire had asked her that a few days ago, Violette blinked in confusion at first. Then she remembered that she'd told her mum she was going to the library to read. Though Claire, ever careful about giving Violette her privacy, wasn't the type to mind where she went or what she did, Violette didn't want to go through the hassle of explaining – besides, there was a chance that her mum might feel hurt that she was keeping secrets, however small and harmless.

So instead Violette had only muttered, 'Good.' She wasn't telling a complete lie – she was doing the same thing she'd be doing at the library, just in a different location.

***

Violette stood before the town's only cinema, located on rue Éomine. The vast car park was empty save for a lonely orange Vega. Violette pulled down her black beanie as she entered the cinema. A caution sign warned of the slippery floor. If somebody were to ask her, 'Why the cinema?' Violette wouldn't be able to answer. At first she'd come to watch a film, a decision she'd made on a whim after spending a dreary afternoon wondering if she should try doing something out of her comfort zone. Out of all the options she could come up with, a solo movie date had seemed the least intimidating. As she stood in line at the box office, she studied the row of movie posters, but none appealed to her. When it was almost her turn, Violette left the queue wordlessly, walking straight past the box office. She didn't want to spend two hours stuck watching a film she had no interest in. The only problem was, Violette had already told Claire and Maurice she was going to see a movie. They had barely been able to hide their surprise – and joy – when Violette, whose only friends were the books in her room, announced that she was going out. If she wanted to keep up the pretence, she'd have to find a way to kill time. That was when she discovered the seats. Upholstered with red velvet, basking in the subtle stench of the toilet, furnished with a single broken bulb and tucked away from the frenzied crowd – a refuge.

That row of seats had become her secret hideout. She didn't know which she liked more, the moderate silence or the feeling of sitting idle while a crowd bustled around her. As gross as it might sound, she also quite liked the musty old seats. Actually, come to think of it, she liked that they were seats that no one but her would look for and love. Today, as usual, she strolled towards them at a leisurely pace. They were all going to be unoccupied anyway.

Little did Violette know she'd find someone sitting there. For the very first time.

The girl had long black hair tucked behind her ears, dense eyelashes and a slender face that was fair – no, waxen. Bloodless, even. Her skin looked colder than the snow that had turned Violette's hands pink. She had a book on her lap and its title was written in a strange language Violette couldn't decipher. She wore a navy blue coat. And she was barefoot.

'Barefoot…'

As if the stranger had heard her, she turned to face Violette, her gaze a vivid gold. She closed her book, planted her naked feet on the icy floor and walked past Violette.

'It's fine,' Violette blurted. Her own words caught her off guard. But it was too late, the girl had stopped in her tracks, and Violette felt compelled to continue. 'Oh, I mean… It's fine if you'd like to read there,' Violette clarified.

But the seats didn't belong to her in the first place, and obviously didn't require anyone's permission to be used. Violette flushed at her own self-righteous tone. Instead of answering, the girl let out a soft laugh before walking away. Violette shifted awkwardly, waiting for the girl to disappear completely, before she settled down into the seat, right where the girl had sat.

When Claire and Maurice returned home at the usual time, past midnight, Violette was lying in bed, staring at the ceiling. She flipped to her side and pulled her blanket over her head. The snow must've gotten heavier after sunset, since her parents were spending ages dusting snow off themselves as they bickered over whether to shovel the veranda now or later. It was funny how her dad would always put up a fight, even though he knew he would end up giving in to his wife. Maurice huffed a dramatic sigh, and soon after the front door clicked shut. Violette heard a single pair of footsteps. She figured her dad had gone outside, getting started on shovelling duty, so that was probably her mum coming up to the first floor. She knew their movements by now. No matter who it was that came to check on her, neither parent would wake her up. Even so, Violette squeezed her eyes shut under the blanket. There was a soft knock on the door. When she didn't answer, the door creaked open. The feeling in the room changed as a little noise coming from the door told Violette that there was someone watching her. After a brief pause, the door was closed again. This time, the footsteps heading downstairs were barely audible.

Violette pulled down her blanket. Gazing out of the window, she saw that the snow had stopped. She listened to the sound of Maurice's shovel knocking against the ground.

The moon was full and radiant. Just like the girl's eyes.

Maybe she's a ghost? Violette chewed over the possibility. There had been an *absence* around her – there was no other way of describing it. She should've felt more of a presence – like the one that had confirmed it was indeed her mum and not a ghost who'd poked her head in to check up on her. But with the girl, Violette had felt nothing. Stranger still, the girl had been wearing a coat that looked far too thin to offer any protection against the harsh weather. And she'd been barefoot.

Maybe she left her shoes somewhere in the cinema? But why take them off? She wasn't even wearing socks…

From the moment Violette had sat down in her favourite seat, she hadn't stopped thinking about the girl. Her train of thought continued to chug on, heading in no particular direction. The brevity of their meeting left very little room for analysing who the girl was, or *why* the girl lingered in her mind.

The next day, Violette was awoken by loud hammering. This time, instead of going back to sleep, she hopped right out of bed.

In the kitchen, Claire was busy making Violette's lunch. 'All done?' she asked, clearly assuming it was her husband coming in from the veranda. But when she realised the footsteps were soft, Violette's mother spun around.

'Up so early?' Claire asked, apparently surprised to see her daughter brushing her hair, toothbrush in mouth. She seemed to think hard, probably worried she'd forgotten an important occasion. Just then, Maurice came in through the front door. Once he'd hung up his jacket, his eyes rounded when he saw Violette standing in the kitchen. 'Whoa, sleeping beauty got up early today,' he teased. Violette rolled her eyes, barely stifling a smile.

'Just meeting a friend,' she answered, mouth full of foam, not yet realising the significance of what she had just said.

***

The cinema was chilly at opening time. Violette was worried she'd draw attention to herself by coming in so early, but thankfully the attendant was too preoccupied with wiping the foyer floor to notice her.

The cinema was doused in the savoury scent of freshly made popcorn. Even though she had filled up on a proper breakfast before coming, Violette's tummy rumbled. In her bag were two sandwiches that Claire had carefully assembled, excited over her daughter's new friend. Violette had resolved to finish the contents of her lunchbox herself before going home. She couldn't bear to dampen her mum's enthusiasm, but even if the girl turned up, Violette knew she wouldn't have the courage to offer her a sandwich. No way.

Violette sat in her usual seat. Since she didn't know if or when the girl might come back, she'd decided to come to the cinema as soon as its doors were open. It was no hassle. She'd brought along a thick book guaranteed to make the time fly by.

The girl didn't show.

Violette finished the sandwiches on her own. She finished the book as well. When she saw an attendant wiping the floor again, this time preparing to close up, she got up.

The next day, too, Violette got up early, packed two jambon-fromage sandwiches, and headed straight to the cinema. Perhaps the girl had only been there that one day. But Violette knew that she had to keep coming, that if she didn't, the thought that the girl might be at the cinema would gnaw at her. The day after she went with two slices of quiche, and the next, bagels and comté slices. All of which Violette finished by herself before going home.

On the fifth morning, she rolled around in bed thinking about the past few days. She considered staying in, but eventually she did get up. *No more waiting after today.* The whole of her winter holiday was going to waste. *Really, this is it*, she made herself promise as she headed downstairs.

Claire and Maurice were experts in the art of waiting – the entire week they'd managed to refrain from asking about their daughter's new friend, though their expressions betrayed curiosity and concern. Violette was grateful for her parents' patience, but still ignored their eager stares while she packed her bag. On today's menu were brioche rolls with homemade apricot jam. Violette popped open the lid of her lunchbox and indulged in a big whiff of sweetness.

Her resolution of 'no more waiting after today' fizzled away before the day even ended.

When she saw the attendant mopping the foyer, Violette gathered her things. She wound her scarf around her neck tightly and pulled down her beanie. L'Épiphanie was the day after tomorrow and she noticed the cinema was selling galette des rois. It was a dessert that most people preferred to bake at home, but Claire made them to sell at the restaurant. Tomorrow, Violette would have to lend her mother a hand. *Won't be able to stop by the cinema tomorrow then*, Violette thought, shaking her head. *Today was supposed to be the last day of waiting anyway.*

Violette gave the revolving door a hard push and exited the cinema. As always, the lonely street light in the car park was blinking. Violette let out an exhale, releasing a cloud of disappointment. Just as she was turning in the direction of home, she stopped short.

Then, she forgot to breathe. The air hung there, undisturbed.

Tightening her grip on the strap of her backpack, Violette watched the person standing under the broken street light. After a moment's pause, her face broke into a smile.

The girl was barefoot.

SUYEON

There. Two holes above the left clavicle. No more than five centimetres apart, each resembling a deep poke left by a fountain pen. Suyeon got out her phone and snapped a picture. She could hear Chantae behind her, busy shooing away gawkers. Suyeon stood up. She had seen enough. Taking her cue from Suyeon, the police officer covered the corpse's face.

The fifth victim was found on the 18 April, a week after the fourth incident. This meant that two suicides by jumping had occurred in the same hospital in the span of one week. Stepping out of the police line, Suyeon went up to Chantae.

'Our victim was fifty-five, a patient on the fifth floor. He didn't have dementia but just like the others, he left behind a note.'

Suyeon handed over the letter that she'd received from the police officer. Chantae looked at the limp sheet of paper inside the ziplock bag before nudging Suyeon towards the road. He squinted at the building.

'At this rate, maybe they should think about installing window bars,' grumbled Chantae.

'Come on. You know something's up.'

Ignoring the look of irritation on Chantae's face, Suyeon pulled up a photo of the fourth victim. Chantae squirmed at the photo, but Suyeon thrust her phone in his face, forcing him to take a good look at the victim's neck.

'Similar wounds were found on the previous victim. We don't know what left them, but we know they were made just before their deaths – see how the flesh around the wound is wide open? There's more. Besides these lacerations, the victim's skin was discoloured in several places.'

She signed and pinched the skin between her eyes. 'Maybe it's time we looked into the possibility of homicide. I mean, think about where the bodies landed. If the victims *had* jumped themselves, they should've landed somewhere near the flower beds. But both – actually,' she turned to face the building, 'the third victim, too – three victims were found at least ten metres off the mark. That's impossible unless they'd sprinted and leapt off the building.'

Chantae turned to look at where the bodies had landed. His expression seemed to acknowledge the possibility of Suyeon's hypothesis. But that was all. He looked at the crowd before grabbing Suyeon's shoulders and steering her in the opposite direction. Standing in front of an abandoned convenience store, he spoke in a low voice.

'Look, we could go on and on about whether or not we've got a case on our hands. So let's ask ourselves the most important question here – *who* is interested in bringing the case to light? Because here's the thing, if the only one interested in finding out the truth is a detective, then it's all pointless.' Suyeon stayed quiet. Chantae continued. 'No one showed up for these victims, kid. No one.'

He didn't have to elaborate any further. Giving Suyeon one last pat on the shoulder, Chantae took his leave. He was right. Annoyingly right. For a while, Suyeon remained glued to the spot.

Suyeon went back to the hospital again that evening. But this time, it wasn't to look for clues. Holding a heavy carton of soy milk, she headed towards the rehabilitation centre on the sixth floor. The patients who'd just finished dinner were gathered in the seating area, watching TV. Upon hearing the soft *ding* of the lift, they turned their heads meekly towards the sound, but lost interest once they saw that it was only Suyeon. As usual, Suyeon walked past them and entered room 608.

It was a six-person ward, but the two neatly tidied and empty beds in the middle made the room look bigger. When the redevelopment had been announced, the number of the patients in the rehabilitation hospital had begun to dwindle rapidly, and the few who remained were those abandoned by the rough tides of change.

Granny Eunshim's bed was right next to the window. Suyeon slid open the curtains encircling the bed and found her leaning against the backrest, knitting away. Perched on the tip of her nose were the trusty reading glasses that she'd relied on for decades. Suyeon walked over to the windowsill and set down the heavy carton. On the ledge was a paper carnation. Granny Eunshim lifted her head. Seconds ticked by while the old woman studied Suyeon's features. Soon, a smile of recognition spread across her face. Folding her knees, Granny Eunshim made space for Suyeon.

'You should've called! Have you eaten?'

Suyeon nodded as she sat down, but the old lady reached for a bottle of yoghurt anyway. She stuck a straw in it and thrust the drink into Suyeon's hands.

'Halmoni, I'm way too old for this!'

Granny Eunshim sulked. Glaring at her visitor now, she mumbled something about how young people didn't know what was good for them. Through the reading glasses, her eyes were as wide as saucers.

'Listen, you, this is much healthier than the coffee you always drink.'

Before Granny Eunshim could get another word in, Suyeon put the straw in her mouth. Granny Eunshim seemed to notice Suyeon's quizzical look at her knitting – summer was approaching. She smoothed out the fuzz on her yarn as she explained.

'That scarf you were wearing for months is basically in tatters, so I wanted to make you something nice. But my eyes have been failing me lately, so I have to start now if I'm going to have it ready by the winter.'

The old woman continued fiddling with the orange yarn. She had always had nimble fingers, so Suyeon had no doubt she'd be sporting a new scarf long before winter rolled around. Once she had finished with the yarn, Granny Eunshim took off her glasses.

'Did the doctor say when I'll get to go home? Who knows what's become of my shop!' she moaned.

'I told you, there's no need to worry. I'm taking good care of things.'

'A shop must be run by its owner or it'll be ruined sooner or later.'

'Well then, you'd better start taking your daily exercises more seriously. You were lazy again today, weren't you?' Suyeon challenged her.

Granny Eunshim raised her eyebrows and glowered at Suyeon, a tactic she resorted to when she had nothing to say or was losing a fight.

Until six years ago, Granny Eunshim had run a small shop opposite a primary school. It was called Youngjin's Mart, named after her son. Although it was registered as a grocer, it was more of a general store. Besides your usual supermarket foods, Youngjin's Mart sold all sorts of knick-knacks like toys, indoor slippers and random things you might occasionally find useful – compass sets, for instance.

When she was in primary school, Suyeon had dropped by at least once a week. That was when she first met Granny Eunshim. Whenever she visited, Granny Eunshim would look up from her knitting project, say, 'You're here!' then take out a bottle of yoghurt from the fridge and offer it to her. It was her way of making sure that the girl who was much shorter than her peers got all her vitamins. *You have to drink this if you want to grow taller. Lots of it!* That was her philosophy. Granny Eunshim may have been right.

Granny Eunshim had always been at the counter, sitting cross-legged while she knitted or sewed. She made all sorts of things – heart-, dress-, star-shaped dish scrubbers as well as the coin purses which she put up for sale in one corner of the shop. All were beautiful and, more importantly, made to last. Hers was the most popular shop in the neighbourhood and she held the fort for decades. It was only when she started confusing Youngjin's Mart with Youngju's Mart that she made the tough decision to close its doors. Suyeon could still recall with clarity every nook and cranny of the little shop.

After Granny Eunshim was diagnosed with dementia, she spent six months living with her son before she was admitted to the rehabilitation hospital. Suyeon helped her move. The old lady's only son expressed his gratitude not only in words, but also in cash. Suyeon turned the offers down, but later found a thick envelope of money in a drawer beside Granny Eunshim's bed with her name on it. A few months later, a nurse informed her that the son had moved overseas. It was only then that Suyeon realised that the money hadn't been to thank her, but to cover his mother's expenses. In the envelope was a brief note saying that he had no choice but to leave, and hoped that Suyeon would look after his mother in his absence. Suyeon had only let out a light sigh; perhaps deep down, she'd seen this coming. Since then, she'd been making sure to visit once a week. Eungyeong sunbae usually came along, too. Until recently.

'That son of mine's always so busy. That's a good thing, of course, but do you think he'll come see me this weekend at least?'

Suyeon snapped out of her reverie right away at the mention of Grann Eunshim's son.

'Yes. And maybe he'll bring you something yummy,' Suyeon reassured her.

'Oh, he's in for a good scolding. Unni's been waiting to tell him off, you know.'

Granny Eunshim was getting things mixed up again. Although Eungyeong sunbae had never once met that son of hers, Suyeon agreed enthusiastically, not correcting the old woman.

'Oh, by the way, that apple you brought me yesterday was delicious.'

'Apple?'

Suyeon hadn't been here the day before.

'You know the one. Red like a ruby. It's been a while since I had something so sweet!' Granny Eunshim chirped, as she popped a few pastel-coloured pills into her mouth.

Wondering briefly if the old lady was confused, Suyeon noticed the apple core on the windowsill. Or rather, what was left of it, sitting in a clean banchan container. Utterly browned. Someone had brought Granny Eunshim an apple. *Who else would come to visit? Maybe her son and his wife are back for a while?*

Suyeon got up and rearranged the crumpled blanket.

'Want me to lower your backrest?' she asked.

Granny Eunshim nodded. Suyeon bent her knees and grabbed the stiff handle. That was when she spotted the paper flower lying underneath Granny Eunshin's bed.

Lifting the flower as she righted herself, Suyeon saw that Granny Eunshim was already staring vacantly at the ceiling. Suyeon pressed her lips together. The old woman's eyes were empty. Before bedtime and right after waking up was when her mental state was the most volatile. During those times, she became a different person. She said things Suyeon couldn't understand and held conversations with imaginary friends from her past. When Suyeon realised that Granny Eunshim was no longer capable of holding a proper conversation for today, she slipped the paper flower into her pocket without another word. She tucked the old lady in, making sure she would be warm throughout the night before turning to leave.

'They're going to a place where the sun doesn't set. Good for them,' the old woman said in an unusually high-pitched voice.

Suyeon turned around. Granny Eunshim continued to mutter at the ceiling.

'We have to wash our bodies clean. That's why that woman spent three hours in the shower, they said. She scrubbed herself so hard she almost tore off her skin… but that's what we have to do. That's what I'll do. Because that's the only way I'll get to go…'

Suyeon realised the old woman wasn't simply asking after an imaginary friend. Standing by the door, Suyeon called out her name softly to try and break the spell that had come over her – but Granny Eunshim shot her a menacing look. In her eyes, Suyeon was nothing but a stranger.

'You wait your turn. They'll decide on the order.'

'What order?'

'What do you think! The order of the hike. That man went first… how much his stomach must've hurt.'

After a few incoherent sentences, Granny Eunshim closed her eyes and drifted off, knocked out by the sedatives in her medicine. Suyeon stood there quietly, watching sleep settle over the old woman's face.

A believer of cold, hard facts, Suyeon told herself she wouldn't jump to conclusions. But she couldn't shake the feeling that the hospital's many deaths and the uncertainty around them was slowly bleeding towards Granny Eunshim.

When Suyeon had first discovered the two wounds on the corpse at the morgue, she'd assumed Violette had simply seen the body beforehand. But she'd found the same lacerations on the fifth body, which had only been discovered today.

Are there holes on the third body, too? What would that mean? Is this the work of a serial killer? What if Chantae sunbae is right about all of this – who am I doing it for?

As Suyeon left Granny Eunshim's ward, regret nipped at her – she shouldn't have sent that woman on her way that night without at least asking for her phone number. Thankfully, Suyeon didn't have to berate herself too long. Violette was right there in the foyer.

She was standing in front of the non-functioning lift, pushing the button repeatedly. Suyeon grabbed Violette's arm and spun her around. When a welcoming smile spread across Violette's face, Suyeon slapped a pair of handcuffs on her wrists.

***

Suyeon led Violette into the empty office. Everyone else in the third detective team had clocked off for the day. The rain had started when they stepped into the police station, and it was only getting harder, its rhythmic tap occupying the silence between the two women. Suyeon studied Violette's expression. She was relaxed, composed.

'Can I see some ID?'

'I have my French passport and residence card. Which would you prefer?'

'You're a foreigner?'

'Yes.'

Well, that was unexpected. Suyeon paused for a bit before bringing her fingers to the computer keyboard. Then she asked Violette if she had any of these documents with her right now. Reaching into her coat pocket, Violette pulled out her passport. Suyeon flipped it open, only to find an incomprehensible string of characters staring back at her. She strained to keep her composure at that point. Shifting her gaze back and forth between Violette's face and the photo in the passport, she proceeded to copy down every piece of information she could make out before asking Violette when she'd arrived in the country, why she came, and what she was doing for work.

'I translate French articles into Korean. Mostly pieces on the economy or politics, but every now and then I'll translate a novel. If you flip to the back of my passport, you'll find my business card. Feel free to keep it. If you look up my name and email, you'll find the articles I've worked on.'

Suyeon kept her eyes fixed on Violette as she pulled the business card out of her passport.

'I came to Korea five years ago. And as for why I'm here… I was adopted and sent to France when I was five, but I've always wondered what it was like to live in Korea. You know, it being my birth country and all.'

'Why do you keep showing up at the crime scene?'

'Did I not mention? It's also my job to catch the bad guys.'

'Who exactly are you referring to? Vampires?'

Suyeon couldn't help but scoff.

The tip of Violette's lips curved into a smug smile. 'You saw for yourself, didn't you? The two holes I mentioned. Isn't that why you were so eager to put me in handcuffs? I bet you were thinking, "How did that woman know? Did she do it? Should I lock her up?"'

Suyeon kept quiet.

'Let's see... Something tells you I'm not the one you're looking for. Because I'm sitting in front of you, telling you exactly where to look for clues. For a detective, I guess at least you're nice enough to believe these old folk didn't just come up with a schedule to jump to their deaths.'

'Is this a joke to you?'

'No. Is it to *you?* You keep insisting I'm pulling your leg.'

Neither Suyeon nor Violette gave in to the other's accusing glare. *What is this woman's deal?* Suyeon frowned. Violette hadn't been the least bit nervous when she was handcuffed and escorted to the station. In fact, it seemed as though she was used to it. Suyeon regarded Violette's nonchalant expression and leaned back in her chair. Although everything Violette had said so far sounded like nothing but bullshit, Suyeon couldn't deny the fact that the bullshit made sense – where the corpses landed, the lack of blood, the curious wounds. Suyeon bit her lower lip.

Step one of solving a case: empty your mind. Turn your mind and heart into fresh, blank sheets of paper, so that every possibility can be considered. Eungyeong sunbae had taught her this. *Don't let your prejudices stain the canvas…*

Lowering her head, Suyeon took a deep breath. *All right, here we go. Blank canvas. No stains. Vampires are real. Werewolves, too. Don't forget zombies.* Suyeon rubbed her temples and wiped her face with her palms. Despite her efforts, nothing appeared on her canvas.

Still, Suyeon played along.

'How are the two holes relevant to the case? Were they left by the vampires?'

'You believe me?'

'I'm trying to.'

Violette flashed a satisfied smile.

'When they feed, vampires use their canines, which act like a snake's fang in reverse, piercing a person's flesh and locating their blood vessels. Once they've found them, the canal in the fang emerges and sucks up the blood. Sort of like a tentacle. They suck on veins sometimes, but I suppose arteries require less effort. Usually, vampires go for the subclavian arteries below the collarbones or the carotid arteries at the front of the neck. Dig up a body that's been killed by a vampire, and you'll see that its arteries are tattered. This explains why two holes are usually found around here,' Violette tapped on her own throat. 'They're canine marks.'

Suyeon felt exhausted, keen to wrap this up. 'What evidence do you have to prove it?'

'Recall the size and distance of the holes, and think about how many mammals on earth have chins. From what I know, only humans do. Maybe primates. A dog bite certainly wouldn't leave two little holes. Sure, we could consider something smaller like a snake or rat, but if they had a chin that big, well, I guess we'd be facing a different problem.'

Suyeon wracked her brain for a creature to counter Violette's argument, but no plausible options came to mind.

'Shall we compare which sounds more ridiculous? Either a wild monkey appeared out of nowhere, bit someone and threw them out the window. Or, a vampire did.'

Was this woman toying with her? At this point, Suyeon decided to give up. Primate or vampire, both were equally impossible.

'So to sum up, you're saying that a vampire is behind all of this. And that those marks were left by a vampire bite.'

'A vampire can toss a human body out the window with barely any effort. And like I've said before, they would've done so to avoid raising suspicion. It was strange to find a body covered in cuts but not blood. In fact, cut wounds aside, the site of any jumping suicide should be a bloody mess. Stumped you, didn't it? Not a single drop of blood anywhere, when their entire skull had been cracked open.'

Suyeon's lips crimped into a tight line. She knew that Violette's words were the key to solving this mystery.

There was just one little problem – everything sounded like a load of crap to her.

'How do you know all this?'

'Didn't I tell you already? It's part of my job.'

'Catching vampires is your job?'

'You catch people who kill people, I catch vampires who kill people.'

The matter-of-factness was at odds with the quiet in the room, and the rush building in Suyeon's ears. She considered three possibilities. One, a vampire really had done it. Two, a human acting like a vampire had done it. Three, the woman before her was out of her mind. And maybe she was too.

'Let's say a vampire did it. Why go through the trouble of staging the victims' suicide?'

'They can't risk exposing their existence to humans. But I'm positive the suicide notes were written by the victims themselves.'

'Do they force their victims to write?'

'No, they make them *want* to.'

Placing both hands on the table, Violette inched closer. The rain outside had let up. The smell of wet soil slipped through the crack of the window. Soon, it would be midnight.

'Vampires obtain human blood in two ways: one, waiting for a major accident where there are many casualties. They are always the first to arrive at the scene. Once they're there, they look for those on the brink of death and carry them off like provisions. Often that's why victims whose presence may have been confirmed at the scene of an accident disappear without a trace. The latest incident would be in 2017, on 19 July. The Guro-dong fire.'

Suyeon remembered that incident – it was not long after she'd joined the force, and all emergency services had found it a sobering tale.

A fire had broken out in a motel. Twenty-four guests in total were staying in the motel, and a short circuit had set the front desk on fire in the middle of the night. The fire had started at the ground-floor entrance, of all places, leaving the guests with nowhere to escape. But something strange happened. Five people survived the fire, while fifteen were found dead. The police checked the CCTV footage several times to tally the number of people staying in the motel that night, and each time they counted twenty-four, meaning four people had gone missing after the fire.

No matter how far they rewound the CCTV footage, no one had left the hotel before the fire. Everyone had checked in by seven that evening, and nobody had left again before one o'clock the next morning.

Violette continued, her voice steely. 'That hotel was one of the area's oldest buildings. There were no security cameras except for the one at the entrance. One witness said he heard a window shattering when the fire started. The story goes that the sound was made by someone who had successfully escaped the fire. But there was no such person. Every single casualty died of suffocation, and no one jumped to their death. The window wasn't shattered by someone who was going out, but someone who was coming in.'

Suyeon gave a hollow laugh. 'So you're saying a vampire swooped in to steal the corpses? Were you there at the time of the incident?'

'I arrived at 5:42 in the morning. Made it to the point of initial ignition at 5:48. The whole place was burnt to a crisp, and on the ash-covered floor there were footprints heading out of the lobby door, but not entering from there. So whoever had entered the building must've used a different entrance instead of the lobby's main door. A window, or the roof, for instance.'

'You were inside?'

'We're expected to act fast whenever there's a major accident.'

'No, I mean, outsiders are not allowed into premises on the day of an accident like that.'

Violette looked as if she'd been thrown a trick question. There was a mischievous glint in her eyes.

'Desperate times call for desperate fake IDs, as the saying goes. As someone working in the same field, I'm sure you're familiar with it.'

Suyeon tried not to think too much about that. She circled back to the main problem.

'There were no statements that mentioned an intruder. Besides, the police also looked into the possibility of arson.'

'There were signs of an intrusion. They just didn't make logical sense, and were therefore dismissed.'

Violette seemed to be telling the truth.

'The window of the fourth-floor corridor was shattered. The glass fracture pattern indicates the window had been broken from the outside… but who could break a window from the outside? And at that height? No matter how much the police racked their brains, they couldn't find an answer, so it was left as a mystery. Check the case file if you don't believe me.'

Suyeon didn't have to. She was familiar with this mystery: it was one of Eungyeong sunbae's cases. After failing to connect any dots, Eungyeong sunbae started to suspect that a gang might have been involved. But since there was clear evidence that a short circuit had started the fire, the case was quickly closed, the entire thing deemed a simple accident.

Suyeon drew another deep breath.

'Alright. Tell me about the other method.'

'Exploiting loneliness.'

Silence again, this time ringing with surprise.

'Loneliness?'

'Yes. Every human's greatest weakness. A vampire can find a way to bury into their victims' hearts, feed them faith and love, all the while consuming them up bit by bit, until their victims just offer up their own blood.'

Suyeon made no reply.

'People who've met vampires become happier afterwards. That's what vampires do. If flowers make themselves pretty for butterflies, vampires do the same for humans. They're angels from Hell.'

A soft chuckle escaped Violette as she watched confusion spread across Suyeon's face. Meanwhile, Suyeon couldn't even bring herself to ask what was so funny. It was as if her mind had shut down after an overload.

The hospital suicides had all been accompanied by a handwritten note, each one expressing their author's desire to leave behind this suffocating and meaningless life. The letters held the certainty that the afterlife was where happiness awaited, and justified the suicides in black and white. But here was the thing: patients attended Sunday service on the second floor on a weekly basis. Some patients joined for the free snacks or because they wanted to be part of the choir, but three out of five of the victims had been devoted Christians. Would all three of those believers who prayed to go to Heaven choose to end their lives in suicide and bar themselves from an afterlife? Believers who had nothing left *but* their faith?

Unless someone had whispered temptations of death into their ears. What if they were led to believe that death was the only way?

Suyeon freed Violette from the handcuffs.

'You're suddenly so sure I'm not your guy?' asked Violette.

Suyeon slipped the handcuffs into her back pocket without answering.

She hadn't been granted proper permission to link the different deaths into one case and carry out this investigation in the first place. She'd only whipped out the handcuffs to give Violette a scare, and buy time to think. She was still unconvinced that vampires were somehow involved. How could they be? But she'd found something else. A new possibility. That someone had been sweet-talking patients into killing themselves. Perhaps someone who had been lurking in close proximity for a very long time. In that case, Violette couldn't be the culprit. She didn't know about the lift that didn't work.

When Suyeon handed back her passport, Violette thanked her with a smile and put the document back into her coat pocket.

'Keep up your investigation,' said Violette, standing up from her seat, 'that way I can keep an eye out for you. They're ruthless beings, you know. Oh, and about not going to the crime scene? Sorry, but I can't promise you that. I have a job to do, too. I hope you won't get in my way.'

With that, Violette left the station.

NANJU

Armed with a messenger bag slung across her shoulder, Nanju entered the building, which was cloaked in tarp. The eight-storey dump was mere blocks from the hospital and comprised six floors of abandoned shops. Signs hung above the ground floor units like gravestones, marking what used to be a convenience store, noodle restaurant and fruit stall. In the corners, spider-webs bloomed. As Nanju walked towards the lift, her heels clicked across grout-lined tiles littered with insect remains.

The uppermost floors housed a goshiwon – cubicle-like rental rooms with a single bed crammed inside. Each window was blocked from the outside with a sheet of blackout film. A stench pervaded the building, but Nanju didn't flinch. With a stony expression, she pressed the lift button.

The lift arrived on the sixth floor silently, without so much as a *ding*. Its rigid doors slid open to reveal a dark corridor, lit only by the handful of bulbs that were still working. Up ahead, a green exit sign flickered.

The clatter of Nanju's shoes ripped through the silence. She walked down the corridor, where the rooms were arranged in a zigzag formation. On her right was room 101, and across from it was room 102. At the end of the corridor was a short walkway leading to the communal kitchen. There were twenty rooms in total, densely pressed together.

The toe of Nanju's shoe collided into something hard. A jjajangmyeon bowl that 104 had left out for collection. Tossing her bag on the floor, she squatted down and fished around for her cigarette pack. She was short on time, but also dying for a smoke. With one hard shake, she grabbed the last stick of cigarette with her lips and flung the empty box aside. The flint of her lighter clicked. A red flame flitted across her face. Crouching right in the middle of the corridor, Nanju took a long drag. Smoke swirled around the windowless alley.

'Fuck's sake.'

Nanju flicked off a bug that was cresting the cap of her shoe. She stomped on it until it was smeared into the ground. Though she had drummed up a ruckus, no one poked their head out to look. Once she'd exhausted the cigarette, she stamped out the butt and lifted the jjajangmyeon bowl. Tucked underneath it was a black plastic bag containing money. Three 50,000 won bills, Nanju counted. 150,000 won in total. She slipped the cash back.

From her bag, Nanju dug out a syringe and vial. Yanking off the cap with her mouth, she sank the needle into the vial. As she drew back the plunger, morphine rose up the length of the transparent cylinder. She threw the empty vial in her bag and banged on the door. This time, too, no curious neighbours came out to examine the noise. The doorknob turned with a creak. A hand, then an arm, poked out through the door's narrow opening. Without seeing her client's face, Nanju located the vein in his elbow and poked in the needle. A low groan followed. Once the shot was administered, Nanju promptly took care of the used needle.

'It'll be fifty-thousand more next time,' she said flatly.

'I… I can't afford that.'

'Then quit.'

'W-wait.'

Uninterested in a random person's sob story, Nanju turned to leave. But the client seized her arm and turned her around. The strap of Nanju's bag slipped off her shoulder and its contents came tumbling out. Without hesitation, Nanju brought down her fists on the man's skull. The first punch alone was enough to make the man lift his arms in surrender, but Nanju picked up her bag from the floor and swung it at him. The hefty bag crashed straight into the man's face, giving him a bloody nose. 'P-please! I'm so-sorry!' the man pleaded, but Nanju wasn't done. She delivered a few more blows to the man's head before she was satisfied.

'You think you can fuck with me just because I'm a woman?' Nanju seethed.

The man didn't answer.

'Fucking junkie.'

The shit I do for a pittance. Nanju scowled. Adjusting her bag, she left the building. The air outside bit her cheeks. She zipped her hoodie all the way up. This was the worst sort of weather. Despite all the winters she'd lived through, Nanju never got used to the cold.

When she arrived at the hospital, it was buzzing with tension.

'Where have you been?' Bohyun asked in an interrogating tone.

'Just out front.'

'Really. Just out front?'

'Yes.'

At Nanju's curt reply, Bohyun swallowed the words threatening to spill over. She huffed a sigh. A few hours ago, chaos had spread in the ward due to the incessant wailing of one single patient. Her crying had been so insufferable that even the quiet patients had snapped and kicked up a fuss. In the end, even the administration staff had to step in as backup to restore peace. Hearing all this, Nanju knew Bohyun must've wanted to tear her hair out, having to deal with the mess alone, but she couldn't be bothered to work up an apology.

The younger nurses never lasted more than three months in this hospital. Even the bright-eyed ones would start looking into getting a transfer after three weeks. Although the workload wasn't bad, the salary was much lower than at other hospitals because the area's council was so poorly funded. But more than anything, it was too dull a place to be. Nanju didn't mind the fact that her colleagues went as quickly as they came. In fact, she preferred it. The longer you spent with someone, the more you knew about them. Except for Bohyun, who was the exception that proved the rule: even though Bohyun had spent half a year working on the sixth-floor ward, she had never shown any interest in getting to know Nanju. Whenever Nanju left her shift for over an hour, Bohyun would show annoyance, but she never asked where she'd gone. From what Nanju heard, Bohyun would take advantage of her absence to ring up a friend or just do her own thing. Perhaps Bohyun appreciated Nanju's random disappearances.

'You've got some dirt on you,' Bohyun said, pointing at Nanju's shoulder.

It seemed the man's hand had been dirty, for there was a dark smudge in the rough shape of a handprint on her clothes. Reminded of the man's violence, Nanju frowned. Then she brushed off the dirt as if it was nothing.

VIOLETTE

January 1983

'Do you really have to go out today?' Maurice asked. Her father's eyes were tinged with disappointment – he'd assumed his Violette would stay at home and help prepare for the holiday.

Claire stepped in, elbowing her husband in the rib.

'Go – have fun,' she told Violette. Strewn around the kitchen were piles of ingredients waiting to be cooked, but Claire flashed a reassuring smile. Violette knew that her parents could whip up a galette des rois with their eyes closed – but also that her dad couldn't imagine spending the eve of l'Épiphanie with one of them not there. Trying not to think about any of this too deeply, Violette kissed them both on the cheek, pausing only to wrap up warm before she ran out the door. Maurice didn't stop her.

In her mind, Violette replayed her last encounter with the girl from the cinema. It had been confusing, to say the least. When she'd seen Violette, the girl had spun on her heels and simply strolled away, long black hair swaying gently in the wind. Either she'd come to look for Violette, or she'd been trying to avoid her and been discovered. Unsure which it was, Violette couldn't bring herself to follow her or call out to her. But she was certain now of two things: the girl was not a ghost. And she would be back. There was no basis for that last assumption, of course, it was just a gut feeling.

At the bus stop, Violette hugged her bag a little tighter. Inside was a lunchbox Maurice had prepared for her. As he had put it in her bag, he had told her that she could bring her friend home if the weather got too cold outside. The suggestion had been a last-ditch attempt to get her to stay. Not wanting to hurt his feelings further, Violette had said she would, knowing full well there was no chance.

While she waited for the bus, Violette daydreamed about taking the girl home. But holes kept poking through the clouds of her imagination. They appeared whenever she pictured a version of herself who was brave enough to extend an invitation, or the look on her parents' faces as they welcomed a friend of Violette's into their home for the first time.

It was difficult to picture in detail something she'd never experienced. It irked Violette to think that she couldn't do something as simple as letting her mind wander. *But first things first. If I ever invite her over, she should at least be wearing shoes, right?* As she boarded the bus, Violette thought about all the unworn shoes sitting in her closet.

As usual, the cinema was empty at opening time. The attendant, who never paid any attention to her, glanced her way for the first time. It seemed he was slowly becoming aware of the girl who came to the cinema every morning to read. If he started to recognise her, Violette suspected that she wouldn't be able to act so freely, and she wondered if she should stay away for a few days.

Working hard to maintain a nonchalant expression, Violette settled down in her usual seat. She took out the book she'd brought and wondered how long she'd have to wait until the girl showed up, if at all. Dreamily, Violette mused that she might arrive when the cinema was about to close, or not at all. Violette flipped open her book. This was going to be easy. Waiting was her forte. But thankfully, she didn't have to do much that day. It wasn't long before the girl came and sat down two seats away.

In her hand was a black umbrella. And like always, she was barefoot. The soles of her feet were speckled with dirt, but otherwise, they were spotless. *Is that black nail polish?* Violette had been so preoccupied with the girl's shoelessness that she was just now noticing her obsidian toenails. Violette slowly lifted her gaze. The girl wore a green sweater and ivory corduroy pants. She flopped a navy-blue coat over the seat, and her silky hair hung long and loose.

Violette stole glances at the empty space around the girl, only allowing herself one quick look at her face. Her skin was pale, her lips red. She had long eyelashes and a finely defined nose. The kind of face you read about in classic novels. It made Violette cringe to think this, but that was just how the girl looked. Like a word that's been overused a thousand times over, but is rarely true – beautiful. Violette averted her gaze. *Wonder what book she's reading. Looks like a vintage copy.*

As the screenings started, people streamed into the auditorium next to them. In what felt like just moments, it emptied again. The cycle continued, and at some point, as they both sat clutching their books, Violette realised: the girl had come to see *her*. She knew it intuitively. Violette's mother often told her, when laughing and describing the start of her own marriage to Maurice: some people are destined to meet, and they know right away.

Violette tried her best to calm the butterflies in her stomach. She crossed her legs to stop them from shaking and kept flipping back to the page where she'd started reading because not a single word had entered her mind. She *had* to talk to the girl. Maybe even share her lunch with her this time. Just as noon ticked by and Violette's stomach was starting to grumble, a shadow loomed above her.

Violette felt a pair of eyes on her. A dark blue cape and a patterned silver belt came into view. She raised her head. A police officer. He didn't look very old, but his hair was streaked with grey. Although thin, he looked strong and, above all, like he'd never been outrun by a thief. Standing at a distance behind the police officer was the attendant who had clocked her earlier. He'd probably called the police after figuring that a girl who came to the cinema to read every morning and a girl who never wore shoes might be up to no good. She tensed. Stooping, the police officer looked at the two girls, seated slightly apart from each other. His eyes were soft and kind, paired with an expression arranged to assure the girls that he was just here to help. But Violette's mind began to race – what if he took them to the police station? She couldn't care less about getting booked, but the thought of disappointment spreading on her parents' faces worried her. The police officer was sure to keep her until her guardians showed up, that is, until he could find someone who could guarantee that what Violette was telling him was the truth. In that case, Claire and Maurice would find out that Violette hadn't been going to the library to meet her friend, but simply going to the cinema in the hope that her friend would show up. They'd find out that she hadn't been honest with them, and worse, blame themselves for it. Violette scrambled to come up with a plan. But just as she was about to open her mouth and try to explain herself, she realised the girl was staring right at her. Their eyes locked and the girl moved her red lips soundlessly.

'Wait,' she mouthed.

The girl stood up from her seat, picked up her things, and walked past the police officer. When the surprised police officer tried to stop her, the girl shook him off and sprinted towards the exit. Now sensing that something was really wrong, the police officer gave chase.

Violette, who was left gawking, felt a breeze coming from the side, and saw that the door to the toilets was ajar. It must have happened right after the police officer had bolted after the girl. *Did someone open a window?* Violette kept a suspicious eye on the door. The moment she noticed a pair of naked feet by the door, Violette sprang up from her seat and stole away to the toilets.

Strange. The girl had just flown out of the cinema a few seconds ago, and now she was by the toilets. As soon as Violette entered, she saw her perched on the high window ledge, as if she'd been waiting for Violette this whole time.

The girl held out a hand towards her and Violette shook off the questions swarming in her mind. This was probably her only way out of the cinema. Violette took the girl's hand, and the girl pulled her up. Before Violette could even scream, she was hoisted into the air and her bottom was firmly planted on the narrow windowsill. Violette caught her breath before mustering up the courage to look outside. She saw an alley around the back of the building. Their way out.

Somehow, waiting outside on the ground beside the staff-only door, was the girl. Violette's chest squeezed at the sight of the distance between them. Although the sky was clear, the girl had opened her black umbrella, its thin shaft balanced on the crook of her shoulder. She held out both arms towards Violette.

'I'll catch you.'

No freaking way! Violette almost shouted. But behind her, she heard a man's authoritative voice. The policeman was shouting, asking people if they'd seen her.

Violette knew she had to act fast. The girl stood, unmoving, her hands outstretched like the branches of a sturdy tree. *Will she catch me? Impossible. She might get hurt. So would I.*

But Violette's worries were quickly silenced. There was a knock on the door, and the police officer announced he was coming in. Violette clenched her teeth and jumped.

As if she was leaping away from a burning fire. Or maybe, straight *into* one.

Her eyes squeezed shut, Violette didn't see how the girl caught her. Or the expression on her face when she did. All she felt was the girl's grip on her waist, which remained firm until Violette's feet were steady on the ground.

They zipped across the empty car park. Violette suddenly remembered that she'd left her bag in the theatre, but it was too late to go back now.

'Lily.' The girl introduced herself, not out of breath despite their pace.

'We're the same age,' she said calmly, while pulling them both along.

Violette wondered how Lily had known how old she was.

Rounding a corner, they slowed their run and, as she gasped for air, Violette noticed Lily was rather tall for a sixteen-year-old. Lily stood at least seven centimetres taller than Violette, and she didn't slouch like most teenagers did. But Violette forced down her suspicions. Even if Lily were lying, Violette was willing to let herself be fooled. At least for now. Violette asked whether or not Lily's feet were cold. Lily wriggled her snow-covered toes.

'Perfectly fine. No worries.' She beamed.

The truth was, Violette wanted to ask *why* she wasn't wearing shoes.

She had assumed Lily would give her an answer if she'd asked in a roundabout way, but Lily had answered with a real full stop. *Maybe it's not my place to ask. Maybe she doesn't like talking about it. At least her feet aren't cold...* With the latter thought, Violette was content.

The pair strolled down the narrow path, tracing the edge of the wheat fields as they made their way towards Violette's home. Her shoeless companion held her umbrella aloft against a grey but rainless sky. It was Violette's preferred route home, the one that made her feel like she was roaming the same pastures as la Princesse in *Peau d'Âne*, a perennial movie favourite. A large cypress tree stood at one end of the field.

When at last the sun sank, Lily folded her umbrella. It occurred to Violette that this was the first time she had walked down this path with someone else, and the thought made her heart thrum. She strolled along slowly, letting her footsteps linger, already sad that this walk must come to an end. Her house came into view, and regret rose in her. She wished she could invite Lily over, but as much as her parents would love to meet her new friend, perhaps Lily's eccentric choice in footwear – or lack thereof – would stir up concern rather than excitement.

When Violette came to a stop, Lily did the same. Lily traced Violette's gaze and took a step back.

'I guess you'll be heading home now?' Violette asked.

Lily nodded.

'Where do you live?'

Lily pointed northwest, towards Pieffe. It was a small town, forty minutes away by car, a two-hour walk through the forest. And they had their own cinema. Could it be that Lily had come all this way to see her? Violette wanted to ask, but shyness prevented her.

'We can't go back to the cinema tomorrow. The attendant will probably recognise us,' said Violette, instantly wishing that she'd been more forthright.

Please read between the lines this time, she pleaded inwardly.

Thankfully, Lily did.

'Let's meet here then. Under this tree, when the sun sets.'

'Tomorrow?'

'Yeah. OK. At night then?'

'Sure.'

Violette wanted to ask why it had to be after sunset, but instead held fast to her impatient heart.

As the distance between them and the house grew smaller, the two said their goodbyes. For a long while, Violette watched as Lily shrank into the darkening distance, swinging her umbrella.

Claire and Maurice didn't scold Violette for her carelessness over losing the bag. Instead, they consoled her, clearly worried that she might beat herself up about it. Their gentleness tugged on Violette's conscience, since she felt more than fine.

Her parents brought out the cake that they'd baked that day. Steam swirled above the leaf-patterned surface. 'Go ahead, pick a slice,' they coaxed.

Traditionally, the cake was to be eaten the next morning, but they seemed to hope that a sweet treat would cheer their daughter up.

After a moment's deliberation, Violette relented. With the fork Claire had handed her, she cut a square of cake topped with almond cream and apple compote and took a big bite.

Out of the four slices, one always held a little ceramic fève. Every year on Épiphanie morning, the three of them would pick out a slice of cake, put it onto their plates, and bet on who'd be the lucky one to find the trinket. Whoever did would get to be king for a day and make a wish.

With her mouth full, Violette studied the surface of her slice. She discerned a slight bump. Smiling, she fished it out with her fingers. It was the size of her thumb – a ceramic angel.

'Lucky you!' Claire rejoiced.

Angel... Luck... As Violette chewed over the words, she thought of Lily.

That night, Violette lay in bed stroking the freshly-cleaned angel. The moon was exceptionally bright. Without curtains in its way, its light poured into the room, drenching every corner. Violette pulled the blanket over her head and pressed her eyes shut. She thought about seeing Lily tomorrow, and pictured them together under the cypress tree. She didn't worry if Lily would show up. She knew she would.

The next day Violette wondered about bringing Lily a pair of shoes, but left the house empty-handed. She ran down the dark path. Lily was already waiting under the cypress tree, wearing a dark coat and a pair of black leather boots, looking as she had the day before: awfully beautiful.

SUYEON

'Out with it,' said Chantae, as if he'd read Suyeon's mind.

The knot in Suyeon's chest loosened. She cleared her throat sheepishly.

'I'm all done for today. May I be excused early?'

Chantae glanced at his watch. Thirty minutes until the end of their shift. There was no reason to keep Suyeon at work if she'd completed the day's tasks, but Chantae knew better than anyone that she was the type to find something to do even if there was less than a minute left on the clock. In other words, she must be running off to dig for clues again. Sensing the incoming questions, Suyeon cut in.

'I'm not asking for a warrant. I'm just going to take a look. I mean, it is an open case, so, you know… might as well.'

Chantae heaved a sigh of resignation. 'Do you think I'm the kind of detective who doesn't give a shit? I've just been through this enough times. Trust me, you'll only wear yourself out.'

'Can I go if I promise not to wear myself out?'

'Why bother asking when you're going to go regardless. But if we get a back-up request from Bucheon you better get your ass there right away. Understood?'

Suyeon was quiet.

'Understood?' Chantae repeated.

Suyeon nodded.

'Whatever. Go.'

Suyeon bowed and sprang out of the office, dashing straight to the car park before Chantae could change his mind.

When the hospital came into view, the first drops of rain splattered on her windshield. On the ground floor, the hospital administrator was slumped over her desk, using the computer as a cover for her nap. At the sound of Suyeon's knuckles rapping on the counter, she stirred, lifting her face to reveal half-shut eyes riddled with exhaustion. Once she recognised Suyeon as the detective from the last few weeks, she sat up straight, rubbing eyes and asking if something had happened *again*. Her face was pure irritation – no fear or worry.

Suyeon's face hardened. 'I need a list of existing patients and members of staff.'

The administrator's face crumpled.

'What for?' she asked, her tone clipped.

'I'm writing up a report on the case and need to confirm a few details. The number of staff members and patients, for instance…'

‘Give me a minute,’ the administrator nodded without even pretending to listen to Suyeon’s made-up explanation. She went over to a second computer and started typing. Suyeon let out a soft sigh of relief.

‘I’m sure you can write your report without that.’

It was Violette, who had appeared without so much as a squeak. Crossing her arms and resting them on the desk, she whispered loud enough only for Suyeon to hear. ‘But since you’ve asked for it, may I suggest you pay attention to those who work nights?’

‘May I suggest you stay out of this?’ Suyeon countered.

After receiving the roster from the administrator, Suyeon left the reception area. The clicking of Violette’s heels trailed behind her. When she made it out of the building, the sudden quiet made her turn around. Violette was no longer behind her. Instead, she was metres in front, standing right where one of the victims had fallen, studying the building’s exterior. Feeling Suyeon’s eyes on her, she spoke.

‘Do you also wonder if, in the moment before they died, they looked up to see where they had fallen from?’

Violette approached the wall. She reached for the long water pipe that ran up to the rooftop and gave it a hard shake. Then she turned to Suyeon. ‘If only we could see the roof.’

Suyeon thought about asking why, but instead gestured for Violette to follow her.

The administrator handed the keys to the roof to Suyeon without saying much this time, only requesting that Suyeon be sure to lock the door before leaving.

Violette was somehow already in the foyer, pressing the same lift button as last time. Suyeon walked over to the other lift and pressed the button.

'That one's always off. They only switch it on during meal times.'

The rooftop was closed off by a gated door. A heap of cardboard boxes lay beside the entrance. As she inserted the key into the lock, Suyeon pretended they weren't there, hoping not to encourage anymore unauthorised snooping, but Violette lifted the flaps of one of the boxes. It contained medical-grade tools for restraint – from mouth gags to ropes. Suyeon's eyes snapped back to the door.

When the stiff hinges finally budged, Suyeon called Violette over, but the woman was focused on the box's contents.

Suyeon cleared her throat and explained, 'They're used when the patients have to be transferred to a different ward. It's to prevent them from hurting themselves.'

The hospital was composed of eight floors. The administrative office and consultation rooms were on the ground floor, the kitchen was on the first floor, and the rehabilitation and exercise room were on the second floor. On the same level there was also a multi-purpose room where the Sunday service and daily classes were held. The remaining floors were wards, divided into two units. The third to sixth floors were rehabilitation wards that housed patients with dementia or those who required physical rehabilitation, and the two uppermost floors were psychiatric wards for patients struggling with mental health issues and alcohol addiction. Entrance to the latter was restricted and lift access was only permitted to those with a key card. With even the emergency stairs blocked, the psychiatric wards were practically entirely separate from the rest of the hospital.

Even after Suyeon's explanation, Violette still couldn't seem to pry her eyes away.

Does she feel sorry for the patients?

Suyeon wondered if she should've added they were used as a last resort.

But then Violette picked up a mouth gag. Her eyes shone as if she were a soldier who'd been reunited with her lost sword on the battlefield. The way she regarded something that was used to restrain people with so much affection made Suyeon frown.

'I've used a couple of these babies myself. They're not so different from what I use to catch vampires.'

Suyeon stepped onto the roof without another word.

The rooftop was spotless and still. No sign of any recent visitors. A security camera was installed in one corner, but its indicator light was off. The rain had stopped, but the concrete floor was still dark with moisture. Any hope of finding a few footprints would've been ruined by the bad weather. It was Suyeon's first time on the roof. There'd been no need to inspect an area that was inaccessible to victims without a key.

Violette strode up to the railing on the edge of the roof, which was surrounded by a barbed-wire fence. It measured up to Violette's shoulder. Suyeon considered the scene. Using Violette's height – 1.65 metres, give or take – as a point of comparison, the structure was flawless in serving its duty of preventing accidental falls. Violette reached a hand through to the fence. Immediately, Suyeon called her back.

'Stop. You'll get hurt.'

Ignoring her warning, Violette touched her index finger to the barbed wire and swiped. Before Suyeon could stop her, she put her finger in her mouth. Suyeon seized Violette's arm.

'What the hell are you doing?'

Violette savoured the taste on the tip of her tongue.

'Here. This was where they fell from, not the ward,' said Violette. 'Since the doors are always locked, we're looking at two possibilities. Either a vampire climbed up the water pipes to the roof, carrying their victim in one arm, or someone let them up here by opening the door for them. Vampires are skilled enough to scale up a wall without help, but it might be a challenge with only one available arm.'

Squatting down, Violette tapped the floor.

‘I’m certain this was where they fell from. See how the cement is cracked around here? Could’ve been caused by someone with tremendous strength in their step.’

Violette stood up, dusting off her hands.

‘There’s blood here. I’m not sure how useful it’ll be as evidence now.’

It was too dark to see. Suyeon turned on the torch on her phone. Her eyes scanned for any barbed wire dipped in crimson. And there it was – a metal thorn pointing skyward, coloured by a drop of red that had slid down its length, leading to a blackened stain on the concrete ground, sheltered a little by the tangle of wires above. *Blood?* Forensics would be able to answer that. If the results came in positive, Suyeon would be able to get a warrant. The problem was, a confirmatory test for blood alone wasn’t enough to turn the suicides into a homicide case. In fact, it might be taken as further proof that the victims had willingly climbed onto the railing and thrown themselves off.

The administrator had said there were only two keys. One that was kept in the office, and one held by the security guard. But if a member of staff were to ask for the key, they could borrow it to go out for a smoke without going through any security procedures.

When Suyeon walked out of the hospital a while later, she found Violette with a cigarette in between her lips, fishing around in her pocket for her lighter.

Suyeon swiftly plucked the cigarette from Violette's mouth and thrust it back into her palm.

'No smoking allowed in front of the hospital.'

'All the patients smoke here,' Violette argued.

'You're not a patient. They're permitted to smoke here because the nurses don't want them running off by themselves,' Suyeon chided.

Violette slipped the cigarette back into her pocket. Without saying goodbye, Suyeon got into her car. After a pause, Violette climbed into her own car, a dark sedan, and left the carpark.

Suyeon pulled out and followed. Violette kept to the main roads. Perhaps it made sense to stay away from small dark roads at such a late hour, but something told Suyeon that her target was altering the route and speed purely for her sake – so that she could keep up.

Since their conversation at the station, Suyeon had typed Violette's name into a search engine and found some of the articles that she had translated. Still, suspicion lingered. This was Suyeon's chance to see if the facts lined up: was Violette who she claimed to be or had she stolen someone's identity? Was the address she'd given properly registered?

The place where Violette ended up wasn't a residence, but a Western bar tucked away from the chaotic, neon-lit streets of Incheon Chinatown, not too far from Violette's supposed home address.

Once Violette's indicator blinked on, Suyeon slowed her car down. The dark sedan pulled over in a narrow alley opposite the pub. Some distance away, Suyeon also braked and switched off her engine. A patchy neon sign gave the bar's name, 1446. It was a tiny establishment that would fit no more than ten people on a busy day.

Suyeon got out of the car and circled the building on foot, taking in its dated architecture. Once she reached the other side of the building, Suyeon walked up to the bar's back door. Seeing the yellow bags of food waste lying beside the bins, Suyeon concluded that this was where the employees came and went. Luckily for her, the alley near the back door was blocked by a wall, and Suyeon was spared the hassle of surveying that area. She returned to her car.

Midnight crept past. Suyeon leaned her forehead against the steering wheel for a while. Exhaustion was catching up with her. Since this stakeout wasn't part of an official investigation, she'd be expected to return to work on time the next day. Before she could give in to the temptation of shutting her eyes, Suyeon scrubbed her face. She picked at the stack of papers lying on the passenger seat.

The roster that the administrator had printed out for her sat right on top of the stack. She'd stumbled upon something from earlier interviews. The nurses in this hospital followed a schedule split into mornings, afternoons and nights. There were no overlaps in shifts – the morning shift ended when the afternoon shift began, and the afternoon shift ended when the night shift began.

Each person could only work up to three night shifts in a week. If a nurse worked a night shift, she'd be given the next afternoon shift, or a day off. There was one exception – Seo Nanju, the nurse in charge of the sixth floor. She was the only one who had regular days off, on Sundays and Mondays. For the rest of the week, she worked night shifts exclusively.

Suyeon's mind was swimming when the door to the bar swung open. Violette stepped out, buttoning up her coat. Forty minutes had passed. Suyeon threw the papers back onto the seat and got out of the car. Violette's place wasn't too far away from here, and since the roads were narrow, it was safer to follow her on foot.

The location matched the address Violette had provided. It was a five-storey building comprised of neat studio flats, and Violette lived in apartment 402. Suyeon loitered for about an hour, but when it seemed like Violette wouldn't be coming out again, she left.

Suyeon retraced her steps back to the bar.

She had to make sure that the bar was real and not a front. Suyeon stared apprehensively at the glowing pink numbers before pushing open the door.

Inside, all the lights were off. Only a few candles prevented the room from being swallowed by darkness. Just as she had guessed, the place was tiny. There was a long bar table furnished with five stools on which customers could sit facing the bartender. Other than that, there were only two small tables, each accompanied by two chairs.

No music played, and no one came to greet her. Suyeon hung around by the entrance, wondering if they'd closed shop for the day. Her eyes drifted to the end of the alcohol shelf, where a sliver of light was peeking through a pair of dark curtains. She heard the faint gush of water. A running tap, she supposed. Before long, a woman stepped through the curtains, drying her hands.

NANJU

When Nanju heard that his stubborn life had finally ended, she pursed her lips to keep them from blossoming into a smile.

But who would call her out anyway? Unless they'd gone through what she had, no one had the right – and anyone who'd shared her experience would understand her joy.

Her footsteps felt lighter than usual. By the time she entered the hospital, she'd lost count of how many times she'd clapped her hands on her cheeks to stop her smile from spreading. Instead of taking her usual route to the wards, she headed for the hospital funeral home. Nanju could barely tell if she was walking down the stairs leading to the morgue or frolicking in clouds.

Her mother was already waiting. She looked gaunt, but Nanju could tell that a weight had been lifted from her shoulders. Following the instructions of a staff member, Nanju took her place beside her father, who had fallen into an eternal sleep. The white sheet covering him looked so lovely. She reached for it, feeling its silkiness on her fingertips.

When her father was still alive, she'd done everything in her power to avoid the sight of his face, but this time, she decided, she would be patient, and try to look at him through the eyes of her younger self.

But as soon as she lifted the cloth to look at his face, Nanju stumbled back with a yelp. The man's face looked as if it had been buffed against a grater. His nape, utterly maimed, dangled on a precocious tendon. This wasn't the death she'd imagined for him. Even though he'd been the bane of her existence, she'd wished him a peaceful death. But the corpse before her was no different from a broken cockroach, smeared into concrete.

Before she could fall backwards, a cold hand steadied her. She forced her quivering eyes to look. A black fingernail pierced through her skin.

Nanju shot up from her nightmare. She rummaged through the drawer for her pills and gulped them down. She pressed the flat of her palms against her cheeks, desperate to erase the searing sensation on her cheek. Strands of loose hair clung to her damp forehead. Her fears were rapidly manifesting into dreams. They took different forms, none of which Nanju saw coming. Relentless, they flaunted their presence, as if telling her that there was no escape, that they were here to stay, and that they would one day become reality.

Nanju strained to recall how her father had looked on his deathbed. His eyes had been closed peacefully, his face stiff. He had looked flawless.

Nanju threw on a thick jacket and stepped out of the house. It was her day off, but she couldn't stand being inside for a second longer.

She headed to the izakaya that she'd recently discovered. It was a small establishment on a dirty street cramped with old bars and fried-chicken restaurants – a newfound haven. They served amazing anju, but what she liked most was how cosy it was. There was no better place to be by herself for a little while.

Although it was a weekday night, the inn was crowded. An employee swiftly led her to a seat by the bar. It was a spot where customers could chit-chat with the chef while they watched him slice sashimi, perfect for those who considered themselves connoisseurs of raw fish. When she had first come, months ago, Nanju had sat by the bar simply because the other seats weren't available. But since then, the waiter, who recognised her by now, always showed her to the same seat.

The chef ran his slender sashimi knife across the belly of a tuna. Recognising Nanju, he nodded at her. She returned his greeting with a slight bow.

'Got the day off?'

'Yes.'

'You should try the tuna today. It's very fresh. I'll cut you a good chunk.'

'Sure.'

Nanju added a glass of beer to her order. A portion of red tuna belly, sliced delicately, was served to her on a wooden board, complimented by rakkyo, pickled ginger and radish sprouts. Nanju poured soy sauce into a saucer and scooped out a small dollop of wasabi. As he watched her, the chef asked how she'd been.

The man was obviously hitting on her. At first, Nanju had thought him friendly, but once he started to bombard her with facts about himself, she realised he didn't give a shit about her. All he cared about was painting a pretty picture of himself. Nanju pretended not to notice. She couldn't care less about obliging him with a reaction.

'You don't look so great these days. I get it though, with everything that's happening. I know it doesn't look like it, but our business has been going down the drain. People just don't want to go out at night anymore.'

Nanju stared at the chef, mouth full, with no idea what he was getting at.

'You haven't heard? Another missing-person report was just filed in Bucheon. The sixth in five days.'

He lowered his voice, enjoying the horror of the story he was about to tell. Nanju set down her chopsticks with a darkening expression.

'You live around here, right? Don't go wandering around at night. If you want, I can walk you...'

'Bill, please.'

Nanju stood up, leaving more than half of her meal untouched. She'd lost her appetite. Flustered, the chef brought her the bill. But when Nanju turned to leave, he grabbed her arm. Nanju slapped his hand away and shot him a daggered look. Ignoring the sting, the chef forced a laugh.

'You haven't finished your food.'

'I have to go.'

'At least let me see you out,' said the chef, untying his apron and making a start for the door.

'Go fuck yourself,' spat Nanju.

Pushing past the dumbstruck chef, Nanju left the izakaya.

The chef had made the wise decision to stay inside and let her be. *What a shame*, thought Nanju. She'd been looking forward to becoming a regular.

As Nanju walked briskly home, she scoffed, recalling what the chef had said. *Does he think he's special? That he can protect me just because he's a man?* Nanju almost felt bad for him. His head was so far up his own arse.

Midnight inched closer. As Nanju walked with her arms crossed, the missing person case occupying her mind, she suddenly noticed the dreadful silence. She stopped in the middle of the empty street. No longer interrupted by the tapping of her heels, the world descended into stillness. Although she sensed no one behind her, Nanju turned around. Not a single shadow on the ground.

Relieved, Nanju turned back, only to find a large figure standing before her. Her breath caught in her chest. But soon enough, she wiped the shock from her face and sauntered towards the figure. They walked together, side by side.

'A lot has happened in Bucheon.'

Her companion remained quiet.

'It's not you, right?' Nanju asked.

'Of course not.'

Although she had heard the answer she wanted, Nanju's heart teetered like a leaf floating on water. She didn't press further for the truth. There was no reason for him to lie. Even if he did, there was nothing she could do about it. She walked on without another word.

They came to a stop before her building. It seemed her partner had no intention of following her in.

'A detective's starting to get suspicious. Although we've done everything perfectly,' he said as he fixed her collar.

'It's just their job to poke holes in everything, even when there's nothing,' replied Nanju in a tone no different from usual. Yet her eyes kept travelling down her companion's coat sleeve. She felt the weight of his gaze on her.

'She's not working alone.'

'Well, they usually work in pairs.'

'Still…' he trailed off.

Nanju raised her head. He'd never once left a sentence incomplete. Her companion pressed his lips together and paused thoughtfully before deciding to leave it. From his silence, Nanju sensed his doubt.

Before sending her on her way, the man caressed her hair. 'You've had a lot on your mind today,' he said, a note of worry in his voice. 'Sleep well.'

His concern was a gift-wrapped threat, another way of saying he knew she was dabbling in useless thoughts. When Nanju got home, she stood in front of her window. She could still see him, taking his time to walk away. Although he'd just made it clear that he was keeping tabs on her, Nanju knew that *he* was the suspicious one. As she watched him disappear into the distance, she picked at her nails.

VIOLETTE

February 1983

Lily had threaded a string through the fève and made a necklace of it. Violette had given it to her as a gift five days before. Since the string was long, Lily could hide the little angel easily by tucking it into her collar. I have something to show you, she said, pulling it out of her sweater, looking like she had made the catch of the day.

The sight reminded Violette of last summer. On a trip to the riverside, she and Maurice had watched a fisherman bring in his catch. The man's face had been rosy with happiness as he admired the golden-scaled fish dangling from his hook. Violette smiled. She could finally let go of the worry that Lily had chucked the gift onto the street on her way home after receiving it.

'It was tricky to make, since I had to do it in secret,' Lily said.

'How come you had to do it in secret?' Violette asked, looking down at the angel sitting in Lily's palm. Lily had pierced a hole through one of the angel's tiny wings.

Judging by the number of chips, putting a hole through the ceramic trinket must've been difficult. Violette liked the imperfections. She imagined Lily holding down the fève, deep in concentration.

'Let's just say my family and angels are not on speaking terms.'

Her answer made Violette burst out laughing. Lily laughed too, though unsure why. The pair could barely keep themselves from tumbling over.

At sunset, Violette always found Lily by the cypress tree.

Sometimes she was by the foot of the tree, sometimes perched on the lowest branch. There were times when she was balanced on its crown. *How on earth did she get up there?* Violette would wonder as she called out her name. But whether she was by the foot of the tree, perched on the lowest branch, or sitting on its crown, her frosty face was always looking into the distance. Until Violette called out to her, at which point she would smile.

There was a world of difference between her resting and smiling face. When she wasn't smiling, she looked like a statue carved from ice, and when she was, she looked like a painting that captured the light of spring. Both expressions were lovely to Violette, but if she had to pick, it would be the latter.

When Lily smiled, Violette didn't know what to do with herself. She wished she could stare at Lily as her lips curved and her eyes bent into crescents, but she could never manage to hold the girl's gaze, and always looked away.

With no better place to go, the two always spent their time under the branches of the looming cypress. Their clothes and scarves shielded them from the wind, but it was still freezing.

After weeks of cold evening outings, Violette developed a harsh cough. Maurice insisted his daughter's excursions were giving her the flu. He began to make her a hot cup of lemon tea every morning. Despite her father's worries, Violette left the house at sunset every day without fail. Still, she knew it was his lemon tea that held the flu at bay.

Violette still knew nothing about Lily. All she had gleaned so far was that she lived in the vicinity of Pieffe with a strict and eccentric family.

Even so, Violette was constantly occupied with thoughts of Lily. Sometimes, after spending too long daydreaming about her, Violette's mind would jolt with realisations. One of them, for instance, was the question of why they only met in the evenings. She wanted to ask Lily about this, but it was clear that Lily didn't want to talk about it. She would've already brought it up otherwise. And so, Violette was left to come up with her own theories. Maybe Lily was working a part-time job. Maybe her family had a farm and she needed to help. Or maybe she had so many siblings that she had to hold the fort until they all went to bed or until her parents came home. The mystery was all just more fodder for Violette's daydreams about her mysterious new friend.

Although she didn't talk about herself, Lily knew so much about the world. She knew far more than Claire and Maurice, especially when it came to old legends or history. Violette couldn't even begin to guess how much history Lily had heard and read. Not only was she familiar with French history, but also the wars and histories of Eastern Europe, Africa, the Americas and Asia. *Perhaps she studies so she always has a story ready to tell her siblings.*

Under the light of the moon, Lily would begin recounting stories in her low, velvety voice, and Violette wished she would go on forever. She longed to listen to her until the sun came up, but the night frightened her. She worried about making her parents wait up for her, and about Lily walking the long road home alone at night.

***

Early one evening, while sitting at the foot of their tree with the fève in her hand, Lily began speaking to Violette about angels. Weaving in history and legend, she spoke about their duplicity, about those the angels abandoned, and all the times they made fools out of the very people they were supposed to protect. In her soft voice, Lily spoke of the way angels took advantage of people's desperation, and how they never hesitated to crush someone's last glimmer of hope. She said that if angels were truly good, they would stop people *before* they made mistakes, before they turned evil and before they indulged in self-interest. It was the kind of talk that would make her mum fly off the handle. Claire had raised Violette to go to church on Sundays and wear a gold cross around her neck, but Violette wasn't fazed. She nodded along, as if to say, *You could be right*.

The truth was, she was more focused on the timbre and grace of Lily's voice than any of the words being spoken.

Violette checked her watch. It was past ten. She stood up, her legs stiff from the cold.

The littlest things eventually turn into affection. When these things become impossible to count, when they become impossible to pinpoint, that's when people find themselves saying 'just because'. This was how Claire described her love for Violette. It had started with the very first look at Violette's picture, sent all the way from abroad, and she had fallen in love.

Violette had always found the love her mother described hard to believe. While she never doubted Claire's intentions, she didn't believe Claire's words. She simply thought that Claire was trying to make her feel better. After all, how could someone love a person they didn't know?

She believed her mum now.

In the short hours they spent together every night, she and Lily talked about everything and nothing at all. There was nothing she enjoyed more – and for the first time in her life, she opened up about herself completely.

Just as her parents had fallen in love as soon as they saw her picture from the adoption agency, Violette knew when she laid eyes on Lily that she wanted this person to have a special place in her life.

And there were so many reasons why. So many, in fact, that they snowballed into a rush that she couldn't put into words.

Falling for someone was easy, Claire would say, but to have someone love you back – that was rare. When Claire and Maurice had flown Violette all the way across the globe from Korea, they had felt guilty and a little afraid: the birth and adoption of a child were actions involving solely the adults. There was no guarantee that the baby girl they'd fallen in love with would grow up to feel the same way as them. Thankfully, Violette did.

When Lily had sat down next to her to read that second time in the cinema, Violette had guessed somehow that Lily might have feelings for her, too. But she'd never been as certain as she was now: when Lily took her hand; when, before they parted, Lily's eyes would beg her to stay another minute; when Violette's heart trilled.

After weeks of meeting under their tree, Violette finally gathered the courage to ask Lily if she'd like to come home with her – and thrillingly, the ethereal girl said yes.

Violette was chattier than usual on the way home. It wasn't just because she was bringing a friend home for the first time. Her heart swelled because it was *Lily* whom she was bringing home. 'My parents are coming home at midnight.'

Lily assured her that she'd be gone before midnight.

Violette hadn't mentioned her parents because she was worried about them. She'd meant to ask if Lily would like to meet them. But before she could clarify, Lily spoke.

'You're cold,' she said gently. 'I should've realised.'

Violette wanted to deny it, fearing Lily would insist they stop meeting until the weather turned warmer. Instead, she kept quiet as Lily wrapped her hands around her icy fists. No warmth ever emanated from Lily's grip. No matter how long she held it. Even so, the girls held hands all the way to Violette's house.

Violette was embarrassed to show Lily her room. Seeing it through her friend's eyes, it was lacklustre, with barely anything interesting to look at. Her decade-old wardrobe, desk and bed were covered in scuff marks. Her chair was nowhere to be seen, buried under a heap of dirty laundry. A little shy at the state of her room, Violette asked Lily to give her five minutes to tidy. But Lily had no complaints. She pushed past Violette and threw the door open.

'Cute and cosy,' she noted, wandering into the room as if it were her own.

Observing that the chair was taken, she plopped herself down on the edge of the bed. Rendered a stranger in her own room, Violette inched inside cautiously and sat down next to Lily. Their hips brushed.

Violette cleared her throat. 'Is your room very different?'

'A little bigger,' Lily answered vaguely.

Lily's answer stumped her. Violette's was the biggest room on the first floor. She used to have a piano in here, and at some other point, a basketball hoop.

'What's that?' asked Lily, pointing suddenly.

'Hm?'

'On the wall.'

Violette traced her gaze along Lily's finger, which was pointing to a wall full of pencil marks charting Violette's growth. Every year on the first of January, her height was measured against the wall. Five-year-old Violette was unbelievably tiny, and a palm separated the distance between her ten and eleven-year-old self. That was the time when Violette had started taking an interest in basketball.

'My height.'

'How often do you measure it?'

'Once a year.'

'You've been growing pretty steadily. I bet you'll be taller next year.'

'Who knows? Maybe I will, maybe I won't.'

Thinking hard for a moment, Lily grabbed Violette's hand and sprang up from the bed.

'Let's see about that.'

'Right now? I just measured my height… on the first day of the new year.'

'You never know. You could've grown in the meantime.'

Violette was taken aback by the request, but it wasn't one she couldn't grant. She stood before the wall and touched her heel, bottom, shoulders and head to it. As she raised her hand to mark the top of her head, Lily drew closer. Violette swallowed. Mere centimetres away, Lily checked her height. Violette's eyes shied away from Lily's neck, her chin, her lips.

'Huh, you're right. Still the same,' Lily declared.

Violette felt her forehead tingle, ticklish from the brush of Lily's breath when she spoke.

'Yup, still the same!' Violette tittered as her awkward fingers stroked her forehead. Emotions, unfamiliar and conflicting, criss-crossed and tangled whenever she was with Lily. So used to being by herself, Violette was at a loss. She didn't know how to act, always stumbling or stuttering, worried she looked like a fool. Just as Violette pushed Lily away gently, suggesting that they do something fun next, the front door clicked open.

Midnight was still an hour away.

Violette went to check the kitchen. It was Maurice, home earlier than usual.

He took out a bottle of wine from the kitchen cupboard. He loved wine, but rarely drank. It had been a few years since his doctor advised him to cut out alcohol. Since then, he only drank on special occasions, and even then, he'd just allow himself a single glass. He usually stuck to that rule at all costs, but right now, he drank as if he no longer cared.

Violette couldn't take her eyes off her father, who was sipping glass after glass of wine alone under the glow of the kitchen light.

She stepped into the room and joined him at the table. Maurice's head snapped up and he smiled at her. A sad smile. Violette asked if something had happened. It was so unlike him to drink in the kitchen when he knew she was home. For a while, Maurice's lips remained still. He fiddled with his cup, lowered his head and ran his palm over his face, as if he were secretly wiping away tears. Violette discerned the hesitation in his eyes. Maybe he thought his daughter needed to know the truth. At last he spoke.

'Arthur is dead.'

A gasp slipped from Violette's lips before she could press them together. Arthur was Maurice's friend. They'd known each other more than thirty years. Arthur had been there for over half of Maurice's life. And so he'd been part of Violette's life as well. He was in the photograph of Violette's first Christmas, he was there when she celebrated her first birthday, and when Violette used roller skates for the first time.

A bachelor, Arthur ran a petrol station, and lived with a golden retriever named Berry. Arthur had a heart disease that he dutifully took medication for. Although he loved children, he had none of his own, and instead had wound up being a parental figure to Violette.

As Violette had grown up, she had spent less and less time with Arthur, but never stopped considering him a dear uncle.

Violette wanted to say something to comfort her dad, but sadness and shock had stolen all her words. In the meantime, Maurice had emptied his glass of wine and was going for a refill. Violette couldn't bring herself to stop him.

Quiet moments passed before Violette asked how Arthur had died. She hoped that her father's friend had at least been granted a peaceful death. Tipsy, Maurice cupped his chin and blew out a sigh.

Claire would've stopped him drinking by now. But she wasn't back yet.

'He was murdered. Someone came looking for him. I don't know much. Nothing was stolen, so the police think it was someone getting revenge. But who could dislike Arthur? Who could hold a grudge against a guy like him? He was the town's handyman, for goodness' sake. He was the first person people looked for whenever they needed a hand. But it's hard out there now. People are desperate, resentful – it makes monsters out of people.'

Violette's heart dipped. It was hard to believe such a thing could happen in this tiny neighbourhood. Violette didn't want to believe it.

Maurice looked at her and suddenly seemed to see her for the first time. He cleared his throat.

'Sometimes the reason behind a person's death can be more shocking than their death itself. That's how I feel right now. None of this makes sense. I'm so angry. But I'm also just… so sad.'

Violette watched her dad.

'Maybe I'd feel better if it was a monster who'd killed him.'

'Monster?'

'It's easier to blame the things you don't want to accept on monsters. Your grandfather used to tell me that. He had quite the imagination, that one. He would always tell me how he'd met a vampire when he was a kid. Whenever someone went missing, or died, or had a breakdown, he'd say that a *vampire* did it.'

Maurice ended his slurred spiel with a chuckle.

Violette couldn't laugh. But suddenly she was reminded of her friend, alone in her room.

Lily!

When Violette returned to her room, she was surprised to find Lily gone. She spun around before she heard a voice telling her to look out the window. Lily was already in the garden, looking up at Violette as she waved goodbye. Violette didn't have to ask how she'd got down there. Other than the front door, past her father, the only way out was the window.

The following week, Violette, Claire and Maurice, all dressed in black, attended Arthur's funeral at the local church. He lay in an open coffin. Beneath his sleeping face was a cluster of flowers.

‘What’s with the flowers?’

‘It’s to cover his neck. I heard it was terribly maimed.’

The mourners’ whispers were hard to ignore.

Berry the dog had been quietly ushered into the funeral and lay at Violette’s feet. As Violette stroked her soft head, she thought about monsters and friendships and Lily.

The next time she saw Lily, Violette told her about Arthur’s death and her strange conversation with Maurice. She expected Lily to console her, to scoff at her father’s use of the words ‘monster’ and ‘vampire’.

But at the first mention of the death, a shadow shrouded Lily’s pale face. Not long after, Violette’s friend slipped away into the darkness.

SUYEON

Suyeon had set her mind on death once. She had been seventeen. The announcer's voice from the nine o'clock news had crept into her room as she sat hunched over on the floor, leaning against her bedroom door with her shoes still on.

Darkness enveloped her windowless room.

Outside, her parents had no clue she was in her room after skipping independent night study. For how long had she stayed like that? Suyeon's stomach burned. She knew it was because she hadn't had a bite to eat, yet bile rose in her throat at the thought of food.

Although she'd decided on dying, she didn't want to die alone. That didn't mean she wanted someone to die with her, just that she longed for someone she could spill her heart out to. In other words, someone who would listen. She went through her contacts list on her phone. There was no one she could call. It felt like her friends would turn the other way – tell her that 'it's just a phase', that she just hadn't found the right guy. As her parents had many times before. Pretending not to hear, not to know.

Later that night, it would occur to Suyeon that what she needed was someone who didn't know her at all. Someone who, after listening to everything she had to say, wouldn't feel responsible for the choice she was going to make afterwards. It was through her search for such a person that Suyeon met Greta.

She found her on the internet.

The website was for adults only, but since it had just been released, its verification process was lax. Its system permitted anyone to sign up and chat so long as they had a suitable-sounding screen name and a decent photograph. That was why Greta had slapped her forehead and leaned back on the wooden bench when Suyeon showed up wearing her school uniform. She later confessed she'd sensed that something was 'off' when Suyeon suggested meeting at the playground.

What Suyeon had thought was simply a nickname turned out to be her actual name. Greta looked like a foreigner. She had shown up to the playground with sunglasses, red lipstick and a long, chic trench coat, looking like an old movie star who'd stepped onto the wrong set. That night, when Suyeon was home, she had peered at her screen in the dark and tried to guess which part of Europe she was from.

***

In the dim light of the 1446 bar, Greta looked the same as she did in Suyeon's memory, even after eleven years. She had the same pale complexion and wrinkle-free eyes.

Greta tilted her head, staring at Suyeon as she finished drying her hands.

It's been eleven whole years, are greetings really necessary?

For a moment, Suyeon contemplated passing herself off as a stranger. Surely Greta would've forgotten her by now. But eventually, Suyeon decided not to pretend.

She had never had the chance to thank Greta.

The worry that Greta wouldn't remember her dissipated when the woman's eyes rounded and she let out a small shriek.

Greta asked her to wait a minute and scrambled back into the kitchen. Suyeon's mind reeled with the coincidence of their meeting as she looked around.

The table was stained, its hardwood surface blemished by a big, black spot. Suyeon's gaze slid across the length of the table. *Was this the seat Violette had vacated just minutes ago?*

Greta came back into the room. After hearing from Suyeon that she was driving, Greta poured a glass of juice. She propped her elbows on the table and cupped her face in her hands. Her thick, yellow eyelashes fluttered.

An inexplicable chill emanated from her. *Or is it just really cold in here?*

Watching Suyeon take a few sips, Greta's crimson lips curved into a wide smile.

'So *you're* the detective who was going to come,' she chuckled.

Suyeon shot up from her seat. Greta waved off her defensiveness.

'She told me a detective would show up, and to take good care of her. Violette, I mean.'

So she did *stick to the main roads for my benefit*, thought Suyeon. Her thoughts darted to Violette's own home. If Violette had known that she was being followed, then maybe she *hadn't* simply returned home as Suyeon had thought.

While Suyeon was lost in thought, Greta stepped out from behind the bar and began to close for the night. She switched off the neon sign and drew the curtains, shutting away the bar from the outside world.

'Why don't you settle down instead of standing like a wooden block over there?' teased Greta. 'Go on, you can ask me anything.'

But Suyeon couldn't bring herself to sit down. While she remained frozen in place, Greta returned to the bar and rested her arms on it.

'Isn't this the part where you ask me what my relationship with Violette is, what grand scheme we're conniving, stuff like that? I'm all yours, so stop dawdling and ask away before I change my mind and disappear.'

Silence.

Suyeon took a seat at last. Laughing to herself, Greta returned behind the bar and faced Suyeon.

'I first met you in 2009, so that makes it, what, eleven years ago? I'd just spent my first year in Korea when you popped up in my inbox. I was living in Berlin before that.'

Suyeon watched as Greta's fingers drew circles in the wood of the bar while she reminisced. 'That was where I met Violette. My God, that girl tells the best stories. She was the one who told me about this country, a country that's been separated into two, just like Germany. I wanted to see how similar it was. I had been there for four years before she came and was bored with my life. I didn't have anyone in Berlin, and though I'd spent a lot of time there, I guess my heart had left the city long ago. Before Violette came to Korea, life was so awfully dull here too that I would meet up with anyone and everyone. It's amazing how easy it is to meet random people in this country. You know what I mean. That's how we met.'

Greta laughed. Suyeon didn't reply. She was overcome with awkwardness, but she was also embarrassed for some reason.

'I won't bore you by going into the people I met, or how I got myself scammed and deep in debt. Trust me, that'll *really* ruin the mood. But Violette found me, and helped me set up this bar. I don't know how she got to know the previous owner, but she said she'd been in contact with him since the time when she still lived in France. Something about the owner wanting to shut down the bar and enjoy retirement looking after his grandchildren. Frankly, I think it was as much because the area was in decline and business wasn't doing so well. Still, I took it. Pretty cosy, isn't it? It didn't cost me a lot. And finally,' Greta clapped her hands together, 'Violette's a translator, did you know that already? She makes a pittance but donates everything she earns to kids awaiting adoption. I suppose I should've started with that to score her points in whatever your investigation is.'

'Donations?'

Greta dipped back into the kitchen. It was a while before she emerged, a card between her fingers.

'Give them a call to ask if you don't believe me.'

Suyeon took the business card. *Future's House*. It was an orphanage located in a neighbourhood in Incheon, not too far away from here.

'I go with her sometimes. I read English storybooks to the kids or teach German to those who are about to be adopted in Germany. This is the director's card. You can keep it if you want.'

Suyeon slid the card into her pocket.

'Oh, and this,' Greta handed her another business card from the same orphanage. 'This is mine.'

Suyeon took the other card as well, her eyes on Greta's smile.

'I'm always a call away, so don't you go around meeting strangers from the internet.'

Suyeon couldn't think of any questions. Head swimming, she drained her glass.

Sensing that Suyeon was done, Greta added one final remark.

'Violette seems to like you a lot. You can trust her. She sees things no one else does.'

It was almost two in the morning. Suyeon got up to leave.

'You're welcome to crash at mine, as it's so late. It's only a five-minute walk from here.' Greta offered.

When Suyeon bowed her head in polite refusal, Greta opened the door for her without asking twice. Suyeon took one last look at Greta – she really hadn't changed at all. Not just in looks, but in the way she spoke, too, with the same warmth and ease. Suddenly, she recalled the image of Greta and her sitting at a table, a tray of junk food between them, talking late into the night. A crisp gale gushed in, snapping Suyeon out of her reverie. Collecting herself, she bowed once more and left.

The first thing Suyeon did when she woke up the next morning was make a phone call to Future's House. The standoffish director perked up at the mention of Violette's name, and confirmed she sent 2 million won to the orphanage every month.

Getting into her car, Suyeon gripped the steering wheel as she sunk deeper and deeper into contemplation. She took out the business card for the orphanage again. According to the director, Violette was their most dependable donor. She visited whenever she could, and read to the kids and taught them French. In response to Suyeon's persistent questioning, the director offered to show her the donation receipts and photographs, and invited her to drop by for a visit. Suyeon ran her fingers through her hair.

What would Greta say if she knew what Violette believed in?

'Vampires, huh?' Suyeon muttered under her breath.

No matter how many times she said it, the word didn't roll off her tongue. But this time, Suyeon didn't scoff. The word weighed heavier on her lips.

***

The passenger door opened and Violette sat down in the seat. She'd showed up at nine o'clock on the dot, despite the heavy downpour. It was Suyeon who'd texted, asking for the meeting. Considering all the clues that Violette had been feeding her, Suyeon figured she couldn't ignore the woman forever. Skipping the pleasantries, and ignoring both protocol and misgivings, Suyeon handed over the case files containing everything on the hospital suicides.

'Here are all five cases. Let's say you're right, and these victims were hurled off the building by a vampire. How would you explain the first two cases?'

Violette perused the documents, taking her time.

'Did you get to see this corpse for yourself?' she asked, holding out the first case file.

The victim had been found in the hills behind the hospital, dangling from a tree with a rope around her neck. She was fifty-seven, a patient on the sixth floor who didn't have dementia. A handwritten note had been found.

'I did. The victim's airways were blocked when they found her. There were no holes on her body. None on her neck, for sure. The neck was thoroughly examined, since she'd died from asphyxia.'

'The vampire must've bitten her elsewhere then. They're not fools, you know. Also, I see here she was initially admitted as a road-accident patient.' Violette tapped a finger on the file.

'She flew off a bridge after her family car and a lorry collided in a high-impact crash. She was the only survivor. The rest of the family died in the accident.'

'So she was alone.'

'No, she had a sister. An older sister. She came to see her on the day of the accident.'

'Were they close?'

Suyeon shook her head slowly. 'She didn't come to visit for over a year. She would call sometimes, but the victim always told her she was fine, so nobody could have known that she was depressed...'

'How serious were her injuries?'

'Her spine was severely injured, and most of the nerves in the lower half of her body were damaged. She stayed in a university hospital before moving to Cheolma, where she underwent physical rehabilitation for three years. From what I've heard, she wasn't able to receive proper treatment.'

'Did she use a wheelchair?'

'Yes.'

Violette frowned. 'This is the hill at the back of the hospital, right? So you're telling me this woman wheeled herself all the way into the woods, threw a rope over the branch of a tree, and then tied it around her own neck? Come on. You *know* that sounds ridiculous.'

The first time Suyeon saw the body, she'd tripped on the same puzzle, but the captain had urged them to wrap up the case quickly, citing lack of evidence for foul play.

'There were no signs of resistance, so we closed the case as a suicide. She was suffering from severe depression as well,' said Suyeon.

Not once had the victim clawed at her neck. Unusual for a hanging. Both her eyes had been closed. Her face had looked serene, as if her death were a feat accomplishable only by those whose mind refused to let them suffer in a world they couldn't bear, or those who found life no different than death. But if it hadn't been a suicide…

A patient who needed a wheelchair to get around had trudged up a hill and hanged herself from a tree. It *was* ridiculous.

While Violette flicked through the papers, Suyeon allowed her thoughts to stray for a bit: imagine if monsters, if *vampires* were the key to unravelling this twisted case? A vampire taking prey to the woods, hanging a rope on a branch for her, feeding on her in her last moments. While breath clings to her still, they wrap the noose gently around her neck and hang her from the tree. Drained of blood and energy, the victim fails to resist.

Suyeon's thoughts felt like puzzle pieces falling into place. It was a flawless line of reasoning, save for the impossible culprit. When Suyeon didn't respond, Violette flipped the page.

The second victim was sixty, a patient on the fifth-floor ward. He had died from an overdose after stashing away a few days' worth of sleeping pills and swallowing all of them in one go.

'This one didn't leave a note?' asked Violette.

'No. He was found in his bed, and he had no blood relations at all. He was not married and didn't have siblings. There was no one for him to write to. He was alone.'

'The kind of blood every vampire loves.'

Hearing that, Suyeon let out a bitter laugh. It drew no reaction from Violette, who continued calmly.

'Did anyone hear crying coming from this patient's ward?'

Suyeon knew that patients whose memories were disappearing sometimes broke down, crying like babies desperate for their mothers. It was a common symptom. Just as people coughed or sneezed if they caught the flu, dementia patients burst into uncontrollable tears. That lonely, isolated wailing was often the only type of crying you heard on that particular wing. Rarely were the tears from empathy, or sadness over a particular circumstance. If a patient was bawling, the other patients would often stare at them for a while, dry-eyed, before averting their gaze.

For the most part, however, these patients lived without a sound, as if they weren't there at all.

What could silence have to do with vampires?

Suyeon told Violette that no crying sounds had been reported.

'Red wine is made by crushing red grapes, including their skin and seeds, and fermenting them,' Violette murmured in a whiplash change of subject. 'That's how it gets its red colour and tartness. Connoisseurs are able to tell the age, vintage and origin of a wine just by looking at its colour. I myself am not a big fan, so I'm nowhere near that level, but my father loved his wine. So I've picked up a few things by listening and trying a few sips for myself.'

Suyeon listened with practiced detective patience, not having a clue as to where this conversation was going.

'They say the more red wine matures, the more it loses its colour and starts to taste of soil. Some even say it can taste like tree bark. The colour of wine doesn't deepen as it ages, it lightens and becomes diluted. People who aren't serious about wine won't think it tastes any good, but wine lovers like my father? They crave that taste. He's the type who would drive eight hours just to have a sip of a particular wine. I suppose people like us will never understand it. Anyway, blood's just the same. As I've said before, vampires are creatures that exploit loneliness. They'll pounce on anyone who smells of loneliness, and they'll do anything for a taste of their blood.'

Suyeon stayed quiet.

'They call it the "taste of lonely blood". There's an astringency that can only be produced by those who are lonely and alone,' said Violette.

Suyeon took a few breaths before speaking. 'And why can it only come from them?'

'People who are driven to the edge of loneliness and solitude don't cry. They've forgotten how, or know their tears would only go to waste. They pass their days staring into nothing with soulless eyes. Crying when you're sad, that is, being able to cry, is a testament to the fact that your will to live still exists. People who've lost their will to live don't cry. Because crying won't grant them release. If no tears are shed, then no moisture escapes the body. Extra moisture dilutes a person's blood, just like aged wine. And since they are creatures with an inconceivably keen sense of smell, they can discern the scent of lonely blood.'

Suyeon found it hard to believe that a person's loneliness and solitude could dilute their blood and turn them into some kind of target.

'How do you know all this?'

'I've tasted the blood of those who've been killed by vampires.'

Suyeon's brows furrowed. Her thoughts flashed to the image of Violette sniffing the floor and putting the blood from the barbed wire to her mouth.

'It doesn't matter to me whether or not you believe in vampires. Because, regardless of your belief, they exist.'

'You've… really seen a vampire?' Suyeon managed.

Violette looked up from the papers, a smug look on her face. 'Seen one? Please. I kill them like mosquitoes. You know, I'm sure you yourself have seen one.'

'Nope, never,' said Suyeon, giving her best dismissive shrug.

Violette turned to Suyeon. Her lips tipped upward as she challenged her: 'You really think so?'

Her dark pupils bore into Suyeon like the lens of a security camera.

'Their eyes have a sheen of gold. They say that God loved them so much, he dropped the most beautiful colour into their irises. They've got skin as white and smooth as fresh dough, but their lips? The most vibrant shade of red. They're tall, even their fingers are gracefully slender. In other words, they tick all the boxes of modern society's definition of beauty. One look, and they'll be forever etched in your mind. Close your eyes, and you'll see them. What's more, they never age. Well, they do, but it's not something we humans will ever get to witness in our lifetime. Half a century for them is equivalent to five years for us, which is why they'll look the same to us even after a decade. So,' Violette threw Suyeon a knowing look, 'still think you haven't seen one?'

For some reason, Greta's face floated into her mind. Suyeon willed the image to disappear, but had no luck.

'Vampires mostly go out at night. Their skin burns easily under the sun. Sometimes they come out on cloudy days or as the sun is setting, but even on those occasions, the sun still hurts their flesh, so most of them are *only* active after sunset. The stories of them being repelled by garlic are bullshit, and they cannot be warded off with crucifixes. On the contrary, they consider red crosses to be a symbol of their kind. They don't operate as a group. They're territorial creatures and hate it when other vampires intrude into their area to hunt. That works in our favour, thankfully. If they banded together, the human race wouldn't stand a chance against them. That's why hunters work in pairs. One person to lure out the vampire and pin them down, and another to drive something through its heart.'

'So… Wait, wait – am I your *bait*?' Suyeon blurted.

'Don't worry. You won't die if they take just half your blood. If you're lucky.'

Violette's attempt to reassure Suyeon fell flat.

'Are you working on your own?' asked Suyeon carefully.

'No. An institution's involved.'

'You mean…'

'There's a place where humans are trained to hunt vampires. There are none in Asia, so hunters are dispatched here instead.'

Suyeon's temples throbbed. 'Is the government aware of this institution?'

'Not a chance.'

'Wouldn't working with the state make your job a lot easier?'

'Let's just say that this is a group that possesses a strength beyond anyone's imagination. They've got a weapon so powerful that they could raze the Americas to the ground in a matter of days. Even if there *were* an organisation who could keep that group under control, would it be useful or healthy to let society at large know of their existence? My answer's no. Most humans steer clear of any dangerous and powerful force, but there's bound to be a handful who would die for a taste of that power. They'd sell their souls for it. I'm sure you'll agree, Detective.'

Suyeon had worked on the force long enough to know that humans were not virtuous creatures. Often they only appeared to be because they didn't have the strength required for evil. In that regard, Suyeon agreed with Violette. A world that knew of vampires would be heinous. Her imagination swam with the prospect of new religions that idolised vampires being created. Some would jump at the opportunity to play sidekick to a darker, predator species. Suyeon had seen plenty of the likes of them.

'Besides, what are the chances of a human coming across a vampire in their lifetime?' Violette asked. 'Pretty low. Out of a village population of five hundred, one person *might* run into a vampire. But there's a high chance that none of them ever will, and less still that they'll know it – or live to report it. We rarely hear about vampire sightings. It's pretty much impossible for rumours to spread. Because, you know, that person would be dead.'

There was a pause.

'What's even rarer,' Violette continued, 'is someone meeting a vampire who not only spares their life, but instead uses them to achieve their own gains.'

Suyeon noticed the slight narrowing in Violette's eyes. She'd been trained to look out for miniscule movements like this. 'There must be someone from the hospital who's helping the vampire then. If, as you've said, there are vampires who use people.'

'What makes you think that?'

'You said they exploit loneliness and drive their victims to the point of choosing death. Wouldn't they need someone on the inside, someone who is constantly around the patients? A staff member or someone who knows the hospital well would fit the bill… If the victims were thrown from the roof, then it's possible that someone from the hospital opened the doors for them. Actually, there *is* someone that I keep coming back to.'

'Impressive line of reasoning. Well done, Detective! Took you forever, but you're finally coming around to it. In your defence, I suppose it *did* take a while for vampires to start showing up in Asia.'

At some point during the conversation, the heavy whips of rain had stopped. The clouds were wringing out the last drops of the storm.

Perhaps Violette was right. This problem had nothing to do with what Suyeon did or didn't believe. Evidence was evidence. Just because she herself didn't believe in a world of monsters or hadn't seen something with her own eyes, didn't mean it didn't exist. If vampires hunted their prey by taking advantage of their loneliness, then… All the suicide notes had something in common. Salvation. The victims all wrote about how they'd been saved. If it really was a vampire who had exploited the victims' loneliness and driven them to their deaths, then the question was: how did they get close enough to accomplish something like that? *Vampires who use people…*

'I'll look for any clues about the holes on the victims' bodies. Vampire or not, I want to know what caused them. And besides, I think that's the best way for me to approach this without drawing suspicion,' Suyeon said. 'There's one more thing I'm curious about.'

Violette nodded for her to go ahead.

'If all it takes is "one look", does that mean you can tell solely from their appearance?'

'Yes.'

'So you *haven't* seen a vampire in the hospital, right?'

If Violette could recognise vampires, the investigation would go smoothly from here. That fact alone took a weight off Suyeon's shoulders. She thought of bringing up the idea of a stakeout to Violette. If vampires did exist, and Violette could recognise them just from their appearance, then solving this case was just a matter of time.

But Violette shook her head. 'Nope. I have seen one.'

This was not the answer Suyeon was expecting. Up until now, Suyeon had believed that Violette was pursuing someone without knowing *who* they were. She'd assumed that all Violette had to do was narrow the search with her help, then find the hidden vampire amongst the sea of people.

Violette continued. 'But I don't know whether or not that vampire has killed a person with their own hands. We're not allowed to apprehend them unless we see for ourselves that they're *killing* for blood. That's the rule. If you've got other questions, maybe you should go ask the vampire *you* know. She'll be happy to tell you everything – oh, but don't bring a gun with you. It won't kill one anyway.'

NANJU

Back at her work station, Nanju checked her appearance in the mirror. The name tag pinned to her uniform was crooked. She adjusted it so that the three characters that spelled her name sat perfectly horizontal. The plastic tag gleamed under the fluorescent light. When she pushed the curtains aside, Bohyun, who was ending her shift, entered wheeling a cart.

'You're still here? Your class is about to start,' said Bohyun.

'I was about to go.'

With that, Nanju picked up her clipboard and box, and brushed past Bohyun. Her colleague, so used to receiving the cold shoulder, only glowered at her for a second before brushing it off.

Nanju entered the multi-purpose room on the second floor. Fifteen patients were already seated around a broad table. Their carers were at the back of the room, lounging in their chairs with their earphones in and heads bent over their phone screens. No one bothered to say 'hello'.

Nanju placed the box on the table. She took out a packet of construction paper and handed it to the first patient on her right, who took out a few sheets for herself and passed the rest along. While the packet was passed slowly down the line, Nanju took attendance. Although the hospital provided a diverse range of classes to help with its patients' rehabilitation, the number of patients who attended those classes were only a handful. Even then, they didn't show up out of interest. They came either for the snacks that were given out after each class, or were sent by their carers, who wanted to catch a break.

'Today, we'll be making *roses*,' announced Nanju.

The patients stared blankly at her. Nanju reached for a sheet of paper and the patients followed suit. Next, keeping her eyes on the paper before her, Nanju slowly recited a chain of instructions while she worked to transform the rectangle into a rose, raising her head every once in a while to check on her patients. Most of them couldn't keep up with their teacher's explanation. When Nanju was about halfway done, she went around the table to help them catch up, completing the rose for those who couldn't get past the first step of folding the paper in half. Calling the session a 'class' was simply the hospital's way of sounding professional. Instead of hiring external professionals, the hospital pinched pennies by having the nurses teach. Nanju's hands worked hastily.

Just then, a patient started to throw a tantrum. He let out an anguished screech and began driving his foot into the table repeatedly. When Nanju turned, she saw that it was Park Mokjun, a patient who was usually quiet. Half of his body had become paralysed after he suffered a stroke, causing his speech to slur. He often had to wear a bib because of his drooling. Up until last year, his children had come to look in on him, but they'd since stopped, only wiring over the hospital fees. It came as no surprise. All the nurses had known the children's visits wouldn't last more than a year. That was how difficult a patient Mokjun was.

But what drove Mokjun's children to give up on their father wasn't the hourly bib changes. It was one of the many complications that came with his illness – aggression. A year ago, Mokju began seizing every opportunity to scream, swear and hurl things across the room. His children slowly grew tired out. They didn't have to say it, it was written all over their faces. Nanju had observed enough carers to recognise that expression, the one that gradually stiffened as people lost the energy to smile, cry or get angry. Drained, these carers became immune to the swearing and screaming of their patients, absorbing every blow while their minds wandered off to a different world. Nanju believed they'd moved on to that new world now, having escaped the reality where the patients lived, the reality with no future nor hope.

The last time Nanju saw Mokjun's children, they were all wearing the same stony expression. Before leaving for the last time, they told Nanju it was all right to prescribe a sedative. While the pills were effective in subduing Mokjun's violent behaviour, it meant he'd be put in a daze for the entire day. Since the drug was meant to prevent self-induced accidents and suppress movement, it was as good as paralysing the patient's entire body. That was why carers who still had hope either refused sedatives or allowed only a small dose. Mokjun's children had done the same, but their father's erratic temperament prevailed. Requesting the drug was perhaps their way of apologising to the nurses who had to take care of him in their stead. Since then, Mokjun no longer kicked up a fuss. Staring vacantly at the ceiling was the most he could do.

Nevertheless, there were times, like today, when he would break out in tears or throw a fit. Mokjun unleashed another ear-splitting scream. Springing out of her seat, his carer rushed to his side.

'*Ayu*, why are you raising hell all of a sudden? Keep still!'

The carer slammed her palm down on Mokjun's back, which only agitated him more. He wailed louder, like a lost child. Flustered, his carer released the break on his wheelchair. Just as she was about to wheel him out of the room, Nanju stopped her.

'Here, I'll calm him down,' Nanju offered evenly.

'It's OK, we'll just head up…'

'Head up and wait for him to stop?' Nanju snapped. 'The patients on his floor shouldn't have to bear this.'

The carer frowned as she surrendered the patient. Without another word, Nanju wheeled Mokjun out of the room and parked him next to an empty mat. She knelt before him. A long thread of saliva dangled from his mouth. He wrapped his fingers tightly around the arm rest. Nanju placed her hands over his.

'Harabeoji, what did we say about losing your temper and raising your voice like that?'

Mokjun's aimless gaze finally settled on Nanju. She held his hands tighter. Her hands turned white.

'Didn't I tell you? If you behave like this, people will think you're going crazy. And then you won't be able to die. A man who's losing his mind can't commit suicide, can he?'

'N… na…'

The old man laboured to shake his head. Nanju broke into a kind smile.

'Now be good, OK?'

'K… ay…'

Nanju flipped up the old man's sleeve. His wrist was covered in dark splotches. Nanju pulled out a roll of bandage from her pocket and wrapped the wrist up, pressing hard to secure the bandage in place.

'Even when you're frustrated, you have to remain calm. That would please him very much. You wouldn't want to get on his bad side, would you?' Nanju beamed, pleased with Mokjun's compliance. 'Now, let's go.'

When she stood up to grab the wheelchair's handles, Nanju noticed the woman who'd been watching her from behind. *The detective's partner.*

Nanju steered the wheelchair away, feeling the heat of the woman's eyes scorching her back. Even after she'd made it back to the multi-purpose room, her heart pounded against her chest. It was as if the woman's watchful eyes had bored into her and seen all the secrets she was hiding.

Nanju tried to carry on with the session, but her peace of mind had collapsed entirely. Around the table, the patients tilted their heads in more confusion than usual, wondering why their teacher had frozen.

Why is she here? Nanju wondered. *What if she came for me?* Then, her mind drifted to *him*. She'd never seen him worry about anything until last night. Those two women must know something, and whatever it was, it mattered to him.

This was new. Whenever someone bothered him, he'd take care of it quickly and find a way to shut them up for good. Nanju would only hear about it after the fact, when they'd already ceased to exist, or were beyond repair. That was why his recent behaviour was all the more strange to her.

As Nanju gathered up the unused sheets of paper, she allowed herself a quick peek outside, but the woman was already gone. She wrapped up the class in a hurry. Once she was out of the multi-purpose room, Nanju dashed to the lift. Seeing that it might take some time to arrive, she scampered down the emergency stairs instead. She didn't know what she'd say to the woman once she caught up to her, but for now, she was simply obeying desperation's instructions.

The woman was nowhere to be found. Nanju checked everywhere. After combing the second level of the basement car park, she slumped onto the floor. She had been shaking this whole time.

She cursed until she was out of breath. Until silence was ringing in her ears. Nanju couldn't lift her head. A spider descended onto her bent knee. For a while, she watched its long legs traverse her thighs. Then, with her palm, she squashed it. The spider squirmed in protest before its legs slowed to a stop. Nanju stood up, possessed by an eerie tranquillity. Leaving the spider's splattered corpse on her palm, she exited the car park wordlessly.

VIOLETTE

February 1983

Lily didn't show up the next day. Or the next. Or the next.

Violette sat alone under the cypress tree, staring out at the dusky street. That was when she learned that if you looked at a certain spot for too long, the rest of the world blurred out. Stalks of wheat swayed and bowed playfully behind Violette's back, resuming their original positions whenever her gaze passed over them. Even they knew. There was no better fun than teasing a girl waiting for someone who wouldn't show up.

As time crawled by, her mind turned over her last meeting with Lily. The things she didn't understand were growing in number. The shadow across Lily's face when she told her about Arthur, for instance, and the image of her running away – these all became pieces of a riddle that only Lily, the riddler herself, could crack. No one else could provide any clues. And so, until she showed up, the puzzle would remain unsolved.

Maybe everything that has happened will haunt me forever, Violette thought. The more she missed Lily, the shorter the time they had spent together felt. *Soon I'll wonder if I really met her.* In the end, she would live as nothing more than a ghost or fever dream in Violette's memory, an ambiguous presence to be yearned for. Violette's brows narrowed at the thought of such an unbearable future. She couldn't let it happen. She couldn't let Lily become nothing more than an afternoon dream.

Violette stood up. It had been four days of waiting for Lily under the damned tree. If she wasn't going to show up, then Violette was left with one option: to go and find her. With a hand on the tree trunk, she mapped out the route in her head. Shipped to a different country when she was just a small child, Violette felt suddenly like she had never been given the chance to exercise her own will. Until now.

After sixteen years of being what others had wanted, she was going to set off in search of something *she* wanted.

She wasn't sure if hunting down someone who didn't want to see her was the right thing to do. Who knew if it might rub Lily up the wrong way? Or if Lily had enjoyed the last four days without her, at peace with erasing Violette from her mind and never seeing her again?

Am I being clingy? What if this dream becomes a nightmare? The consequences of her decision weighed heavily on her shoulders. Nevertheless, the desire to find Lily continued to burn. Better a nightmare than endless yearning.

And so, Violette set off, ignoring the sinking feeling that somehow she'd get hurt.

Was this how they felt when they gave me up? For the first time in her life, she thought of her birth parents.

Pieffe was a forty-minute bus ride away. At seven in the evening, the roads were dim and desolate. The only passengers on the bus were Violette and an old lady in a fuzzy purple hat. From the back seat, Violette observed the old woman, who was sitting right behind the driver's seat. Her knitted hat was embellished with yellow butterflies and rainbow flowers. Although the colours were gaudy, they suited the granny.

Last winter, Claire had taken up knitting as a hobby. She gave up after completing one lousy blue scarf. She sulked, muttering how being good with a spatula didn't make you any good with knitting needles. Violette suddenly realised she hadn't once worn that scarf this winter – it was buried somewhere in her closet.

I wonder if Mum's upset about it.

Violette made a mental note to put on the scarf tomorrow.

Feeling Violette's attention prickling her neck, the old lady turned around. But before Violette could look away, the lady smiled and nodded at her. Violette's ears burned. She returned the old lady's greeting with a slight bow and turned to look out of the window.

Once she'd reached her destination, Violette was at a loss. The streets of Pieffe were so wide. Besides, Lily had said she lived in the Pieffe 'vicinity', so Violette was unsure she was even in the right neighbourhood. For a while, she lingered helplessly. The late hour tempted her to turn back home, but she eventually headed towards a block of ashen buildings. She'd come all the way, after all. Might as well have a look around.

Pieffe was a much gloomier town than the one where Violette lived, and it was practically deserted that night. A woman clutching a bottle of alcohol tottered towards her.

The woman wore a grey coat and a beret, stealing glances at Violette as she staggered forward. Violette straightened her posture and held her chin high. She kept her eyes to the front and walked as if she knew exactly where she was going. When the woman paused to get a good look at her, Violette forced herself to continue on coolly, unaware that she would soon learn why the woman had gawked at her. Her bold feet had led her to a street lined with factories. She recalled then that Pieffe had a textile district. With no lamp in sight, the district was swathed in darkness. It was after work hours, but the factories also looked like they had all been shut down.

Out of the row of abandoned buildings, Violette picked a random one and peered in through a dust-coated window. She could see nothing except some large desks and a mountain of rubbish piled in one corner.

Feeling cold and hungry, Violette turned to leave. There was no way she'd find Lily here. She knew almost nothing about her, and this place was way too big. She thought she heard someone behind her, but turned to find only darkness.

On the bus home, Violette stared at her own reflection in the dark mirror of the window. There was an unfamiliar feeling stirring in her chest. *Could it be…*

Before all this, Violette had been lonely, but she had never been resentful.

Not even when she was forced to move to a country where she looked like none of the other kids, or when she found out that Claire and Maurice weren't her biological parents. Those events didn't warrant her anger, they were simply roads that she had travelled.

Violette squinted hard at the image before her. She recalled what Maurice had said about resentment – *it turns people into monsters.*

But can you resent someone you barely know?

Violette squinted hard at her image in the window.

It seemed to be turning into a beast.

***

Violette had two birthdays. The first was on the date of birth written on her adoption papers, and the second was the date when she first stepped into her current home.

For birthday number one, Violette would always have seaweed soup, a Korean traditional birthday dish that Claire always bungled despite her best efforts, and for her birthday number two, she was indulged with cakes, pies and chicken. She much preferred the latter. She could always count on having a feast.

It was on birthday number two, when Violette was seven years old, that Claire and Maurice had broken the big news.

That day, too, had been filled with the usual good food and presents. There was only one thing that was unusual – an album. Violette's parents had presented her with the book, containing pictures she had no memory of. There was a photo of her slouching listlessly amid a hoard of toddlers, of her brooding in undergarments printed with animal faces, of her bawling her eyes out. In every picture, she wore a name tag. The pictures were taken in the place where she'd lived before meeting her parents. Violette took the news well. Partly because she had always been aware of how different she looked from her parents, and mostly because the truth didn't change the fact that her parents loved her more than anything.

But occasionally, there were people who would create problems out of nowhere. At school, Violette's form teacher had been a kindly old lady. On their first meeting, at least. In a cheerful tone, she presented Violette's story to the class. *No looking down on her because she looks different, no teasing her, be good boys and girls and treat her with kindness,* the teacher said to her students.

From then on, there had been trouble. There were the kids who were nice to her, and those who were mean. And there were times when their meanness had been cloaked in kindness.

Even though the good outweighed the bad, that didn't cancel out the hurt.

But who should Violette resent?

She didn't know what her biological parents looked like. Sometimes, when she stared into the mirror, she tried to conjure their image, but that habit eventually passed. It wasn't that she had found peace or got over her curiosity. She'd simply borne it long enough for it to become a thing of the past.

In the days that followed the search for Lily, Violette spent too much time moping in bed. Her parents began to fret. They gave her space for the first two days, and on the two days after that, they came into her room and planted kisses on her forehead. Maurice went through the ordeal of putting on a happy face and asked her to hang out with him day after day, but he always ended up leaving the room quietly.

On the fifth morning, however, Maurice patted her on the shoulder and said they should talk. Violette wanted to ignore him, but, worried she'd hurt her father's feelings, she pushed herself up. Maurice took her hand in his and stroked it, gently signalling for her to go first. *Where to begin? Should I explain how badly I'm missing a girl who runs around barefoot in the winter?*

'Did you and your friend get into a fight?' asked Maurice.

Violette nodded. It felt something like that. Her problems suddenly felt so insignificant and trivial. Nothing worth making her dad upset.

'Sorry, I shouldn't make you worry over such a small thing...'

'Listen, I'm like that, too. I can't sleep a wink after I've had an argument with a friend. Bet you didn't know that,' said Maurice.

But Violette knew already. She'd often catch Maurice pacing the living room in the middle of the night, sipping water from his cup.

'I had no idea,' she replied, feigning ignorance. She didn't want her dad to feel like his attempt at consoling her was going to waste.

'Sometimes we make up, sometimes we don't,' said Maurice. 'That was how things were for Arthur and me.'

'What do you do when you don't make up?'

'I pretend nothing happened. It can be a little awkward at first, but after a while, it really does feel like we never fought at all. I might find a way to sneak it into a conversation much, much later. There's always a way to put things behind you somehow, though I suppose that makes me a coward.'

Would Arthur agree? Violette didn't think Arthur would have ever called Maurice a coward.

'But you can only be a coward if you have someone to be cowardly with. The last time I played chess with Arthur, I was annoyed by how quickly he made me concede. I could've just expressed my frustration, but instead I got petty and pretended that the game was no fun. Arthur suggested we play table tennis or pool, but I said I was bored and left without even looking at him. What I *should* have said was 'I'm jealous of how good you're getting at chess.' I thought I would get to see him the next day. That I could pretend nothing had happened and start a new game.'

Maurice smiled sadly.

'But that was the last time I saw him. Only when I was at his funeral did I realise that it was too late. What I'm trying to tell you, love, is – whatever you have to say, no matter how hard, make sure to say it while your friend can hear it.'

'What if she doesn't want to see me?'

'Hmm… You could write a letter? Do whatever it takes to tell her how you feel.'

To show that she was grateful, Violette pulled her dad into a tight hug.

She decided to make another trip to Pieffe. She wouldn't give up. Just like how she hadn't when she'd waited for Lily at the cinema.

The factory district was less daunting during the day. The streets were spotless, and there were no homeless people or stray dogs wandering around. There was a pine forest at the far end of the district. The pine trees were huddled in clusters, yet Violette had somehow missed them the other night. As she walked, she craned her neck to get a good look at the towering trees.

Since Lily had said that her room was as big as the entire first floor of Violette's house, Violette assumed that she didn't live in the residential area, where all the houses were similar to those in her neighborhood. In fact, she could be living in one of these factory buildings.

Is that why she's so used to the cold?

The red-brick factories were a maze. At the end of every alley stood yet another factory. Failing to find the pattern in which the buildings were arranged, Violette had no choice but to memorise the block number of each building she passed. She was sure to lose her way otherwise. She peered into every building, hoping to find one that was inhabited, but most of the doors were tightly locked with metal chains. She skipped those doors whose chains were caked in the thick rust of neglect. When her shadow began to lengthen, she promised herself she would return the next day. Just then, she spotted a length of metal coiled more loosely than the others.

This chain was tied into a knot. She pulled on it with her full force, but it refused to budge. Violette scanned her surroundings. About a foot above her was an unlocked window. Gripping onto the windowsill, Violette scaled the wall. The soles of her shoes provided barely any grip and she almost slipped off a few times but, eventually, she managed to hook her elbow over the ledge. The factory was flushed in a red glow. There was a pile of rubbish in one corner, just like in the other buildings, but something was different – here, the desks were stacked with books. Violette's eyes gleamed. She had to go in. With one final push, she heaved herself up, forgetting all about the window's height in her excitement. The next moment, she was falling. A sharp jolt of pain tore through her back. Darkness swooped in.

Violette must have lain unconscious until the sun went down.

Ever since Maurice had mentioned monsters, her mind had orbited nonstop around Lily. She wanted to raise it with her.

She'd tell her: *My grandfather believed that vampires are behind all the inexplicable things that happen in this world. You know, if they were real creatures, I think they'd look like you.*

She'd wanted to tell her but hadn't had the chance. Because Lily had taken off. Like a creature of the night, she'd disappeared.

Something was burning.

Violette felt her face crumple as she pried open her eyes. A red light hung from the ceiling above her. It wasn't the sun.

The light flickered.

Warmth tickled the left side of her body. When she turned her head, she saw a fire burning inside a drum can. Violette scrambled to get up. Sitting behind the makeshift fireplace was Lily, her nose stuck in a book.

'You'd make a great detective,' said Lily. Without looking up, she flipped a page. 'How'd you find me?'

Not believing her eyes, Violette blinked. When no response came, Lily closed her book and looked straight at Violette.

'Why'd you come after me?'

What should I say? Violette wasn't prepared for this either. All she had known was she'd regret it if she didn't.

'Why not?'

Sometimes you had to be a bit shameless. Be blunt. State the obvious, even when the other party knows full well what you want to say without you saying it.

Violette was sure that Lily already knew why she'd come looking for her.

A memory rose in Violette's mind:

Stars spilled across the night sky. Some shone brighter than the rest. They somehow managed to stand out amongst all those countless stars. 'They're not stars, they're planets,' said Maurice. Violette wondered if there was any big difference. They all looked the same anyway. Though they might look vastly different up close, from this distance, they were all alike. That was how Violette liked to admire them. It was also how she liked people to look at her. From afar.

She turned to Maurice, pouting. 'Can't we just pretend they're the same? That's how they look from down here anyway.'

In response, her dad said, 'Sure, they might look the same from far away, but some stars can be particularly bright. And even amongst those, you might spot a single star that outshines the rest. You won't want to shut your eyes. And even if you force your eyes shut, you'll still see it. That's its afterimage. It'll linger in your mind's eye and you won't be able to ignore it. You'll want to get out a telescope and have a proper look.'

True enough, Violette was looking through the telescope right now. On the other side of the lens was Lily. The brightest star.

A strange one, no doubt.

What if, like Maurice had said, Lily was not a star, but a planet? In any case, she was *something*.

A special something that could put Violette on her back, scale up the brick wall, and set her down on the roof.

Violette wished she could ask her outright, but her lips refused to part. It wasn't the answer she was afraid of, but the fact that Lily might disappear again. As she lay on the roof staring up at the sky, Violette mustered up the courage and turned her head. Her eyes met those of Lily, who'd been watching her the whole time.

'I've been lying to you,' said Lily.

'About what?' asked Violette.

'We're not the same age. I'm two hundred years older than you.'

'And?'

'*And?*'

'What else are you keeping from me?'

Santa had once existed. He died when Violette stopped believing in him. Every year, millions of Santas are born and killed at the same time. Every child must kill Santa on the road to adulthood.

Little do children know, Santa is just the beginning.

There are plenty of others after him, whom children kill without a sound. Without knowing. That is why every child gets lonelier and lonelier as they grow up. The vacancy cannot simply be filled by another human being.

People are not as kind or loyal as those creatures of imagination whom the child has killed. An empty heart is the penalty for killing those who've stuck with them.

But Violette's heart was not yet empty. She still believed in certain things. And so, rather than the fact that her friend was two centuries old, she cared about the fact that she'd lied.

'You lied. You're not human,' said Violette.

Lily shook her head.

'I never *said* I was human.'

'True. What are you then?'

Lily sat up. Her long hair brushed across the roof tiles. Stretching out a hand, Violette fiddled with the wispy ends. She waited for an answer, but Lily changed the subject.

'Why did you wait for me in the cinema?'

What does that have to do with the question? Violette wanted to argue, but swallowed her irritation.

'I just wanted to see you again,' Violette answered.

'Why?'

'Just because. Do I need a reason?'

'I'd like one.'

'OK, well, you were sitting in my spot.'

'What kind of a reason is that?'

'I've been going there long enough to know that I'm the only one who has ever sat in that spot. It's dark, it's cold and it smells like shit. No one ever goes there, and that's why I like it so much. But that day, there you were, in my seat. Once you saw me, you got up to leave. I found myself wishing you'd stayed and sat beside me or something.'

'I'm a vampire,' said Lily. 'I feed on human blood.'

When Violette didn't reply, Lily continued.

'I went to the cinema because I was starving that day. I was going to kill whoever sat on that seat. But I couldn't. You showed up, and for some reason, I couldn't kill you.'

'Why not?'

'Just because.'

'Good enough for me.'

'I'm telling you I'm a monster,' Lily insisted.

I see a monster in the mirror too, thought Violette.

And so she said at last, 'That's OK. I'm a monster, too.'

Monsters lived inside closets, under beds, in the mirror, on the roof. She loved that she was on the roof with Lily now. Just two monsters. Together.

The blood-sucking monster carried the monster who lived in the mirror on her back and ran. Because the monster who lived in the mirror had to get home before her parents did. The monster who lived in the mirror wrapped her arms tightly around the blood-sucking monster, who told her a story to keep her entertained.

Once there lived a human being. But for a human, he had too much hair, his hands were too big, and so were his ears. People thought he wouldn't fit in, but because he was earnest and kind, he was well-liked by the village folk. He was blessed with a green thumb, and the flowers he grew bloomed bigger and more beautiful than everyone else's. When asked if he had any special tips, he always gave the same answer – all you have to do is pour your heart into it. Despite following his instructions, no one could grow flowers like him. One day, a gentleman visiting the village fell in love with his flowers and bought a bouquet. Word spread, and the man slowly grew famous. He received a rush of new orders, enough to make him rich, and the village became known for its gorgeous blooms. The villagers put aside their jobs to help the man with his business. Soon, the village had a booming flower industry and began exporting flowers to the rest of the world. The village flourished, and everyone was wealthy.

Then, the people decided to name their flowers. They wanted names that set their flowers apart from those of the rest of the world, a name that was unique to their village. There were at least three hundred varieties of flower that came from the village, and they named each one. While everyone was busy doing that, the man quietly went about his work. Alas, the village's peace and prosperity couldn't last. Like all fairy tales, this one had a cruel ending. A lord who visited the village was frightened by the man's looks and fired a bullet at him. The villagers were devastated. Now that the man was dead, there would be no more special flowers. The alluring blooms that had captivated the whole world disappeared within a day. One by one, the names of the flowers were forgotten too. Eventually, there was no one who remembered what the flowers had been called. And since it had forgotten those names, the world was left with nothing but the memory that there had once been something beautiful. And it is because of that lasting memory that reality feels so cruel.

Lily set Violette down in her own bed, in her own room.

'But why did they forget the names of the flowers?' asked Violette sleepily. 'All they had to do was remember.'

As Lily tucked the wild strands of Violette's hair back into place, she explained, 'Words die. Once enough time passes, they all do.'

SUYEON

Seo Nanju was born in 1986, Nowon-gu, Seoul. She graduated with a nursing degree from a university in Gyeonggi-do and started working in Cheolma three years ago.

But something wasn't adding up.

Seo Nanju had finished nursing school without any leave of absence, but her record showed an empty gap between her graduation and her first day of work at Cheolma. Eight whole years of nothing. Maybe she'd had a different job? Or struggled to find work? But there were only so many paths open to someone who was trained in nursing. Frustrated, Suyeon pulled at her hair.

The phone on her desk rang. Jiseon from forensics. The caller ID reminded Suyeon that she'd ghosted Jiseon after promising to check up on something. *Now what was it?* Right. *There was no trace of blood on the suicide victims.* Wincing, Suyeon answered the phone. As expected, Jiseon asked if she had any updates on the case.

'About that...' Suyeon rubbed her neck as her mind scrabbled to form a sentence. Preferably something that didn't go along the lines of: vampires are involved, apparently. Thinking back on the day she'd called Jiseon, Suyeon remembered the rain.

'It was raining that day, so no luck. And sorry for not calling back, my mind's been all over the place.' Suyeon let out an awkward laugh.

'There was another suicide, right? I heard the news after our call.'

'Yes.'

'Do they hold Sunday service in that hospital?'

'Yeah. A priest drops by every weekend.'

'OK, my advice is to look over the bodies again. Suicide victims of religious cults are often found with marks on their bodies. Something like a cult symbol or bruises from heavy beatings. If not those, then you should also look into the possibility of substance abuse.'

'Substance abuse?'

'You remember the plastic surgery patient who killed herself five years ago?'

Suyeon did. The case happened in a hospital located in Nowon-gu. It fell out of Suyeon's jurisdiction but the case had been a hot topic amongst her colleagues and in the news.

'I know the one. I don't remember the specifics, though,' said Suyeon.

'She died because of a drug overdose. There were other victims, too, all regulars at the same hospital. That was probably how they caught the suspect, by tracing the victims' hospital records. The drug in question was morphine. Some patients died after experiencing severe hallucinations, while some ended their lives because they were addicted to the drug. I guess in terms of accessibility to opioids, there's no place like a hospital.'

Suyeon thanked Jiseon and hung up in a rush. A whole new explanation for the two holes on the victims' bodies was right in front of her.

As soon as she keyed 'Nowon-gu incident' into her search engine, a number of related articles appeared on the screen. She clicked the first link. Nowon-gu, Sanggye-dong Cosmetic Clinic. It looked like the clinic had illegally dispensed morphine shots to their patients in exchange for money, causing three patients to take their own lives after falling into depression because of their hallucinations and addiction. Ten staff members, including two doctors, had been detained, but only the doctors and two managers who had an active role in the incident were eventually sentenced. The identities of the nurses involved were kept confidential. After a bit more digging, Suyeon found the police station in charge and closed her laptop.

It was already past one in the morning. From her pocket, Suyeon took out Greta's business card. She fiddled with it for a while.

Go ask the vampire you know.

Recalling Violette's words, Suyeon let out a sigh. She leaned back into her seat, and stared up at the ceiling.

Lining the edges of the plasterboards was a splotch of brown. Directly above was the police chief's office and the complaints office, and the toilets were at the end of the corridor, same as the first floor. *Where could that stain have come from?* Suyeon narrowed her eyes at the spot.

Although it had dried to a crisp, it seemed to be crawling, spreading itself wider. It reminded her of the black spot on the bar table, and how deeply it had seeped into the wood. Suyeon grabbed her jacket.

***

Greta was waiting for Suyeon in front of the bar. She brought up a hand to block the blinding headlights of Suyeon's car as she squinted at the passenger seat.

Underneath furrowed brows, the gold in her eyes glimmered. Suyeon gripped the wheel tighter. She took a deep breath and switched off the engine. Then she pulled out her gun and opened the door. Once the headlights were off, Greta smiled in recognition.

'Well, hello to you too,' Greta joked, looking towards the weapon pointed at her.

Suyeon stayed behind the car door, using it as a shield. Although Violette had said that vampires couldn't be killed with a gun, she wasn't going to walk into the lion's den empty-handed. She kept her eyes fixed on Greta's.

'Violette told me.'

'Ah.'

Greta simply gave an acknowledging nod. She stepped closer and closer until the barrel of the gun was touching her chest.

'Told you *what*?' Greta asked.

Suyeon didn't answer.

'Why? Too embarrassed to say it?' Greta teased. 'Yet here you are, dying to know the truth… What a dilemma.'

Greta tapped on the gun.

'Didn't Violette tell you this won't kill me?'

'She… she did,' Suyeon managed at last.

'So you believe. You just need to hear it from me? You'd be the first of your kind. Humans tend to get a kick out of ridiculing me. Can't say I'm a big fan of, you know, having your existence *denied*.'

'I just want some evidence.'

Greta looked around. Her eyes landed on a five-storey building. Without a word, she walked towards it with Suyeon's gun still pointed at her back.

Curving her fingers, Greta put her hands to the wall and began to climb. She looked completely human, yet her movements were reptilian. As soon as she had made it up the smooth wall, she settled down on the roof's edge. She dusted her hands off and waved.

Suyeon awkwardly lowered her weapon, which, she realised now, truly was useless. Greta leapt off the roof. When her feet touched the ground, Suyeon felt her throat dry up. Holding back laughter, Greta approached her. The click of her heels echoed.

The pair sat in the car, staring straight ahead. Suyeon tried to ignore the fact that she was sitting next to something that wasn't human. Drawing long breaths, she found her composure again. She brought up the hospital suicides. Greta listened without interrupting, although it seemed from her expression that she'd already known about the incidents.

Greta was now right at the top of the suspects list. Because if every vampire in the world was a suspect, then Greta, who was closest to the crime scene, was the most likely one out of all of them.

But Greta was innocent. Suyeon knew it in her heart.

When she had first met Greta at seventeen, Greta had spoken to her in slow yet coherent Korean. She had insisted they delete each other's numbers and pretend the whole thing never happened, but the look in her eyes had told Suyeon that she felt sorry for the young girl who had come all the way in the late-autumn cold without so much as a jacket.

Heaving a perplexed sigh, Greta had asked if Suyeon had eaten.

'No, but I'm not hungry,' Suyeon had said. But Greta had dragged her to a fast-food joint where she ordered her a hamburger set and nuggets. Cupping her chin, her eyes had bored into Suyeon's, digging around for her life story. Suyeon had turned away, failing to hold her gaze.

'Don't kill yourself,' said Greta.

Her tone had been indifferent, but it had made Suyeon want to cry.

'I'm serious. You might meet someone who will make life worth living. Maybe not right now, but you never know.'

Do you think I'll live to meet someone who understands me? Suyeon had sunk her teeth into her hamburger to stop herself from blurting out. She didn't want to get her hopes up by believing it.

As she sat next to Greta in the car, Suyeon remembered their conversation almost ten years ago: the first time words of comfort had been offered to her. Greta had been a stranger, but she'd listened. It had taken Suyeon a moment to delete this stranger's number.

And it had taken a while for her to believe. But she did start to believe.

And because she did, she lived.

And while she lived, Suyeon kept an eye out for the kind of person Greta talked about. Then she met Eungyeong sunbae.

Can someone who saved a human life be a killer? Suyeon clung tight to her memories of the past in the selfish hope that Greta wasn't the culprit she was after.

'Violette knows a vampire's behind this, but she isn't doing anything about it,' said Suyeon.

'I suppose she's not sure the vampire actually killed someone,' replied Greta, as if she'd known all along.

Suyeon didn't miss a beat. 'What would she need to be sure?'

Greta paused for a bit. She flashed Suyeon an apprehensive look before telling her all about the treaty.

Forged a long time ago between vampires and humans, it was a contract full of clauses which Suyeon assumed were most likely written in haste. She wondered who'd considered themselves fit to speak for the whole human race.

The treaty, albeit nothing more than a scrap of paper, was still in effect to this day, upheld by the vampires, and therefore by their human hunters, too.

One of the clauses stated that 'blood feeders shall not kill by drawing human blood' – and was the reason why Violette hadn't yet apprehended and killed their culprit.

Greta explained that unless a vampire had sucked someone's blood until the human had drawn their last breath, the loss of a human life couldn't be attributed to the mere act of feeding.

It all came together now and made a strange sort of sense – although bite marks were found on victims who'd jumped from a building or overdosed, there was no way to ascertain whether the victims had died from these causes, or from a vampire's appetite. That was why Violette had reached out to her. She needed someone who could help her gather solid proof.

Suyeon stepped out of the car to see Greta off. When the detective stuck out a hand to thank her for cooperating,

Greta's eyes shifted back and forth from her face to her hand. She laughed before taking the hand.

'Did you get to meet that person I said you would?' Greta asked. 'Someone who makes life worth living?'

'Oh… Yeah. I did.'

Greta's face lit up. She was genuinely happy for Suyeon.

'Really? What are they like? We should've talked more about you.'

'She was amazing. Someone who truly understood me, just like you said.'

'Bring her to the bar next time. I make a mean cocktail.'

'I don't think I'll be able to do that. She's dead,' Suyeon answered. 'Thanks for today. I'll stop by for a drink next time. And I won't drive.'

As Suyeon drove away, she watched Greta in the rear-view mirror. Greta was standing in the same spot, watching her car shrink into the distance.

The person who'd saved her was dead. *Should I follow*? Suyeon used to wonder, but those days had flashed by.

It had been Eungyeong sunbae who had pushed Suyeon to join the criminal division.

***

Suyeon remembered that day. Eungyeong sunbae had been watching her pace back and forth around a crime scene, reluctant to leave. Eungyeong had then sat down on the concrete floor of the building and lain down, right beside where the body had been.

Startled, Suyeon asked what she was doing. Eungyeong replied that she was picturing the victim's final moments. After hesitating, Suyeon settled down beside her without a word. The two women lay side by side, the wisps of their hair intertwining. But Suyeon's imagination had always been limited. No matter how much she tried to recreate the victim's last memory, the only thing she saw was the mouldy ceiling.

'Our division could use a keen observer like you,' said Eungyeong. Suyeon asked if becoming a detective would help her find peace of mind.

Victims always looked at police officers like they were their saviours, but Suyeon couldn't think of one instance since she joined the force when she'd *saved* someone. In fact, all she'd learned up until then was that all police officers operated within the parameters of their organisation, and that an officer's proactiveness could achieve very little. She had become depressed. Colleagues in her unit tried to comfort her by saying that everyone went through the same rite of passage. That everyone eventually put to rest the fantasy of becoming the neighbourhood hero. But instead of comforting her, those words only wore her out.

Suyeon was, at that point, seriously wondering whether it was too late to call it quits and start a new career. That was when Eungyeong sunbae brought up the suggestion of moving to the criminal division.

Suyeon had thought that the only difference between a police officer and a detective was the clothes they wore, but Eungyeong sunbae managed to convince her: she told her that although detectives couldn't go entirely wherever they wanted, at least they could linger at the crime scene for a bit longer. Plus, they were entitled to yell whenever they found something, and were listened to when they did. Once in their career, they might get to keep a case from being dropped, and if they were really lucky, get to solve it. 'Above all,' said Eungyeong, 'you'd get to work with me.'

Suyeon burst out laughing. 'And what's so great about that?'

Rolling her eyes, Eungyeong insisted that once a month, at the very least, Suyeon would be happy to have her around, since she always had pads and painkillers ready. Suyeon pretended she was sold.

Mun Eungyeong. Her name was usually accompanied by 'the one who graduated top of her class', and then, 'the one with a stick up her arse'.

Suyeon hated the names people had for women who were good at their jobs, but Eungyeong never seemed to mind. In fact, she probably took them as compliments.

'If I cared about what people say then I wouldn't have the bandwidth to listen to what actually needs to be heard.

Whatever anyone says, take it with a grain of salt. The same goes for your victims and suspects. People will say anything to sway your decision or spit in your face. If you take in everything, you could miss crucial hints. So, in a way, letting things slide can be a skill.'

Hearing this, Suyeon realised that most of the police officers she knew were already experts at letting things slide. Drunken insults, curses searing with resentment, sarcastic laughter, degrading actions… No matter what was thrown at them in the process of taking down a criminal, her colleagues never seemed to let it bother them for long.

It was only when she experienced first-hand the difficulty of brushing things off that Suyeon fully appreciated Eungyeong sunbae's ability to block out the teasing and insults. Police officers simply didn't bother with phrasing things nicely. At the end of the day, having 'a stick up one's arse' meant that you never let a clue go unnoticed, that you were good at your job. Nothing more, nothing less.

It was also thanks to Eungyeong sunbae that Suyeon was able to quickly adjust to her new work environment. Eungyeong often stopped by Suyeon's apartment, where she lived alone, and left traces that made the house look lived in. Sometimes she bought containers of food from the banchan shop to stock up Suyeon's fridge, insisting that nothing was more nutritious than handmade food. In many ways, Eungyeong sunbae was special. She was the only one whom Suyeon willingly let cross the boundary she'd spent her life guarding.

Of course, Suyeon hadn't dropped her defences easily. Although she'd moved divisions because of Eungyeong sunbae's recommendation, for a while at least, she kept her at a distance, the way she did with everyone. Eungyeong sunbae respected her space, but one day during work, she loitered around Suyeon more than usual, and when their shift ended, she asked about Suyeon's plans for the evening.

When Suyeon said she was just going to head home to wash up and sleep, Eungyeong asked if she'd like to go out for dinner. Suyeon said yes, thinking they'd be having kimchi jjigae or something simple in the neighbourhood, but Eungyeong drove her all the way to the Chinese restaurant where their squad always held the annual company dinner.

Suyeon stared, nonplussed, as Eungyeong ordered chilli shrimps and yangjangpi. But when Eungyeong added a bottle of kaoliang liquor to the order, she finally yelled, 'OK, enough! Why are you doing this?' Eungyeong sunbae broke into laughter and congratulated her.

'Happy birthday.'

As soon as she heard those words, Suyeon's soul slunk out of her.

'How did you know?' asked Suyeon, her voice drooping in resignation.

'Looked through your personal records. Duh.'

'You could've just *said* you wanted to buy me dinner.'

'If you were the type who'd let me buy you a birthday meal, you would've told me it's your birthday when I asked about your plans. But *you*, you're the type who keeps your birthday a secret, aren't you? You don't ask for things or for help. You're always trying to settle things on your own. You don't feel lonely when you're dealing with your own problems alone, or living by yourself. Always Little Miss Independent… Am I wrong? Feel free to correct me.'

Suyeon thought Eungyeong sunbae cruel, asking questions that she knew the answers to, just to make Suyeon admit them with her own mouth. When Suyeon caved and asked, 'How did you guess?' Eungyeong said she'd known since she first saw Suyeon inspecting an empty crime scene alone.

How could she tell with just one look? Suyeon was dying to ask. But the words caught in her throat, and so she shut up and ate her first birthday meal in ten years.

From then on, the two ate together more and more often. Eungyeong kept an ever-growing list of the best restaurants in the area, and Suyeon, who had always eaten for the sake of survival alone, followed along on her gastronomic adventures. As their tastes became aligned, their conversations grew longer.

Eungyeong sunbae was curious about everything. When Suyeon said she didn't like kimchi, she asked why and since when. When they had jjajangmyeon together, she wanted to know if Suyeon liked having pickled radish with her noodles and whether or not she liked dipping her onions in chunjang. Although Suyeon couldn't wrap her head around why someone would be curious about such trivial things, at some point she found herself thinking through her answers. Sometimes she even anticipated the questions, wondering what Eungyeong would ask this time.

One day, months after the birthday dinner, Suyeon and Eungyeong sat side by side in the car, watching the rain draw patterns on the windshield. The case they had been working on together had gone through its final hearing. Eungyeong sunbae said nothing, only sighing over and over again. As the atmosphere stiffened, Suyeon felt her chest tighten, as if they were submerged underwater. The rain blurred out the rest of the world. The defendant had pleaded guilty and had been dealt a sentence, but instead of prison, he was sent to a mental institution. He'd been drunk at the time of the incident, was known to exhibit unstable behaviour, but most notably, he'd bawled his eyes out as he swore he hadn't meant to kill his girlfriend.

Eungyeong sunbae had worked harder than anyone to uncover the meticulous scheme of the accused. Never in a million years had she thought he would burst into tears, admit to his crime, and weaponise his erratic behaviour to victimise himself. Eungyeong had dug her nails into her palms until they bled, and upon hearing the judge's verdict, stormed out of the courthouse.

Suyeon wished she could say something to make Eungyeong feel better, but she had never properly comforted anyone before. She chose to ask a question instead, just as Eungyeong sunbae had done with her so many times before.

'Do you like the rain?'

'I used to, but since I joined the police, I don't any more.'

'How come?'

'The rain washes away evidence. It's as good as an accomplice.'

'Hmm… you like the snow then?'

'Sometimes. Keeps evidence fresh. I hate the cold though.'

'What about windy days?'

'They sound like the cries of the dead.'

'I see.'

'You didn't ask me if I like sunny days.'

'Who doesn't?'

'Me.'

'Why?'

'How can the sun shine so brightly, right in front of someone who just died without knowing why? It's so cruel.'

'Yeah. I'm not a big fan of sunny days, either.'

'You? Why not?'

'I've cried in parks on sunny days.'

At last, Eungyeong turned to look at Suyeon.

'So, what kind of weather *do* you like?' Suyeon continued. 'You seem to hate everything.'

'Hmm… I like the kind of weather that threatens to put me out of a job. Days that are so still that you might wonder if anything's happening at all. Come to think of it, those days are always foggy, strangely.'

Suyeon thought about the number of times in the last year that she'd seen fog. She could count on one hand the days when it had been too foggy to see anything.

'You don't regret choosing a job that has made you hate every weather?'

'Nope. Not really. I don't think I'd like every type of weather even if I had a different job. I'm sort of a weirdo.'

'I can tell.'

Suyeon leant her head against the car window. The cold nipped at her forehead. A long while passed before she spoke again.

'But I like that you are. You look at the world through your own messed up perspective. You tilt things that are perfectly balanced to find what others might've missed. You always do, and it's incredible. You're amazing at it, but I regret it, sometimes. Choosing this line of work.'

So, please, stay beside me as my partner, Suyeon wanted to add, but her awkwardness stopped her.

She should've just said it.

***

The person who answered Suyeon's call didn't hide his annoyance. His voice was hoarse with sleep. While Suyeon waited patiently for the detective to wake up a bit more, she looked out of the window, watching people stream into the police station for a new day of work.

To avoid Chantae's grumbling, she'd snuck out of their cushy office and into the emergency stairs.

He had told her to request a warrant if she was going to pursue this case properly, but at this stage, it was clear that the court wasn't going to approve one. Of course, Chantae must've known this. He probably figured that a denied warrant would drive the message home – that this case wasn't worth pursuing and that Suyeon should take her hands off it. Suyeon had obliged with a brief nod before scurrying away. Thankfully, Chantae let her go.

'What did you say you needed?' the detective on the phone asked again.

'The names of those working in the hospital at the time of the morphine scandal.'

The detective muttered under his breath, something about how his beauty sleep was being ruined by some busybody. Through the receiver and his laboured groans, Suyeon discerned the sound of someone rummaging through a stack of papers. She suddenly felt bad for making him unearth a five-year-old case file.

As he continued to look, the detective asked, 'Why the sudden interest in this case?'

'A series of suicides have taken place in a rehabilitation hospital in our jurisdiction. There's a nurse who has a huge gap in her records, so I'm wondering if the two cases might be related. Do you have any insight into the judge's verdict in your case? Pretty unusual.'

'The nurses were investigated as accomplices, but as it turns out, they'd been heavily coerced by a doctor. The judge decided they hadn't acted on their own accord and suspended the case. Did you find any bruises on your victims?'

'Bruises?'

'If the victims' addiction was advanced enough to drive them to suicide, they could well have been receiving injections on a constant basis. Overuse of an injection site can cause veins to blow or collapse, meaning the next needle would have to be stuck somewhere else. The bodies of heavy drug users are often covered in an unbelievable number of bruises.' A faint sigh escaped from the detective as he found the file. 'All I've got is a list of names. Who am I looking for?'

'Seo Nanju. Born in 1986.'

The detective repeated the name to himself as he scanned the list. He came up empty.

'No Seo Nanju here. But there is a Seo Yeongeun, born in the same year. Do you have a photo?'

Suyeon texted him the photo on Nanju's CV. At first the detective said that it looked similar to the one in his file, but then he corrected himself and concluded that they weren't lookalikes, but the exact same person. Phone gripped tightly in her hand, Suyeon stared at the slice of light by the window frame and considered the possibility that Seo Nanju had changed her name after the scandal.

Violette was sitting on the hood of her car in the car park, waiting. Suyeon had had no choice but to call her to the station since she was only free during her lunch break. Just as Violette was about to light a cigarette, ignoring the police officers around her, Suyeon snatched the stick from Violette's lips and thrust it into her hand. They both got in the car. Hoping to wrap up the conversation within thirty minutes, Suyeon fired question after question, without sparing Violette a single glance.

'I met her. The vampire I know. I've got questions.'

'This wasn't the reaction I was expecting.'

Suyeon was about to ask what kind of reaction Violette had expected, but caught herself before the conversation could veer off course.

'Even if you were to see a vampire feeding on a human being, you can't catch them unless they've killed the person? Is killing a human by feeding the only grounds for capture?'

'There are humans who choose to offer their own blood to vampires. A cup's worth is more than enough. It's because such people exist that we aren't allowed to apprehend a vampire just because they've fed on someone.'

'Why the hell would anyone...'

'Out of envy? Perhaps out of love.'

There was a pause.

'But that doesn't mean we leave it alone completely,' Violette clarified. 'If we can prove that the person was influenced by fear, or manipulated while they're not in the right mental state, we consider that murder as well.'

'Right. When they have no choice but to give up their blood.'

'That's the power of their terror.'

'I suppose driving someone to suicide would be a piece of cake once you've ripped away their desire for life, or their agency. In that case, what if a vampire were to convince their victims to commit suicide after they've fed on them? Or if they only choose people who are about to end their lives?'

A dull ache spread across Suyeon's chest. The horror of the words she'd spoken was starting to sink in. Violette nodded.

'If we can prove that they planned the whole thing, we're allowed to apprehend them.'

'I suspect they have someone on the inside helping them. There's a nurse whose whereabouts in the eight years prior to joining Cheolma Hospital remain unknown. It's also odd that she only works night shifts. It's just a hunch, of course. Nothing is certain right now. I don't even know why she would help a vampire...'

'She's probably delusional. Getting close to a vampire will do that to you. They toy with people's hearts,' said Violette. 'Be warned: never fall for a vampire's words.'

Suyeon's phone rang. It was Chantae, meaning her lunch time was up. Violette left the car without having to be told.

'You're proving to be more useful than I thought, Detective. You're looking out for someone, aren't you? That old lady?'

Suyeon nodded.

'Lucky her,' sighed Violette. 'She has someone reliable on her side.'

Violette chuckled and shut the door.

NANJU

It was early in 1998 when Nanju's father lost his entire life savings during the Asian financial crisis. At the time, he ran a company that was subcontracted by a conglomerate. Once his business partner saw the first signs of parent companies going bankrupt, he took off with all their money.

Nanju's father spent a month hunting him down until the creditors came knocking. To make ends meet, Nanju's mother sold her wedding ring, her first-birthday ring, the family's expensive porcelain, and anything that could fetch cash.

When her mother went to work at the twenty-four-hour bathhouse, which was nearly every day, Nanju was expected to cook for her older brother. During mealtimes, her father would call and ask if her brother had eaten. Nanju believed herself to be a good daughter. But she'd later learn that she was the only one who thought so.

Her mother said the family should work together to overcome such trying times. Nanju abstained from buying the things she wanted, scrimped on school supplies, wore her clothes, no matter how worn out they were, until she could no longer squeeze into them – that was her way of helping her family stay afloat. Her mother, too, wore tattered clothes, and so Nanju believed that every member of the family was sharing the same burden. But no.

One day, she spotted a new pair of shoes on her brother's feet. When her mother told her that it was because his shoes were old, Nanju hurled her own trainers, the soles of which were practically dangling off, at the wall and ran out of the house, bawling. That night, to appease her daughter, Nanju's mother took out a packet of instant ramyun – a luxury that they were allowed only occasionally – and made a pot of noodles just for her while her brother was sleeping. That was all.

Nanju had spent too long taking her parents' words at face value. By the time she realised that something was wrong, it was too late. Her body had grown accustomed to a certain way of life and had lost its ability to rebel.

In her third year of middle school, Nanju dreamed of attending a foreign-language high school that was quite far away from home. Her form teacher was confident she'd get in, given her stellar report card. Since her parents had once mentioned that they'd like to send her brother to a foreign-language high school, Nanju had thought they'd be happy to hear about her decision. Instead, they threw her a look of disapproval and asked why on earth she'd want to attend a school so far away. *You'd have to live in a dorm, and that's spending money we don't have. Besides, girls your age who live away from home are bound to get themselves into all sorts of trouble.*

Rage coursed through her veins, but she couldn't pinpoint its source. *Where's all this anger coming from? And what's this piercing emptiness?*

The year her brother retook the entrance exams for the third time, Nanju, who was taking the Suneung for the first time, placed first-tier in every subject. When she burst through the door singing about her achievement, her parents put their fingers to their lips.

'Quiet,' they said. 'Your brother is studying in his room.'

Seeing her parents on tenterhooks, so desperate to protect their son's dignity, Nanju scoffed.

'You're fucking kidding.'

The words had slipped out without her realising. It was only when she heard it that she realised she'd just sworn at her parents. Yet she felt no regret or guilt, only annoyance and contempt.

***

Nanju wanted to go to medical school, but couldn't afford the tuition. Her father had barely managed to set up a fried-chicken restaurant with the tattered financial remains of his business, but the opening of his new venture coincided with an implosion of fried-chicken franchises, against which his restaurant didn't stand a chance. There were times when Nanju stayed up thinking about her family's pathetic state, and she'd burst into an uncontrollable laughter.

In the end, she decided to enrol in nursing school for its promising job prospects. It was more affordable than medical school, and she managed to find a job straight after graduating. She was happy to have a role in the medical industry.

Nanju never could have known what life had in store for her. She began paying off her student loan and even gave her parents pocket money. She scraped together every penny and stashed them into different savings accounts. Still, she often felt empty on the inside. It was as if there was a monster living in the pit of her stomach, consuming everything. She tried telling herself everyone was in the same boat, but she fell into depression too often and suffered terrible luck. There was no way everyone lived like this.

She could've quit the hospital in Nowon-gu whenever she wanted, but she stayed, becoming a little more disillusioned with medicine every day.

She watched as the hospital fattened its wallet by doping up their patients, and she was rewarded in the form of bonuses. Nanju was finally able to buy the things she hadn't been able to afford before. She wasn't planning on staying for long. She figured she'd stick it out for another two or three years, and move to a different hospital in a nicer neighbourhood once she made enough money. Somewhere far from her family.

Needless to say, shivering on a rickety plastic stool in a police station hadn't been part of her plan. As the hospital patients began to die, one after the other, the police were called to investigate. The very first time she was brought into the police station, every detective's breath reeked of nicotine and coffee, and they couldn't be bothered to use the polite form when they spoke. To avoid the stench rippling from their mouths, Nanju bowed her head as low as she could and apologised profusely.

'I had no choice,' she squeaked. 'They threatened to fire me.' She was promptly let off with a warning.

News of the scandal spread like wildfire within the industry, and for a few years, no hospital would take her on. Thankfully, she was able to get by with the money she'd saved. Around that time, she was informed of her brother's death. She didn't know much, only that he'd died in a motorcycle accident. She was a little surprised that her cowardly brother had dared to get on a motorcycle, but that was all.

At the funeral, her biggest challenge was trying not to doze off. When she walked out of the funeral home, the realisation that she'd never have to see her brother's sickening face again made her heart sing. She moved back to the family home and things stayed like that for a while, with Nanju and her parents living like strangers. That was until her pathetic father was cursed yet again in his latter years, this time by disease.

***

The people in the goshiwon lived no differently from rodents. Like her brother, every one of them clung pathetically to their textbooks, stewing in the regret of not taking school seriously when they had the chance. Their hunched backs and nerd necks were indicative of the copious amount of time they spent shut in their rooms, studying. With half-shut lids, they'd stare into space as they smoked cigarette after cigarette.

At first, she charged 30,000 won a pop. Then, slowly and steadily, she began to raise her price. By now she was charging more than five times the original amount, but those who relied on her injections for the only taste of pleasure in their lives were willing to fork out the cash by borrowing recklessly from different places. They looked like zombies, monsters who'd given up on any last shred of human decency. And then, Nanju met him.

Pitiful and starving. But his beauty outshone his fragility. He was charming and wise, and had benevolently concealed himself and sacrificed everything for the sake of humans.

He opened up to her with such ease, recounting the story of how a stake had been driven into his father's heart, how the rest of his family had hidden in a warehouse for two long months, how his sister had wrestled with an unknown skin disease and withered away, and how his mother had cut off and sold off her gorgeous long hair to make ends meet. His name was Ulan.

She had thought he was her saviour. Later, Nanju would realise it was the world, not her, that needed saving.

And so, Ulan could never be her saviour. She thought again and again of the detective who had looked up from the ground floor that day. *Is she different? Could she be my last fighting chance?*

***

Ulan showed up without a sound, sitting on the windowsill like a child perched on a jungle gym. Nanju hid her surprise. She threw her towel into the laundry basket and opened the fridge, forgetting she'd emptied it of food a few days earlier. Thankfully, she wasn't that hungry. She uncapped a bottle of water and gulped it down.

It had been a while since he last came to the apartment. She didn't know what he'd been up to in the meantime.

Sometimes he'd tell her he was going away, but he never said where and for how long. When he showed up again, she'd play coy, hoping to pry some information out of him, but he always kept his answers vague. For a while, Nanju had wanted to know every little thing about him. That was no longer the case. She stopped asking where he'd been, and now she cared less about his whereabouts than about the soiled hem of his coat brushing against her precious bed.

Ulan turned away from the window. Despite everything, his beauty always had a hold on her.

***

Nanju remembered the first time she met him with great clarity.

She'd just started her gig at the goshiwon. He'd appeared silently back then, too. It took a while before Nanju realised that someone was watching her from the middle of the corridor. Her first thought wasn't that she'd been busted dealing drugs, but that he was beautiful. *Where did he come from? He doesn't look like he's from this part of town.*

The next day, she found him wandering around the hospital. At first she was on edge, thinking he might report her to the police, but at some point, when that report never came, her worry dissolved into anticipation. He'd bloomed out of nowhere like a carmine rose, a splash of colour in her monotone life. The thought that she might see him after work got her through the day, and his beauty alone was more than she could ask for.

He would come to her only after sunset. She wished they could meet in the day, since she worked nights. But whenever she brought up the idea, he would refuse. Nanju was left to speculate. Maybe he had a wife and kids, and that's why he couldn't meet her during the day. Yet if he had a regular office job, he couldn't be staying up until the break of dawn. *So what does he do during the day? Is he a handsome butler who's at someone's beck and call?*

Nanju knew jobs like this no longer existed in this day and age, but there was something about his pale, delicate face that kindled the idea in her imagination. She thought he'd suit a quiet role from the past.

Everything about him piqued her curiosity, and Nanju worried she'd never be able to learn anything about him. Not even his name or where he was from.

But she did find it all out eventually.

One day he showed up at her doorstep, his jaw and cheekbones jutting out beneath his skin. She learned his name, where he came from, and why he'd collapsed at her feet like a sack of bones.

She thought back to that day from time to time. She should've feigned ignorance, kept living in her little fantasy. Left him on the floor to starve, too weak to even lift a finger.

***

'It's so easy to resent someone. That makes me sad,' he said as he stared into Nanju's eyes. His gaze, which had once been filled with tenderness, coiled around her throat like a serpent. 'Perhaps if such an emotion didn't exist there'd be no tragedy in the world.'

Nanju sat on the edge of her bed. Ulan was sitting on the windowsill, his legs dangling near her bed. Nanju watched his shoes closely, worried that they might dirty her bedsheet. He'd moved to Korea a long while ago, yet never learned to remove his shoes inside the house.

'Hating someone can be agonising. You can't stop it. It's perhaps the best method of self-torture,' said Ulan.

'What's with the sudden philosophical talk? Did someone cross you?'

Ulan's lips twisted into a thin smile.

'A long time ago. Before you were even born.'

'That's odd.'

'What is?'

'It means you've let the person you hate live.'

'What makes you think I *haven't* killed them?'

'If you had then you wouldn't be saying all this.'

Ulan burst into laughter. Nanju waited for his laughter to settle. After a while, Ulan continued.

'You're right. I haven't killed them. I wanted to, but I was stopped.' He smacked his lips regretfully. 'Trust me, I wanted to, very badly. And not because I was ravenous. Never had I been seized with such a desire to kill. To inflict pain. The feeling was new to me. Before that, I'd only slaughtered for the sake of the flesh.'

'Why did you want to kill them?' Nanju asked, knowing it was what he wanted to hear.

A moment passed before Ulan spoke again. He didn't look at Nanju, gazing into nothingness instead.

'I was only a child when I was stuck in that warehouse with my dying mother and my sister, their faces oozing with pus. Even then, I could easily kill an adult myself, but not if I was outnumbered. Factories were erected in our city, and as the buildings grew taller and taller, the population grew in proportion. Like this place, there were very few places to hide. If it wasn't for *her*, I might've caught my sister's disease and died beside her. Starved to death while humans held banquets and feasts.'

Her.

A word and a tone Nanju had never heard together from him before. He wasn't referring to a human being, she was sure. He'd never once spoken about a human with warmth. Not even when he called her own name. He tried many times to treat her with tenderness but never succeeded. Nanju noticed a spider climbing up the wall. It stopped for a while, searching for a hiding spot. Then, it scuttered in between the crevices of the wallpaper.

'"Be wise and live." That was what she told me. "Don't just sit like a fool waiting for death," she said, "because survival is the only way to prove strength." I'm sure you'd agree with that sentiment. No matter how dreadful a human being is, they become nothing when they're dead, reduced to a mere parasite scuttling about in the memory of the living.'

When Nanju didn't reply, Ulan continued, 'She taught me everything. She showed me how humans perish on their own if we just let them be. How they'll kill one another if we sit back and watch. She told me anger is the only thing that can chew us up from the inside, and that as creatures physically superior to humans, we mustn't let them get under our skin. What words of wisdom! She saved me from heading down a dangerous path. I guess you could say she was my... benefactor. Indeed, she was. In all my life, no one else had reached out to me like she did. But at the same time, she's the bane of my existence. She occupies my mind as a memory I can't forget, discard, or extinguish. It's truly remarkable how the one who saves you can be the one who kills you. She's claimed both roles for herself. The thing about resentment is that you become so obsessed with one thing, it turns you into a fool. Before you know it, you're heading down the path of self-destruction.'

'She must've been very important to you.'

Ulan nodded without hesitating.

'Yes. She saved my family and took us in. Us vampires, we try not to bother one another. Once we've decided on a home ground, we settle down permanently and do our best to maintain peace. That's the nice way of putting it, of course. It also means we turn a blind eye to our neighbour's misfortunes. You see, interfering in someone else's affairs can get you hurt or killed, and that's detrimental to maintaining the population of our kind. But that woman, she didn't adhere to such callous norms. She was the only one who ever reached out to help us. When I asked her why she didn't simply turn a blind eye, she just said, "Well… let's see… let's see…"'

Ulan's voice droned on softly as he repeated the words. His eyes were still fixed on nothing at all.

'If only I'd known then that being different wasn't something to admire. But, oh, I was so beguiled. Being different is a double-edged sword. It can protect you, but also harm you. And naive little me, I embraced her difference wholly and was stabbed in the end. It was bad. Just the thought of it rouses an ache here.'

Ulan pressed his palm onto his torso and chest.

'That betrayal must've really stung.'

'I don't know if betrayal is the right word. Will you be the judge?'

'Sure. Tell me.'

Nanju was inching closer to Ulan's motive.

'It must've been a century after I'd begun to follow her around. Word had spread that humans had drawn up a set of regulations that were to be imposed on us, so we retreated deeper and deeper into darkness, where we wouldn't be found. I wasn't particularly happy about our new circumstances, but I put up with it to avoid trouble. I was very good at making myself small back then. It was her belief that we should do whatever we could to maintain peace between us and the humans. And her beliefs were ours, because she was our core, our centre. Her judgement was always correct. We upheld it as such, even when it was not. Because it was impossible for an individual to overcome the entire clan. If our existence were to be revealed to the world, we wouldn't be captured, we'd be subjugated and exploited and turned into weapons. So even when we thought her unreasonable, we obeyed. We saw it as the last means of protecting our kind. I gave up the last bit of our freedom and cuffed a shackle around my own neck, while I watched her put my brethren in manacles. You see, I couldn't care less back then, for I would follow her wherever she went.'

After a pause, Nanju asked carefully, 'You must've been let down since you trusted her so much. Did she betray your brothers?'

'She killed one of them.'

Nanju pressed her lips together.

'Twisted his neck. She strangled him so hard, her nails tore through his skin.'

'When he'd done nothing wrong?'

'He did, of course. He was going to harm a human. One whom she loved.'

'*Loved*?'

The unfamiliar word tickled the tip of her tongue. Ulan nodded.

'It was a very young girl. Practically a toddler walking on two feet. She would've died on her own soon enough. Especially in that godforsaken town of ours. I've seen too many of her kind, with frail roots. They can't hold their own. They appear free but are the quickest to bend and break. I don't know how the two of them met. But the girl was dear to her. I know it for a fact. Of course, I do. I never once left her side. And that was why it baffled me. How did they meet? And where? But it was already too late for those questions, and nothing else matters if you're too late. I'd taken my eyes off her for a while, and in my negligence, she went to see the girl. She went often. I kept quiet even though I knew. Humans aren't our enemies. We might tear at each other's throats sometimes, but there aren't many other creatures – perhaps none – whom we can communicate so well with. It goes both ways. Not all humans see us as other. Before we were forced into hiding, many humans and vampires worked hand in hand. It wasn't uncommon. At least, I tried to see it that way. But not everyone agreed. That was the tragedy. Loving a human at a time when we needed to stay away. Timing truly is everything. You never know how the tides are going to turn, or when something that isn't wrong will be considered as such.'

'Did she kill your brother because he found out?'

'Yes. He tried to kill the girl she loved. What a fool he was. She believed he'd approached the girl to kill her. She warned him several times but, still, he crossed the line. He couldn't help his appetite and went in for the kill, just for a taste of fresh human blood.'

'He killed the girl?'

'No. He had killed the person who showed up before the girl did.'

'Someone else?'

'Yes. Someone else. But she felt it then. My brother's desire to kill the girl. She had to do something, and so she killed him. Ended both this thirst and his interminable existence in one go.'

Nanju assumed that Ulan resented 'her' because she'd killed his brother. It was understandable, given what he'd shared with her. But it was someone else that Ulan had in mind.

'We banished her. She was our leader, but she was cast out in an instant. We wrote her name out of our history. The person I treasured most was driven out, and I was forced to look the other way. All because of one stupid little girl.'

The person Ulan resented was the girl she had loved. The one who was responsible for the banishment of the person he held in the highest regard. Ulan sank into contemplation for a while. Then he broke into a chuckle. Nanju didn't ask what was so funny. His laugh chilled her.

Instead, she tried to give a name to the ambiguous dread lurking in the pit of her stomach. Ulan's anecdote sounded like both a recollection of the past and a warning of what was to come. He had never before talked about his past in such detail.

'Pure hatred craves annihilation. Not an accidental end, but one so meticulously planned and executed that the person being destroyed knows exactly why they're meeting their doom. In the same way that your father's eyes latched onto you before he died.'

'Why bring him up all of a sudden?' Nanju snapped.

Ulan let out a relaxed laugh. 'Perhaps so that you'll understand me.' Ulan picked himself up and stood on the windowsill. 'I'm settling my affairs and leaving this place. I've stayed here for too long.'

At that moment, realisation struck Nanju: the girl was alive, and Ulan was going after her. Whether he had always known or if he had just found out recently didn't matter. Right now, he was pulsing with revenge and out for blood.

What about me? Nanju wanted to ask. *Will you take me with you?* It was customary for someone leaving to specify the date, but Ulan didn't say anything. It was as if he was planning to leave alone, as if Nanju had never been a consideration in the first place. Why was he leaving her? He never spared the humans he met for fear of exposing his kind, he'd told her this himself. What would happen to her? Nanju refused to let her worry show.

Maintaining a casual tone, she said, 'Fine. But as you do that settling, you know the granny who hands out yoghurt? She's off limits.'

Ulan gave her a quizzical look.

'Her son is overseas but she has a weekly visitor. It's the detective who's been loitering around the hospital. I'm sure she's suspicious, so let's not do anything that might get us on her radar.'

Although she was his willing accomplice, Nanju adhered to her own moral code – no unjustified deaths.

The victims had not been chosen at random. Nanju picked patients who hadn't had a single visitor in at least a year and were tired of living. Patients who stared into space while they received injections, patients who'd completely lost their appetite and ate no more than two spoonfuls of rice at mealtimes, patients who slept without care for the time of day, and when they did, slept as though they were dead.

Ahn Eunshim didn't meet any of the criteria. Although no family member of hers came to visit, she took life in her stride. Nanju had wondered how she could be so different from the others, but now she knew. It was because of the detective who came to see her as if she were her own grandmother. Nanju hadn't realised it until now.

'Really?' said Ulan. A smirk flitted across his face.

Then he took off. Nanju's legs gave in. She hugged her knees. Keeping her head low, she focused on taking deep breaths. When fear loosened its grip around her body, a chill surged in to take its place. She shivered uncontrollably. *He's going to pack up and leave.*

Time was running out for Nanju. Had she known this was coming, she wouldn't have let him get close in the first place. But what were her chances to begin with? If she hadn't made herself useful, got close, perhaps she would already be dead. A single woman living alone, crushed by debt, her orchestrated suicide would've gone unquestioned. She'd been the perfect prey.

VIOLETTE

March 1983

Violette had been a bundle of nerves. The police officer who showed up at their door that afternoon was the one from the day she'd first spoken to Lily. When she'd lost her backpack and made a friend.

Thankfully, the officer had completely forgotten her face. She sat on the stairs and watched him interview her father. He was asking what Maurice had been doing at the time of Arthur's death. Maurice told him that he'd been at the restaurant with his wife. The police officer, however, brought up a witness testimony which suggested a twenty-minute gap during which Maurice had been absent from the restaurant. Maurice said he'd gone to fetch a few ingredients at the grocer's, but the officer looked as though he wasn't listening.

The conversation angered Violette. Maurice was Arthur's best friend. Everyone in the neighborhood knew that the two would spend hours together, chatting about the future while playing chess. Violette herself had sat watching them play many a time, nibbling on chocolates or trying not to fall asleep. Arthur won most of the time. *Could Dad have killed Arthur over a game?* Violette almost laughed at her own ridiculous theory. She wanted to kick the police officer out of the house. Why couldn't he just leave them alone to be with their sadness? And why was her father putting up with this bullshit? How could he so calmly give an alibi when someone was insulting their friendship? *Arthur's heart would be broken.*

If people found out that her dad had been questioned by the police, the word 'friends' might never be used to describe Maurice and Arthur again. Violette stormed up the stairs and slammed her door.

The tears she'd kept back at the funeral gushed out at last. Violette yanked the blanket over her head, biting her lip to stifle the sound of her sobbing. She was hurt by how her father was acting. She despised him for being servile and weak. It was as if she didn't know him at all.

This new side of him was scary and disappointing. An hour had passed since Violette was supposed to meet Lily, but she remained curled up under the blanket, letting the hours slip by.

A cold draft rushed into Violette's room. She felt a tender hand rest on her back. Surprised, she threw off the blanket. Lily was sitting on the edge of her bed, looking at her.

Lily told her another story that night.

Once there was a chameleon who lived in leaf litter and never had to change its colours. One day, it lost its ability to camouflage. Stripped of its powers, the outside world became more dangerous than ever, and it was destined to remain on the forest floor forever, until death. Lily explained that this was why Maurice had been so subservient before the police officer. If he'd fought back as Violette had hoped, the police officer might've marked him down as violent and impudent, which was enough justification to drag him to the police station. Maurice had made the best choice, given the circumstances. Hearing this, Violette's fear dissipated a little. Still, there was a difference between being convinced and really understanding, and Violette felt for the first time that she might never understand her own father.

'But Arthur and my dad were best friends. Everyone knows this. Dad would never do such a thing, he shouldn't have sat there and let himself be accused,' Violette argued.

'Closeness is not very good evidence for innocence,' said Lily.

Expanding one's world view isn't so different from getting stitches. People whose skin is so thick they don't bleed when they're pierced with a needle aren't afraid to keep expanding their world. As their world grows, they master the art of adaptation. They observe their environment, adjust to it, and learn to rule it. In the process of expanding their world, they mustn't pore over the finer details. Who cares if their land is barren, a wasteland where not even a single stalk of grass can grow? All that matters is that their world is getting bigger.

Most adults in this world have skin that keeps thickening. That's because they've bled out completely, or have stolen someone else's skin to protect their own. There are some who, sickened by the sight of grotesque scars, throw away their skin, choosing instead to lay bare their red muscles, scaring away others.

And just as they've made it impossible for others to get close, they themselves do not touch others carelessly. They do not steal the skin of others. They stand on the periphery, watching the world thicken into a callus of skin and blood. However, boys and girls who wish to grow up must hold up their needles and put them to their skin. They must sew up their wounds ever so slowly, as beads of sweat collect on their foreheads. The first prick will sting. It will last longer than any memory. The process of expanding one's world is one of pain.

Lily's honesty hurt, but Violette saw it all clearly now.

That the chameleon had only kept quiet to survive. That appearances didn't reflect one's thoughts, and that no one but the heart's bearer could know what it holds. It was time for Violette to apply needle and thread to her skin. Her needle wouldn't be the possibility that Maurice had killed Arthur, but the truth that she'd so badly wanted to deny – that a person was capable of killing someone they loved.

'Love is the most despicable excuse, Violette,' continued Lily.

'But people are always sad to see their loved ones go. I've never met anyone who wasn't.'

'A person can still feel sad after killing someone.'

'Why?'

'Because they're watching someone they love die before their eyes.'

'Why kill them in the first place then?'

'The reasons can be many.'

Love doesn't always remain as love. Love turns into familiarity, betrayal, yearning, resentment, comfort, hate, dependence or even destruction. Love can morph into as many shapes as there are words in the dictionary. Oppression and freedom, truth and lies, idolatry and hatred – love embraces all. And because it does, it embraces hate. It was out of love that Violette believed in Maurice's innocence, and it was out of love that Lily told Violette about the shape of love.

Wrapping herself in the blanket, Violette sat up. *Is abandonment another form of love?* If you could throw someone away, not because you didn't want them, but because you loved them so much, then perhaps Violette could come to understand the two-faced monster in the mirror. The needle was now between Violette's fingers, resting on the surface of her skin. From it dangled a thread – the possibility that her dad could've killed his best friend.

Reading Violette's mind, Lily added, 'No one can say for sure that it was your dad who killed Arthur. All I'm saying is we can't deny the possibility.'

'Then I suppose it wouldn't be wild to assume that someone thinks I'm the killer.'

'Yes, but let's not jump to that conclusion just yet. You look a bit too scrawny to rip off a man's neck. Even if your name makes it to the list of suspects, it will be at the very bottom, no bigger than a chicken scratch.'

Violette imagined scanning a list of names and finding hers at the bottom. If everyone before her was found innocent, then wouldn't the police come looking for her anyway? What if, when they showed up, they whipped out her lost bag as evidence, and badgered her to admit she'd killed Arthur because he'd stolen her bag? As her imagination ran wild, she lightened up. The feeling of unease, too, vanished. Lily's revelation had been cruel but it restored her calm. Perhaps she'd even grown up a little.

No sound came from the living room. There was no sign of the police officer or Maurice now. Violette and Lily were left alone in the house. It was unlike her father to leave the house without going upstairs to his room first, but Violette didn't think too much of it. The interrogation must've taken a toll on him.

Violette's eyes landed upon Lily's pale feet. She stood up. Lily might be immune to the cold, but the sight of her bare feet always made Violette shiver. Going to her drawer, Violette took out a pair of socks. They were long and mustard yellow. A present, Violette explained when Lily quirked a brow in confusion. I thought you'd pull them off well, said Violette. Lily hesitated for a moment before she thanked her. She slipped on the yellow socks and giggled at how, paired with her green trousers, they made her look like a forest pixie.

Violette didn't tell her that they were her favourites. That she loved them so much she hadn't worn them once since she'd received them from Claire as a birthday gift. She thought Lily would feel pressured, somehow, if she knew.

***

Five grey wolves lived in the forest of fir trees. It was snowing heavily, as if winter was putting on a final show. Careful not to startle the wolves, Lily climbed the tree stealthily, coming to rest on a branch higher than the clock of the cathedral. Too afraid to look, Violette wrapped her arms tighter around Lily's shoulders. The branch shook precariously in the wind, but Lily maintained a relaxed grip on the tree trunk. 'Don't worry, we won't fall,' she said, as if she knew Violette's eyes were squeezed shut. Violette opened one eye, and then the other.

Against the full moon, the firs stood like arrows pointed at the sky. Ash-like snow slept on their branches. The forest stretched on without end. Violette breathed into the crisp air. 'Wow,' she sighed, before catching herself. Thankfully, the wolves only lifted their ears slightly and stayed where they were.

‘They say these wolves have gone extinct,’ whispered Violette.

Grey wolves hadn’t been seen in France for fifty years. That was what Maurice had told a young Violette when she had pointed at her junior encyclopaedia, saying she wanted to see one in real life. ‘Why did they disappear?’ she had asked. Maurice had shrugged and said they probably didn’t fancy living in France any more.

‘There aren’t many of them left, but they’ve always been here. Hiding, so they don’t get caught by humans.’

‘So it’s people they don’t like, not the place.’

What if all the creatures we think have disappeared are still alive and well? Just hiding from humans? What if they’ve only disappeared from the world which we can see, and humans are just going around pretending we know and see it all?

Violette was suddenly in awe of all the creatures in the universe. *They’ve outsmarted us.* If this were a game of hide-and-seek, the wolves of France were winning by a mile.

The wolves ambled away. Their paw prints were immediately covered by the falling snow. Violette hoped nobody would ever find them. It didn’t matter how sad humans were about not seeing them, so long as the wolves could continue to live in peace.

The two girls strolled through the forest together, surrounded by silence.

Violette told Lily about the monster who lived in the mirror.

'Sometimes when I look into the mirror, I see a monster. Not very often, and especially not recently. I think I know why it's slowly disappearing. It's because I'm starting to understand it.'

In return, Lily told her a story about Korea.

Violette knew a little bit about Korea. A peninsula divided into two. The capital of South Korea was Seoul. The traditional dress was called a 'hanbok.' Their national treasure was the Sungnyemun Gate. The peninsula was shaped like a tiger. The Korean alphabet was Hangul. Historical figures included Sejong the Great and General Yi Sun-Shin.

Violette had learned all this from Claire, who studied everything she could because she felt it was her duty to educate her daughter about where she came from.

Violette's biggest takeaway was that South Korea was just another country on the map. Out of the two of them, it seemed Claire was the person who felt an affinity with the country.

While Violette had no memories of Korea, Claire did. After all, she was the one who had travelled there to meet Violette. It was also Claire who hoped Violette would one day get the chance to visit, even though Violette saw no reason to do so.

Lily's voice was soft against the cold night. 'It's warm and lively. How to put it… there's always a savoury scent in the air, as if every house is cooking up a feast.'

Claire had made Korea seem like a boring place of obligation and learning. Lily's version of Korea was vivid and compelling.

'It's been twenty years, so I'm sure a lot has changed, but I'd like to go again.'

Lily had crossed France, Germany, Austria, Slovakia, Ukraine, Russia, Kazakhstan, China, Myanmar, Thailand and Cambodia to get to Vietnam. Back then, the country was engaged in a civil war. Rife with violence and air raids, bombings, weapons of mass destruction and chemical weapons, it was a land of havoc and death. Soldiers and civilians were indiscriminately attacked, and the ground was littered with bodies and mines. Violette didn't ask why Lily had gone to such a place. She knew the answer, and didn't want to hear it.

While she was there, Lily met soldiers who'd been dispatched from South Korea to go to Vietnam. Five strays, separated from their unit. While they scoured the wetland hoping to reunite with their comrades, Lily and other vampires followed them. The other vampires lay in wait. Although they could've gone in for the kill at any time, they held out, waiting for exhaustion and fear to drain the men of their energy, until they were too weak to even scream.

'Did you kill them in the end?' Violette asked. Lily shook her head. A sigh of relief escaped Violette.

When the five men split up, Lily went after one of them. The young man – a child in Lily's eyes – was a fool who didn't recognise Lily as one of the monsters who had been chasing them. He hid behind a rock and urgently waved Lily over, mistaking her for a civilian living in the area. When he warned her to watch out for dangerous enemy soldiers, Lily lost her appetite and told him the truth.

They had spent about thirty minutes together.

'How old was he?' Violette asked. Lily complained that it was always so difficult to guess how old human beings were, but she said he had looked very young, too young to be sent to a place like that.

So very young, she repeated, again and again.

'Well, at least he lived because he met you.'

'He died. He was shot before he got the chance to reunite with his unit.'

When Lily went to Korea, she crossed the South China Sea as a stowaway. There were thirty or so Vietnamese people on the same boat who saw the chaos as the perfect opportunity to sneak into Korea. Had there been other vampires on that boat, perhaps the boat would've arrived at the dock with no one on board, Lily said with a chuckle.

So Lily went to Korea to return the boy's pouch. The boy who'd chatted to her nonstop for thirty minutes, thinking he was easing a young girl's fright. He'd reached into his uniform and pulled out a palm-sized little bag. Lily knew immediately what it was. A gift from your mother? You need to make it back to her safe, she'd said to him.

When Lily got to the boy's home, no one answered the door. She left the pouch on the windowsill.

'How did you get his address?'

'I had memorised the number written on his uniform. Once I was in Korea, I was able to track it down.'

Violette pictured the moment when the mother found her son's pouch sitting on the windowsill. *Did she cry? Or did she smile?*

Seoul was like an ant cave, said Lily. The roads were crowded with rickshaws and bridled oxes, rows of street vendors, and cars coughing up black exhaust fumes at all times of night. Children meandered around the bustling maze with yokes or bundles on their backs. It was noisy and chaotic, yet filled with life and warmth. Despite Lily's evocative descriptions, Violette struggled to picture anything.

'You should go one day,' Lily urged.

Violette almost said she didn't want to. That she wouldn't even if she got the chance. But after a short pause, she nodded reluctantly. Anything Lily said was worth at least trying.

They wandered back to Violette's house. The two of them said their goodbyes.

Waving to Lily at the door, Violette asked, 'Are there really people who'd wish death on the person they love?'

What is it like to lose a loved one? How can anyone kill someone they love with their own hands? Did they bottle up their love so tight that it exploded into a million pieces?

Violette wanted Lily to lie and say no, that such people didn't exist, and so there was no need to worry. But Lily was stubborn. Older folk tend to be, Claire had once told her. They had a strength rooted in their will to live.

'Yes,' Lily replied.

Violette watched Lily melt away into the night before heading inside. As she took off her clothes, got into the shower and put on her pyjamas, Violette tried to imagine a person killing someone they loved. The mere idea of Claire killing Maurice, or the other way around, was simply inconceivable to her.

When she slipped into her bed, buttoning up her top, she imagined herself pointing a rifle at Lily. A shadow flitted across the bedroom wall, cast by the moonlight. Violette smiled as she turned around. She thought it was Lily, but there was no one at the window.

SUYEON

Suyeon struggled violently against the police officers. The harder she resisted, the more they tightened their grip. She was seething with rage, yet could do nothing but stomp her feet like a distraught child.

Suyeon was not the detective sent here to inspect the scene this time. Today, she was the one who needed protection, the most unstable person on site.

Chantae crossed the police line on Suyeon's behalf, squeezing her shoulder as he passed her.

Suyeon looked at the spot. But when Chaetae lifted the white sheet, her eyes flew shut. Still, she had to look. She couldn't afford to miss anything. Her nails dug into her palms as she forced her eyes open.

Her gaze drifted between Chantae's back and the tarmac, and her stomach churned. A bead of cold sweat trickled down her forehead. That was when she saw her, sprawled out on the ground. Granny Eunshim.

Why is she lying on the cold, hard ground?

In the winter, Granny Eunshim would roll out the electric heating pad over the square wooden bench. She always made Suyeon sit in the middle, claiming that it was the warmest spot. *Weren't you the one who always insisted that being in the cold could mess up our digestion and joints? You told me that no matter how terrible life gets, I should always make sure to eat well and dress warm, so why the hell are you lying dead on the cold ground right now?* Suyeon wished she could yank Granny Eunshim's ghost by the collar and scream at her.

But Suyeon knew it was impossible. The living couldn't talk to the dead.

All she could do now was look for traces that Granny Eunshin had left behind.

Suyeon stopped struggling. The police officers took their hands off her.

Granny Eunshim's hair, which she usually gathered into a neat ponytail, was tangled in clumps of dark crimson. Her blood flowed all the way to Suyeon's feet, a stubborn pool above the tarmac.

Suyeon walked up to the body and dropped to her knees. Chantae called out Suyeon's name, but she ignored him and gently closed Granny Eunshim's lids.

Suyeon stayed there for a while. As neither a detective nor a blood relation.

***

Granny Eunshim's son told Suyeon that even if he left Toronto right away, he'd only arrive just before the funeral cortège. It sounded like he wanted Suyeon to tell him to save himself the trouble of coming. 'Would it kill you to come?' Suyeon had asked instead. After a short hesitation, he'd said no. The call ended. Suyeon folded the yellow armband into a neat square and placed it on the chief mourner's spot. That was not her place.

Chantae returned to the funeral home carrying a plastic bag. Inside was some bread and milk. He tore open the carton of milk and slid it towards Suyeon, who was staring vacantly at the swirls rising from the incense sticks.

'So she wasn't your real grandmother,' said Chantae, pulling at the hem of his trousers.

Suyeon turned to look at him.

'Is that why you're not wearing that?' Chantae pointed his chin towards the armband. 'She's that halmoni, isn't she? The one Eungyeong knew.'

Suyeon answered with a small nod.

'*I'd* say the saddest person should be the chief mourner. Didn't know you were such a stickler for gender roles and tradition. Go put that on,' said Chantae, gently tapping her arm.

But Suyeon only stared at the perfectly folded armband. Taking matters into his own hands, Chantae grabbed the armband and set it next to the milk.

'I'm sure you know only direct family members can apply for bereavement leave. But I will pull some strings. Take as much time as you need.'

'Thanks.'

Suyeon fiddled with the bread wrapper. After giving her a final pat on the back, Chantae took his leave, but he didn't take more than a few steps before turning around.

'Suyeon-ah. We found her suicide note.'

Suyeon's fingers froze. She raised her head.

Scratching the back of his head, Chantae continued. 'Don't think too much about it. It's not what she would've wanted.'

Suyeon wanted to know what was written in the note, and whether forensics had confirmed that the handwriting matched Granny Eunshim's, but she could barely move her lips. Chantae waited for an answer before eventually turning to leave. It was then that Suyeon spoke, struck by the sudden realisation that she might never get to speak of this relationship again.

'She ran the shop opposite my primary school,' Suyeon said, smoothing out the crease on the armband. 'She took care of me. Like I was her favourite. I didn't get along with my parents, and whenever I fell into a dark place, halmoni was always there to comfort me. She showed me that I didn't need anyone's approval, that violence was never the answer.'

It pained Suyeon to know that their relationship couldn't be proved by blood or writing. The depth of their relationship could only be displayed when the both of them were together.

Now that one of them was gone, Suyeon was left to reminisce on her own, holding onto one end of a severed string.

'Every day, she'd give me a bottle of yoghurt and tell me to hang in there, to keep on living. She made me who I am.'

'Sounds like an amazing person.'

'She saved me,' said Suyeon. 'Thanks for the bread. I'll put this on, too.'

Suyeon looked down at the armband. Chantae nodded at her with a smile. After he'd left, Suyeon turned her attention to the funeral portrait.

It was a photograph of a much younger Granny Eunshim. She'd had it taken before checking into the rehabilitation hospital. Back then, Suyeon had scolded her, asking why on earth she'd rushed to do something like that. The early funeral photo had unsettled her. It had felt like an omen calling out to the grim reaper. But Granny Eunshim had told her she wanted to have her photo taken before she got any older.

'Why would I want a photo of me looking old and pruney? I'm going to die sooner or later, so I might as well give the people coming to my funeral something nice to look at. A funeral portrait captures our last moments, you know. I want them to know I was happy.'

Granny Eunshim was right. The image of her bloodied body lying on the ground was washed away by the photo of her in a pretty hanbok with her cherry red lips curved into a graceful smile. With the armband clasped in her hand, Suyeon hugged her knees to her chest. Sadness, tinged with regret, was starting to peek in like the break of dawn. Only when the funeral home emptied out did she allow her tears to fall. They trickled onto the floor without end.

Then, she gathered the thoughts she'd postponed, and began to sieve through them.

***

Granny Eunshim marked the hospital's sixth death. The means of suicide was nothing new, but her death stood out from the preceding cases. Fresh, crimson blood. Gushing out from her cracked skull, soaking the floor. Its viscosity had clung onto Suyeon's shoes.

There were no holes on Granny Eunshim's body. Unlike the previous cases, hers was a flawless, straightforward suicide.

Suyeon yearned for nothing more than to have one last conversation with Granny Eunshim.

Written with neat penmanship, the suicide notes made no mention of fear or bitterness. Instead, they expressed the victims' relief in knowing that they'd be escaping this cruel life at last. Suyeon knew this very well. She'd just been denying it all this while. *Was death really their last hope?* She recalled the patients' blank faces, dotted by as many age spots as years spent in the hospital, their hazy pupils, soundless mouths and stick-thin bodies. People who used to be full of life, but were now only alive due to their laboured breathing. If, for the victims, the pain of living was indeed too hard to bear, then Suyeon could no longer say with confidence why she was working so hard to uncover the truth. Agony was a tenacious thing. It devoured people and wore them down. For hours, Suyeon sat still as she watched over the funeral home.

Granny Eunshim's son arrived before the cortège in the end. He brought with him his two kids, whom Suyeon had never seen before. The children stole shy glances at their grandmother's portrait. Once it dawned on them that this wasn't a place of fun, they whined about wanting to go somewhere else. As the son handed Suyeon an envelope containing a token of his gratitude, he begged his kids to behave for just a while more. Suyeon politely declined his token, but the son insisted and tucked the envelope into the pocket of her jacket.

Is it that easy to get rid of your guilt? Suyeon forced herself to swallow her words. Before leaving the funeral home, she quietly dropped the envelope into the donation collection box.

When she arrived home at dawn, Suyeon plopped down on her bed without washing up. Sleep evaded her. Deafened by the silence, she curled up into a ball and hugged her blanket. The emptiness around her swelled.

And so it would continue for the rest of her life. She might forget about it after a while, but one day, she'd be struck by an unbearable melancholy, and some nights, she'd be haunted by forgotten memories. In the face of such great yearning, Suyeon could only see herself growing smaller and smaller, weaker and weaker. But wasn't she already well-acquainted with this emotion? Eungyeong sunbae had assured her she'd toughen up in no time, but sunbae was wrong. A strong heart was something you were born with, not something you could train. Suyeon had only been pretending to be strong, and had fooled herself in the process.

Suyeon hovered a finger over Violette's name in her phone, but didn't click on it. Violette would know. That another person had died in the hospital. That it was the halmoni Suyeon loved most.

Flashes of Granny Eunshim thrashing in a vampire's bony grip hounded Suyeon. Why did her imagination choose this moment to break loose?

It pained her to think that there was a fate worse than death. She had always sought comfort in natural deaths. This feeling had grown with every homicide case she took on.

Weary from staring at the sliver of light streaming through the curtains, Suyeon's eyes fluttered shut at last. She made a futile wish, and hoped that she'd wake up to find that everything had been a bad dream. She longed to hear that nagging voice again.

You're all skin and bones, it said, as a pair of rough, chubby hands offered her a small bottle of yoghurt.

Suyeon slept fitfully. Too tired to fully wake up, she slipped in and out of consciousness until she couldn't tell if the light pouring in was the sun or the street lamp. Sadness was heavy. If it needed a shape, it would steal a human's. A tar-like substance, it would drape itself over their silhouette, covering them from head to toe, not leaving out a single strand of hair, so that if they stopped paying attention to their breathing, they'd soon realise they were slowly being smothered. Even in her sleep, Suyeon felt every cloud of breath warming the back of her hand. *I should get up before this room suffocates me*, she thought.

If she hadn't forced herself, perhaps she might've never got out of bed. It seemed her sadness had fully transformed into lethargy. A colleague begged her to take a few days off, but Suyeon refused. She had to go get Granny Eunshim's things.

At the hospital, all eyes were glued to Suyeon. Carrying a cardboard box, she hurried through the seating area and into the ward.

The room was dark and empty. Granny Eunshim's bed had already been stripped of its covers. Suyeon sat down on the edge of the bed. The size-four box that she'd bought at the post office looked massive beside the pathetic sum of Granny Eunshim's things. All she'd left behind were a few winter sweaters, socks, her reading glasses and a couple of towels. Suyeon packed everything into the box without knowing what her next step was. Technically, she should hand them over to her son, but something told her that he'd accept them begrudgingly and burn them in a heap before flying back to Canada. If Granny Eunshim's son agreed, Suyeon wanted to keep everything.

She would chuck the box in a corner, leaving it to be forgotten until longing found her. Then, and only then, would she take out the box and sort through its contents until every item lost its essence.

After she had finished packing the things away, Suyeon sat on Granny Eunshim's bed, staring into space. At some point, this ward had become a place she'd miss. Who would've thought they'd make so many memories in a place like this? Suyeon forced herself to stand. Just as she was about to pick up the box, she stepped on something. Bright orange yarn, threaded onto circular knitting needles. Setting down the box on the bed, Suyeon knelt down. Underneath the bed was a half-completed scarf still attached to a skein of yarn. She reached to grab the scarf.

That scarf you were wearing for months is basically in tatters, so I wanted to make you something nice. But my eyes have been failing me lately, so I have to start now if I'm going to have it ready by the winter.

'By the winter...'

Suyeon ran her fingers along the crisscrossing threads. Just then, a carer entered the ward, wheeling in a patient holding a paper sunflower. After helping the patient to her bed, she placed the sunflower on the tray. She threw Suyeon a sidelong glance as if to say, *I know you're staring*. Suyeon gave the bottom of Granny Eunshim's bed a quick scan. No paper flowers. She righted herself and approached the carer.

'Sorry! Sorry to bother you, but – where did you get that sunflower?'

'She made it in class just now,' answered the carer.

Leaving the box on the bed, Suyeon rushed out of the ward. There was a noticeboard in the sixth-floor lobby, and her feet were rushing her there as if they had a mind of their own. On the noticeboard was this month's menu, a set of rules for the prevention of infectious disease, a list of visiting hours and emergency contacts, and right in the corner, the information for 'This Month's Classes.' Singing, drawing, Bible reading...

'And origami.'

Suyeon moved her finger up, following the column of the timetable. She stopped at the top, then slid her finger to the side.

'Seo Nanju.'

The nurse in charge.

The name seemed to be haunting her.

Suyeon retrieved the box and dashed out of the hospital. After setting down the box on the back seat, she jumped into the driver's seat and whipped out her phone, swiping to the gallery app. She scanned the suicide notes.

Excluding Granny Eunshim's, all five suicide notes mentioned a hill of flowers. This whole time, Suyeon had assumed they were referring to Heaven or the afterlife, but what if there was somewhere else?

She dialled Chantae's number. When he answered, the gentleness in his voice made her cringe. Suyeon shuddered once and cut to the chase.

'Could you send me Granny Eunshim's suicide note?'

'Oh, what's the use of looking at it now? You should be taking time off—'

'It's not what you think, so could you just send it. You took a photo, right? Please tell me you did.'

'Give me some credit!'

'Great, send it over. There's something I have to check.'

For a while, there was no response. 'Hello?' Suyeon called out. There was an audible sigh on the other end.

'Just the photo?'

'Yup.'

'Is that all?'

'Yup,' replied Suyeon, but she quickly backtracked. 'Actually, could I have a few more days off? Maybe two or three?'

'Three days?' Chantae sounded stressed. Since Suyeon didn't qualify for bereavement leave, he was running out of excuses to grant her any more days off. Suyeon knew this. But she also knew that Chantae had a soft spot for her.

'Never mind if it's not possible,' said Suyeon.

'How about this? We'll say you're working from home, and if anything comes up, you get your arse to the scene immediately. Deal?'

'Deal. Thank you, sunbae.'

'Well, that's something I don't hear often.'

'You haven't done much to warrant my thanks before.'

'I'm hanging up. Rest up, kid.'

A message from Chantae arrived shortly after. Suyeon clutched the phone to her chest. Fear was starting to sink in. She rested her forehead on the steering wheel.

It's not her suicide note, it's just another piece of evidence, she chanted inwardly. On the other hand, she was terrified that the note might indeed turn out to be just another piece of evidence. In the event that Granny Eunshim's death hadn't been a suicide, but rather a homicide, Suyeon wasn't sure if she'd be able to confront her rage.

But first she had to read the note. Even if it meant that anger would be curling its thick hands around her neck and twisting it, she had to read Granny Eunshim's last words. It was her duty. The duty of the living.

As the sun descended, its golden rays splashed onto her car. Feeling her forehead heating up, Suyeon straightened her back. Sixteen minutes had passed since Chantae's text.

She clicked on the photo.

***

My head feels cloudy. It's like my senses are dulling, and I can't tell if I'm alive.

When I was a little girl, my eomma would give me a glass of water mixed with black sugar to wake me up. When that sweetness tugged on my tongue, my eyes would fly open. I haven't had anything like it in decades. I've always thought eating was one of life's greatest pleasures, but now that I've forgotten that sweetness, life has lost its meaning.

Eomma visits my dreams a lot these days, and she always brings me something good. The nurse was right. Eomma has always been waiting for me. She's waving to me, telling me to hurry up because she misses me.

My son's all grown up and has built a life overseas. What more could I wish for? I suppose I'm worried for that daughter of mine. She's tall and pretty, but hasn't found someone to marry yet. I'd love to see her walk down the aisle or at least find someone she likes before I leave. But she's a strong girl so I shouldn't worry. She gets cold easily, so I'll knit her a warm scarf before I go. I've had such fun thanks to her and unni.

What a relief. After spending my whole life at the mercy of life's whimsy, at least in death I'm given a choice.

I've made so many flowers for eomma. The thought of her standing there, with a glass of sugared water waiting for me, has kept me hanging on. Even after all the beautiful moments I've experienced, nothing compares to my mornings with her.

Will she tell me that I've been good? That I did my best even though I was bored and lonely?

I can't wait to tell her about Eungyeong unni and my lovely Suyeon.

NANJU

It had been love once, but only for a while. His sharp fingernails were a turn off when they cuddled, and God forbid he should scratch her by accident.

Still, during the period when she believed it was love, she had been just as giddy as any girl in love. No, she had been the giddiest. The person who'd found her was nothing like the others, and that made him special. He empathised with her rage. Instead of saying empty words like, 'Hang in there, it gets better,' he asked if she wished death upon those who wronged her. The word 'death' was light on his lips, as if it weighed nothing at all.

He told her that to live was to accept that death would come knocking at any time, and that some people's deaths were worth more than their lives. People whose pure existence was torture for others, whose breaths sucked the life out of others. It sounded like he was talking about her father.

Nanju was connected to the other end of her father's ventilator. He breathed through her. Ulan said he would climb through the window of the hospital ward and remove her father's ventilator, he said the old man would die, clueless, in the middle of a dream, and that the hospital staff would say he died in the ward, alone. His words exuded warmth and brought her peace. When he left at dawn, Nanju tossed and turned in bed, worried he wouldn't keep his promise. When she finally fell asleep, her father came to see her in a dream.

It was a long-forgotten version of him, one before all the trouble, when he had still treated her like a proper daughter.

Nanju's eyes flew open. It was already morning. Her phone rang. When she answered, she was informed of her father's death. She stared out the window and broke into an absentminded laugh.

Her father had died as easily as falling asleep. No sign that his blood had been drained.

But why didn't Ulan take his blood? The question slowly started to choke her.

Once she had learned that he was just a fucking bat who killed for sport, she should've made a run for it. But she couldn't. He'd freed her from her father's ventilator. Of course, what she'd believed was love, and what she'd given up everything for, turned out to be a mere hallucination, a symptom of breathing in the poison he exhaled.

When Ulan sensed she was withering under the burden of the loan sharks, he asked again if she wanted them dead. She did. She wanted it more than anything but refused to ask him to make it so for two reasons. She wanted him to be more than just her personal avenger, and she wanted herself to be strong and smart enough to overcome those bastards herself.

That confidence soon turned into fear.

As the love passed, it began to feel like she had accepted a service without knowing the cost. Like Ulan would come to her one day with a vile request.

Now, Nanju was once again made to face her complacency. He'd always been willing to kill for more than just blood. *But why? Why that granny? Old and lonely…*

She suddenly remembered what Ulan had told her.

That person he resents… could it be her? Considering how long he lives, is it possible that the person he resents has become old and grey by now?

But something didn't add up. Up until their conversation, he hadn't been watching the old lady, nor had he approached her. She practically hadn't existed to him. So then… why? Why kill that granny out of the blue?

She thought back to the day the lady had died.

A patient wearing a cardigan had called out to her. 'The wind is too strong.'

Whenever the older patients needed something, their first instinct was to look for a nurse. They didn't get up to shut the windows if the room got too cold. Instead, they'd call a nurse over and tell them that the windows were open.

Indifferent, Nanju had gone into the ward. The room was indeed freezing. Noticing the swaying curtains, she assumed a patient had forgotten to shut the windows before bed. But no one was in the bed beside the window. *Maybe they're in the toilet*, Nanju thought, as she duly shut the windows.

But then, she saw the paper carnation that'd been knocked over. When Nanju finally recalled that the bed she stood by belonged to Ahn Eunshim, she returned to her station and got the keys to the roof.

She moved cooly, ignoring her heart banging wildly against her chest. No way. She'd specially told him that the granny was off-limits. But just in case, Nanju did a quick check to make sure the bathroom lights weren't on before hurrying to the roof. That was when she saw it, in the last shadows of darkness before the morning. The face of someone who killed without greed, temptation, rage or hatred. *Roaches,* Nanju thought, *that's all we are to him.*

As that face floated into her mind, Nanju's suspicion grew. His face had been completely blank. How could he be so calm when the moment he'd been waiting for had finally come? When the object of his resentment was withering in his grasp? If the old woman wasn't the one he was after, then why did he kill her? Was his real target the detective?

When the police had arrived at the scene, the detective that came to visit was nowhere to be found. Nanju supposed she'd been taken off the case because she was close to the victim. Since Nanju had been on duty during the time of the incident, a male detective called her over and asked a routine set of questions. When he asked why she had been on the roof, Nanju said that with everything that'd been happening lately, she'd simply gone to make sure that everything was fine. The detective looked tired and confused and jaded.

Before he left, the male detective said he'd call if he had any other questions. Nanju knew there'd be none, and so she considered: should she at least say something to him? That although she couldn't explain it, there was something weird happening in the hospital? That all the nurses were suspicious?

Nanju's lips twitched, but she got up quietly. One wrong word and she might end up causing more trouble. They were dealing with a monster who had no reservations about murder. Nothing would stop him from getting rid of everyone involved in the case.

As Nanju sat in her room hugging her knees, she felt like a shell-less snail writhing on a hot pavement, waiting to die. If there was a God, she had some questions for him. About why salvation never came at the right moment.

She thought back to the time when it had been love. He'd come to her every day after sunset and shown her just how beautiful a world draped in darkness could be. She learnt that the magic of amusement parks came to life after hours, that a deserted highway beside the sea could be turned into a beach, that the best view of the city was from the top of the 63 Building, and that even in the city, there were unlit alleys where you can gaze at the Milky Way. He had taught her everything.

Their love had been perfect. For the first time in her life, Nanju was no longer screaming in frustration, but sighing in awe. Her nights shone brighter than the day.

That was all in the past now. And although Nanju knew that none of it had been real, only a hallucination, she was scared. If she snapped out of it, she'd be surrendering herself to a life of monotony and banality, a life that had suffocated her for too long, where she was thrown curveball after curveball, forced to walk on thorns until her feet were numb to the pain.

A different thought flashed through her mind. What if Ulan was drawing up a future *with* her? What if her reckless judgement had ruined something good? After all, he'd always been the secretive type. What if all this negativity was just in her head?

The waves in her heart instantly settled. Her body suddenly slackened, and she could breathe again. Nanju tucked herself in and sank deeper and deeper into her mattress.

A gentle touch on the back of her hand woke her up. Ulan was sitting on the edge of her bed. 'You're awake,' he murmured, without looking at her. Nanju pushed herself up. Ulan's thick, silky lashes fluttered as his gold-tinted irises found her. He always looked at her like that, as if he knew what it meant to be tender.

He knew that Nanju had seen him on the roof. Of course he did. They'd made eye contact. But instead of acknowledging her presence then, he'd simply left. In fact, he'd fled. From the emerging sun.

'Was there a reason?' Nanju asked.

Ulan paused, then nodded. His eyelids drooped apologetically. Nanju barely contained her laughter. He was putting on a show. Why was he acting like that when he had never been sorry for anything? When he knew Nanju could never be a threat?

Why? If not love, then there must be another reason.

Nanju couldn't figure it out. Ulan leaned in, resting his head on her chest.

'She didn't react when she saw my face. I thought maybe she'd forgotten me,' he said. 'Though... after all this time, not a single thing has changed. Her eyes were as shrewd as ever.'

'She's the girl you mentioned?'

Ulan nodded. Like a needy child, he burrowed deeper into Nanju's embrace.

'Humans grow old so quickly, and they become so stubborn when they're old. They never react the way I want them to.'

There it was. He was just curious about her reaction. Was that a reason worth killing for? Again, Nanju stifled the laughter bubbling inside her. She wished she could snap the neck she was caressing. If he could be killed so easily, she would do it in a heartbeat.

'Aren't you risking exposure?' asked Nanju evenly.

'Don't worry. I'm going to get rid of that woman and her detective friend,' said Ulan. 'Those people… I've watched them long enough to know they've got no one.'

Nanju knew it then. She had to speak to the detective as soon as possible. Because she herself would be next to die. She would not be leaving with him. Of this, she was certain.

Because she, too, had no one.

***

After Nanju sent Ulan off into the night, she caught a glimpse of the woman.

The one who had been watching her in the hospital last time. The detective's partner. Though Nanju could only see the top of her head from her bedroom window, she was sure it was her. And that she hadn't screamed when she saw a man jump from the twelfth floor.

Nanju considered pretending she hadn't seen, but her resolve came crashing down within minutes. She threw open the curtains and poked her head out. The spot where the woman had been standing was empty. Nanju scrambled to get her jacket. She might still be able to catch her if she hurried. Nanju needed her. Luckily, she was spared the chase. When she burst out of the front door, the woman was already waiting outside.

Wordlessly, Nanju invited her in.

Upon entering Nanju's apartment, the woman locked the windows and drew the curtains. Nanju watched as the woman sauntered freely around her house with her shoes still on. The woman didn't feel human, but she didn't look like Ulan either. Her footsteps were completely silent. If Nanju hadn't had her eyes open, perhaps she wouldn't have known there was somebody in the house.

As the woman stared at her without a word, Nanju forced herself to hold her gaze. She realised soon enough that this woman knew everything. That Ulan survived on human blood, and that she'd been helping him hunt for it.

Does she know he's coming for her and her detective friend? Nanju wondered. If she did in fact know, then had she come to stop him? She seemed to be hiding something. Something sharp. When at last the woman spoke, the words that came out of her lips sounded like music to Nanju's ears. Nanju rejoiced.

'We could kill him with your help.'

But that happiness didn't last for long. Killing Ulan didn't mean saving her life.

The woman asked if Ulan had promised her anything. Nanju explained their arrangement – he killed for her, and she helped him find his next prey.

Was love a promise?

After some thought, Nanju concluded that it couldn't be. Their love only existed in the present. He'd never once promised her the future.

The woman didn't question her further. She turned away as if her work was done. Nanju rushed to grab her arm, but the woman shook her off. Her dark pupils held no sympathy for Nanju.

'Your eyes tell me you want to live. Want to know how you can save yourself?' she asked.

Nanju kept quiet.

'There's only one way. If *he* chooses to spare you.'

Nanju began to shake. As rage manifested into hot tears, her wide eyes struggled to deny the reality inching closer towards her. When she spoke again, she stabbed each syllable.

'The only way to save myself is to not have been born in the first place.'

'But you were, and lived for as long as you have. You, too, had a choice to save lives.'

'That...'

'Save your excuses.'

Wasn't life one big excuse? People bored her to death with all their excuses. Life had never once been on her side. Instead, it hid behind people and forced them to spit out excuses.

'Oh, and about love,' the woman smirked. 'You've got it all wrong.'

Leaning in, she whispered in Nanju's ears.

‘They know how to love. As much as humans, or more. They’ll even kill their own kind just to protect the humans they care about.’

Nanju couldn’t believe it. And as a result, she couldn’t stand the way the woman was tearing her excuses to shreds.

‘If your selfish heart still wants to live, then stay still when the bastard goes for your blood. Don’t resist and don’t put up a fight. Don’t fall for anything he says. Make him believe you’re letting him have you,’ she said.

But what Nanju heard was this:

Be good and die.

VIOLETTE

December 1983

Clouds are prettier at night. You can't look at the sun, but you can stare at the moon, and while the sun steals the spotlight, the moon shares it with the stars. At night, birdsongs can be heard with your heart. Still trees shudder awake, while mice scuttle about, freed from the sharp eyes of cats, as the new season settles upon their little steps. Petals and leaves, too, peek out of their buds. The night was kind to such shy things, those that could not bloom under harsh light and prying eyes. Violette was one of them. She grew up so quietly, she sometimes wondered if she was really there at all. She wouldn't have noticed she'd grown taller if not for Lily.

After giving Violette a piggyback ride up to her room one night, Lily pointed out that she had got heavier. At first, Violette thought she'd put on weight, but she quickly realised that her legs were longer. On Lily's back, her feet used to come up to Lily's shins, but now they hovered around her ankles.

The way humans felt about the lifespan of cats and dogs was how vampires felt about human beings, said Lily. If humans felt sorry about how most dogs only lived to see twelve Christmases, then vampires felt sorry about how most humans only saw seventy. That meant only seventy Christmas cakes in a lifetime, and dogs that grew up with babies never got to see them become adults. It was worse for vampires. Their time with humans never felt longer than a season. That's why we don't have pets, said Lily. It would be no different from caring for something for a few days and spending the rest of your life missing it. Their relationships were unfair from the beginning. To the one who lived longer. That was always the case.

Violette wondered what it would be like to miss something. Missing something meant wanting to go back to the past. Wanting to go back to the past meant that something was missing in the present. Something missing in the present meant that there was an empty space where something should be. And an empty space could only be bitter and cold. Did that mean that the more things you missed, the more bitter and cold you felt? If that was the case, then some people's worlds must be made up of only winters.

Maybe that was why vampires were immune to the cold; their skin turned icy from the unending longing. They must've said goodbye more times than there are dead drain flies under a lonely light bulb. Violette felt sad all of a sudden. One day, she'd be just another drain fly in

Lily's memory. *Is there a way to make someone remember you differently?* she wondered, not knowing then what a childish and selfish thought that was.

Violette was growing up, and she was learning more and more about Lily. In the summer, they went to the sea at night, and in the autumn, they visited festivals. Sometimes they'd sneak into libraries, and compete to see who could read the most books in a night. But what mattered to Violette wasn't the sights and places.

It was finding out what ran through Lily's mind when she saw the sea, what her first memory of the water was, when she had learned how to swim, what foods she seemed to enjoy, what kind of books she liked reading, and what feelings stirred in her when she read those books. Lily's life was long and wide and deep. Violette could hardly believe some of the things she said. Like that time at the museum, standing in front of a Van Gogh, when Lily said that the artist had looked more handsome in person.

'You've seen him?' Violette asked.

'Yeah. Once when I went to boarding school in the Netherlands. And again, later, at a psychiatric hospital.'

'Wow.'

'Miss a moment and an entire world disappears. Scary, isn't it?'

For a long while, Lily hadn't been able to move on from the painting. *Were they close?* Violette wondered. *What does it feel like to discover a trace of someone who is gone?*

As Violette chewed over the question, she wondered if Lily was just pulling her leg. After all, things that couldn't be verified could just as easily be false as true.

Lily's world was wider than her own. In that world, there were rows of graves for those who'd departed before Lily.

Perhaps widening one's world meant making enough space for yearning. Violette wanted to give Lily a hug, but her chest seemed too narrow to hold such an enormous universe. Still, she wanted to hold her. So what to do? She mulled over it for days until an idea struck – in a world full of graves, she would build a giant cinema. A place Lily could visit whenever she felt cold or bitter, where she could play back old tapes of happy memories put together by Violette.

Violette held this plan close to her heart and waited for the right time to execute it, but it was surprisingly hard to find the opportunity. School occupied most of her days, and when summer came, the family decided to go on a short holiday. She'd asked Lily to join them, but Lily had turned her down. And just like that, time slipped by. When Christmas approached, the first she'd be spending with Lily, Violette tried again.

'Would you like to come over this Christmas?'

Lily's eyes widened in surprise, but she nodded. When she asked what she should wear, Violette said it didn't matter, so long as she put on some socks and shoes.

Claire and Maurice were just as surprised as Lily.

They had stared at their daughter, eyes wide in disbelief, when Violette asked if a friend could come over. Their reaction made Violette shy, and she said to forget she even asked. But her parents immediately shook their heads and insisted that they loved the idea. They were practically bouncing off the walls, as if they were the ones who'd made a new friend. Immediately, they got to work, starting preparations two weeks in advance. They gave Violette a task: make a list of Lily's favourite food.

'Let's see… Favourite food…'

It had been a while since the two had sat under the cypress tree, chatting as they gazed out at the moonlight-dappled field. Lily thought long and hard about the question. Her tastebuds weren't as delicate as Violette's, she explained. If they were any more well-developed, vampires wouldn't be able to survive for long. There were times when they had to eat things that could barely be considered food. Surviving meant sucking it up and swallowing stale bread without so much as a drop of water, and a refined palate would make that unbearable. Lily ate for the sake of eating. She couldn't tell the difference between white chocolate and milk chocolate, baguettes and croissants, onion soup and potato soup, tomato pasta and carbonara. To her, they were just chocolate, bread, soup and pasta.

'Well, there's something I'd like to see… Not taste.'

'What is it?'

'Bûche de Noël.'

Violette laughed delightedly. A chocolate cake, iced to look like a log and served at Christmas. Her mum never left it out of the spread.

Since that moment, the thought of Christmas made Violette's heart beat like hummingbird wings.

Claire and Maurice didn't have a clue, but Lily had taken part in decorating the family tree. She'd looked at the tree from outside the window, and leaped onto Violette's windowsill to tell her where to place the ornaments. Violette dashed up and down the stairs, heeding every one of her requests. The Christmas tree had never sparkled so bright.

On Christmas morning, Lily appeared in a black velvet suit. She brought a chestnut tart and a bottle of wine. 'From my parents,' she lied, beaming. Claire and Maurice fell in love instantly. They led her to the dining table, where a feast awaited them.

The bûche de Noël was longer than last year's, and there was a wider variety of food. Claire and Maurice had been in the kitchen since the morning, whipping up a meal that could feed at least ten. Violette hoped that Lily wouldn't feel burdened. She didn't want her to force herself to eat anything she didn't like, or stuff herself to the point of getting sick.

But Lily appeared comfortable. She was chatty as she ate spoonfuls of everything. Holding her utensils with grace, she made eye contact with whoever was speaking and answered every question right on cue. She looked so like an adult, the way she carried the conversation so naturally.

If anything, Violette was the awkward one. She couldn't seem to get a word in. Her parents were showering her new friend with attention, and Lily was so busy answering their questions that she hadn't looked at Violette once.

But, in fact, Violette quite liked sitting back and watching the three of them interact. The dining table felt wider than usual. Her parents looked happier, and Lily...

Looked human.

After Lily said goodbye to Violette's parents, promising them she would visit again soon, she climbed into Violette's bedroom through the window. When Violette came upstairs after helping with the dishes, she found Lily asleep on her bed. She tiptoed through the room, trying not to wake her, but Lily's eyelids fluttered open.

The single bed was small for two. Especially since Violette had grown in the last year. Her shoulders and hips had widened, and she was taller. And so they lay horizontally on the bed with their legs dangling over the edge.

'Was the food OK?' Violette asked.

Lily replied, 'Best human food I've ever had.'

Violette couldn't tell if she meant it, or if she'd said it just to please her. But she decided not to obsess over the truth. It didn't matter anyway. Whether Lily was being sincere or not didn't change the fact that Violette was the happiest she'd ever been. 'Did I mess up? Or do anything that would offend your parents?' Lily asked. No, she hadn't. On the contrary, Lily had handled herself so well that Violette felt like a stranger in her own home.

'You...' Violette hesitated. 'You were so human.'

Lily didn't say anything. The air was muddled with silence, unspoken words and mixed emotions. Lily sat up. Violette kept her eyes fixed on the ceiling. 'Thanks for inviting me. I had a really good time,' said Lily. She kissed Violette on the forehead and left.

Alone in her bed, Violette sobbed. The tears kept on coming. She didn't know why, but one thing was for sure – she'd hurt Lily's feelings.

In books, humans turned into vampires after getting bitten. Last autumn, when they were in the library reading side by side, Violette showed Lily a paragraph and asked if it was true. Her voice rose with hope. Had Lily said yes, Violette would've asked her to bite her right there and then. But Violette was still human. Lily had shaken her head, giggling. We're not some disease you can catch, she said. Violette's cheeks flushed as she blurted out an apology.

Why would writers make up such a thing?

To capture the romance of spending eternity forever.

Violette could see how that was true. If cats and dogs wrote novels, they'd probably write about biting their owners to lengthen their lifespan, and about living together for a long, long time.

Violette assumed Lily wouldn't be back for a while, but to her surprise, Lily came the next morning. She arrived early, before Claire and Maurice were out of the house. Fat drops of either snow or rain drummed on the windows. Holding an umbrella, Lily greeted Violette's parents at the door. Violette had just thrown on some clothes and was heading downstairs when she saw Lily. Embarrassed by her dishevelled hair, she scurried back into her room. *This is so not a good time!* she squealed on the inside. Lily had never come to see her in the morning.

Vampires weren't the only creatures who avoided a certain time of day. Humans used to be the same way when it came to the night. They returned to their homes in the evenings the way vampires stayed inside during the day. But since humans had discovered a way to light up their homes and streets, they'd temporarily forgotten about their fear of the dark. They thought they'd conquered the night. Such arrogance. If all the light in the world disappeared, they'd be forced to face darkness. And the earthly creatures from whom they've stolen the night would come to take back what was theirs.

According to Lily, vampires could roam around in the day so long as they had something to block out the light. In fact, on days like this, when the sun couldn't squeeze past the clouds, a simple hat would suffice. But in general, vampires rarely came out during the day, just because they rested then, and came out later.

Not long after Lily's arrival that morning, Claire and Maurice left for work. They put out cereal and leftover cake for the girls, but Lily didn't go near the food this time.

It was as if Violette had dreamed up the girl at dinner yesterday. Warily, Violette spooned a piece of cake into her mouth in silence. That was when Lily took out a glass bottle from her bag. The liquid it contained looked like wine.

'Meet my breakfast. Human blood,' said Lily flatly.

Violette stopped chewing and looked at her.

'You should know that without it, I'll fall ill. First, exhaustion hits. Ten days later, I won't be able to get out of bed. It's like coming down with a burning hot fever, or a terrible case of the flu, only worse. My pillowcase will be covered in tufts of hair, I won't be able to breathe, and my body will be so inflamed that it'll be torture just to lie down. Pus will leak from every pore, until eventually my heart stops. Ten days is all it takes. See this? It's about as much as your dad had to drink last night, but I can survive on this for a whole week. One tiny bottle. What do you think? Less than you thought?'

Violette nodded.

'We drink blood, but not always. Even though our sense of taste isn't strong, we still eat food. But no food in the world can give us the nourishment we need. And so, we drink blood. Pigs or cows will do, but they're harder to hunt now that most of them are trapped on breeding farms. The quality of blood has worsened as well. Humans feed their livestock trash to fatten them up. Meanwhile, they keep the good stuff for themselves. That's why animal blood can't compare to human blood.

'The amount we need isn't so much that it would kill a human. But if we let them live, they might come after us with pitchforks and torches, the entire village thronging behind them. They set us on fire, drive stakes into our chests, cut off our heads… Once I saw my friend's head being paraded like a trophy. We couldn't find her body. Trust me, we don't enjoy it. We kill because it's the only way we can survive. So what do you think? Now that I'm sitting at the same table as you, drinking this, do I still seem so human? Do you think I could ever be one?'

'I didn't mean it like that,' said Violette.

'I know. But I want to make this clear. I hope that when you feel close to me, when you see me as your best friend, or when you want to spend forever with me, it's not because of how human I seem, but because you like me, as I am. You and I are different. We shouldn't expect to see ourselves in the other. That's the only way we can refrain from hurting each other. So promise me that if the day comes when you find my existence too frightening or heavy to bear, you'll tell me. I'll go away then.'

Violette thought Lily was cheating. What else could she say when Lily was threatening to leave?

'OK,' Violette conceded, 'but I get one do-over. One chance. If I say something like that again, by mistake or not, promise me you'll come back one more time.'

Lily agreed. But it was a promise that would have been better not made.

That night, Violette heard someone knock. She hurried towards the window at first, but something stopped her in her tracks. It hadn't been more than two hours since Lily left. Did she forget something? But surely she could wait till tomorrow.

Violette crept towards the light switch beside her door. She flicked it on. Perched on the railing of her balcony was an unfamiliar silhouette that didn't belong to Lily. She inched closer to the strange figure. 'Who is it?' she asked. No answer came. She stopped in front of her window, before wrapping her fingers around the handles.

Whatever was outside wasn't human – Violette felt it in her bones. She hesitated before throwing the windows open. In a flash, the stranger leapt off and vanished into the darkness. Violette's eyes trailed after him. When she tore her gaze away, she noticed a boy standing at the front door. He looked too mature to be called a boy, but his cheeks were too full to consider him a young man. His irises shone as brightly as the moon. He slowly took in Violette's face before strolling out of the garden.

Violette planned to tell Lily. *Your friends came to visit*, she would say.

But Lily didn't come the next day, or the day after.

Lily returned after a week. By then, worry and anger had passed, and only sadness lingered. Still, Violette thought she'd pull Lily into a hug before either of them could say anything. But before she could spread her arms, Lily collapsed onto her bedroom floor. Her skin was boiling, and her clothes were drenched in cold sweat. It was as if she'd caught an awful cold – or as if she hadn't had blood in ten days.

Violette recalled the museum they'd visited together last year. There had been a painting where a woman is holding a parasol, with her back facing the sun. She is showing the left side of her face, which is not rendered in detail. The blue sky is covered with clouds, every blade of grass has been dappled into place, and her blue scarf and white skirt are flowing in the wind. Violette found the title at the bottom of the frame: *Essai de figure en plein-air: Femme à l'ombrelle tournée vers la gauche*, by Claude Monet.

Out of all these paintings, why did I stop in front of that one?

Compelled by an invisible force, Violette had studied the painting for a while before looking at the artist's other works. Something was different. But being no art connoisseur, Violette couldn't put a finger on what it was.

'This painting's kind of different,' she'd said to Lily.

'What makes you say that?'

Violette had become thoughtful. Then she had said, 'It says here she was his favourite model.'

'Her name's Suzanne,' Lily had replied, reading the label. 'She's his stepdaughter from his second wife's previous marriage. There are many other paintings of her.'

Violette had nodded silently, as if she'd known it all along.

'Did he paint her in a special way because she was his favourite? There's a clear difference.'

Lily had said that perhaps Monet hadn't intended to.

'That's not something you can control. It just happens. If you love someone that much, your heart pours out of you. From your eyes, your fingertips, your tongue…'

Violette focused on the floral pattern printed on the crimson wallpaper of her bedroom – a repeating pattern made out of one yellow leaf that followed after two purple leaves. The ivory blanket resting on the headboard of her bed was embroidered with green leaves. Her entire room was the handiwork of Claire and Maurice. She didn't have to ask, her body knew.

And now, her heart was spilling out from her fingertips, guiding her hands to Lily. She brought her arms around Lily's shoulders and pulled her into a hug. Trusting her fingertips to do the talking, she stroked her back. *Pat, pat.*

'It'll hurt,' Lily rasped.

Violette lay Lily down on her bed. Clumps of Lily's hair littered the bedroom floor. Signs of her death. Clinging onto Lily's scorching body, Violette cried.

Lily looked as if she might stop breathing at any moment. She could barely open her eyes. Speaking, of course, was out of the question. Lily had come here to save herself. She must have escaped from somewhere to come here, to a place where she wouldn't be attacked, where someone would protect her. Violette knew that it was her duty to save Lily, and the only way to do that was to feed her. But the kitchen wasn't stocked with bottles of blood. She had three choices. One, let Lily die. Two, go out and hunt an animal. Three, offer up her own blood. The first wasn't even an option. The second was illegal, and love would be a weak defence in court. It was no question, really.

Pulling Lily in, she whispered, 'Drink. Drink my blood.'

Violette knew. That this was why Lily had come. That once she realised she needed blood, she'd thought of Violette – the only person whose blood she could take without killing. Seeing that Lily couldn't respond, Violette lowered her neck towards Lily's lips. She climbed on top of her, and pulled her into a tight embrace so that Lily couldn't throw her off. Lily held onto Violette's waist. Her fingertips trembled with hesitation. It felt like love.

'I know you won't kill me, but even if you do, it's losing you that I fear more.'

'It could hurt,' Lily gasped again.

'That's OK,' Violette replied.

But she worried, not knowing what to expect.

But no pain could be greater than the pain of losing Lily.

At last, something sharp pierced her skin.

Once, the wind had banged the door shut, tearing off the nail on Violette's middle finger. The blood gushed out at once, but the pain only came after a while. Violette didn't even know she'd hurt herself until she saw blood dribbling to the floor. Violette couldn't remember a more savage injury.

Violette's finger prickled as she winced at the memory. Compared to then, the pain that Lily was inflicting on her was barely a pinch. It stung, but it was warm. Ticklish.

Lily's heart spilled out from her canines. Ever so tenderly, so Violette wouldn't hurt or be afraid.

I won't be telling anyone about this. No one would believe me anyway. Is there a support group for people who've been bitten by a vampire? Her lips are freezing.

Lily's hand hovered in the air for a second before it found Violette's head and stroked her hair. Her sharp nails left a small graze beside Violette's eye, but neither of them realised.

Violette drifted off to sleep, staring at the petals on the wall.

***

When she stirred, Lily was sitting on her windowsill, looking just as pretty as before. Violette couldn't speak. It looked like Lily was deep in thought, and the emotion on her face was one Violette couldn't read.

Violette thought about the grey wolves living in hiding. She'd asked Lily to take her to see them again, but they had since vanished. How could something that definitely existed never be seen again? And why did thinking about it make her feel so empty? *There is a difference between not being able to see something because it no longer exists, and not being able to see something even though it is still around*, Lily explained. The head and heart agreed on the former, and clashed on the latter. When the head fails to understand the heart, it denies its sadness, ignoring it and letting it fester.

How do you know all this? Violette wanted to ask, but she knew the answer. It wasn't possible for Lily to watch over the passing of every human she knew. Surely there were human friends of hers who were still alive, but whom Lily wouldn't be able to see again. She wondered how that made Lily feel. At the same time, she didn't want to know.

She had hoped she'd never have to know.

But looking at Lily now, sitting by the windowsill, Violette felt like she knew. Her throat felt tight.

Lily returned the necklace to her. The one with the angel fève.

'I want you to have it. Keep it safe for me?'

Violette took the necklace without a word.

***

Claire thought that Violette had caught a cold, and Violette let her think so. Better than being tired from losing blood.

Worried sick about his daughter, Maurice took a day off work to look after her. He came into Violette's room with painkillers and soup, but she wouldn't respond when he called her name, keeping her eyes shut and listening as he set the pills and food on the table. But her father didn't leave straight away. He sat down beside Violette quietly, seeming to know that she wasn't actually asleep. 'My daughter never sleeps so gracefully,' he muttered, loud enough for her to hear.

Caught out, Violette considered getting up, but stayed under the covers instead. Maurice didn't insist.

'Even the best of friends fight every once in a while,' he said. He thought the girls had fallen out.

It was fair for him to assume this was more than just a cold: Violette had spent the last ten days in her room, waiting. But she didn't sit up to correct him.

Maurice continued, 'Sometimes the problem solves itself. Sometimes, a brave soul plucks up the courage to solve it. But when things become too difficult and the other person starts dragging you down, it's OK to stop trying, and just let them go.

'Because someone *new* will come along later. It's not good to depend too much on one person, my love. Beneath all that dependence and love is loneliness. Everyone has their own loneliness to bear, and so we can't expect anyone to take ours away. At least there's comfort in knowing we're alone together.'

Her parents had always known that she was often lonely, but they'd said nothing before, and watched over her quietly. Because, as Maurice said, no one can take away our loneliness. We simply learn how to deal with it over time.

'If people were numbers, we wouldn't be ones but zeroes. Two zeroes cannot become another number. Just a zero beside another zero. I guess what I'm saying is, we have to recognise our loneliness without letting it defeat us. And maybe one day we'll be able to embrace it.'

Violette said nothing.

'Did I get too carried away?' Maurice chuckled sadly.

Violette almost nodded. She squeezed her eyes tighter. If she didn't, she would have thrown off the blankets and burrowed into Maurice's arms while she poured her heart out. Everything Maurice had said was right, and that terrified her. She was afraid that the day would come when Lily stopped showing up, that Lily was already prepared to say goodbye. And that was why she hadn't been able to say anything when Lily was sitting on the windowsill. How odd. Lily had bared her heart to Violette, so why was she afraid of Lily never coming back? Why was she panicking as if she'd seen the future?

Sleep tight, Maurice whispered before leaving the room. He promised to bring something delicious home. Violette wanted to get up, leave her room and say goodbye, but she missed the right moment. Instead, she whispered her thanks as she watched him leave through the front garden.

That was the last time she saw him.

That day, Maurice left the world, and became someone she'd never see again.

SUYEON

'Time and time again, I thought I was going to call it quits. Life felt like a burden I was forced to carry. But I'd come so far, and I wondered if better days were ahead. They say life's made up of emotions like happiness, fear, sadness and anger. If any one of them went missing, life would be thrown off balance, and without all of them we're as good as dead. But in a place like this, it gets harder to laugh, cry, or even get angry.

'I was the biggest fan of soap operas, you know. I could watch one episode and talk about it on the phone for two hours. Somehow I never ran out of things to say. I could yap until the sun came up! When I lived in Hwagok-dong there was this seamstress ajumma I was close to. Was it when I worked as a cleaner? Hm, anyway, while I worked I'd replay the soap opera in my head, and once I was done for the day, I'd hurry back to meet that ajumma.

'The two of us would chat through the evening as we nibbled on sweet potatoes or corn. You know, those memories are fresh in my mind, but I can't for the life of me seem to recall why we had so much fun. Drives me crazy, I tell you. Like having something stuck in my chest. But I don't crave that feeling anymore. Because it's dead now. My heart. I can barely bring myself to eat. And when they turn on the television, I just stare at the screen.

'I've lived long enough, so it's high time I went. I mean, what's the point of breathing when I don't even see my kids anymore? I don't blame them, of course, none of us here do. We're just deadweight, another hospital bill to pay. So we keep our mouths shut. They're already struggling to feed themselves in this world, why should they have to take care of us, too? The world's only getting harsher.

'We've lived through wars and watched our country go to shit, but *nothing's* worse than watching your own kids suffer. I know they wouldn't treat us like this if it were up to them. So it's not their fault, really. I just wish someone would come and take me. *Please*, I'm *begging*! And that selfish husband of mine, he should've brought me *with him*!

You know the old people in this hospital always wear a smile on their faces before they die? They beam, knowing that they're about to go. They sleep well, eat well, they laugh, oh, how they laugh! Come to think of it, they must all know exactly when they're going.

'Where do they get such courage? I myself haven't been brave enough to actually do it. It makes me jealous. Really, I envy them to death.

'Talking to a young detective such as you today has got me all excited again. I guess I'm still chatty old me. People don't change just because they grow old. Being old simply means you've been on this planet for longer, but people always treat us like we're from the past. Trapped there. But really, we live in the present, just like everyone else. Wouldn't you agree, Detective?'

The old lady handed Suyeon the rose in her hand. She said she'd made it herself in class, and hoped Suyeon would keep it, since it would never wither.

'If only people could be like this flower. But there's nothing we can do about it. Nothing that can stop us from wilting. Still, the fact that we're only wilting because we've bloomed… that's quite beautiful, isn't it?'

Suyeon nodded. She left the hospital with the paper rose in her hand. Was that granny a target, too? She had bruises on her body and attended the origami classes… Suyeon caught herself.

Bold of her to assume she could protect these patients. After all, these people were much stronger than her. Like pillars, they'd supported the weight of their own lives until the very end.

Violette was waiting for Suyeon in front of the hospital. Surprisingly, there was no cigarette in her hand as she waved. With the car parked in an alley, the two sat there, side by side.

Granny Eunshim's final words were big and sharp. They had pierced Suyeon's heart, and from the wound flowed previously forgotten memories.

She remembered the people from her life who had made life worth living. People who had been there to embrace her after she'd been hurt and was learning how to trust again.

Even in jest, she regretted ever saying, 'I'm an adult now,' or 'I'm fine on my own.' Instead, she should have been brave enough to cry. To say, 'I can't live without you.' Maybe then, in their last moments, they'd think of her, unleash a superhuman strength, break through death, and stay by her side.

A feeling she'd long forgotten enveloped her, as if telling her she was once again alone in this world, on top of this mountain of endless snow.

Suyeon calmly recounted Granny Eunshim's death and the suicide note she left behind to Violette.

'She was preparing for the winter. I know this alone isn't enough to prove anything, because turning your back on the world means letting go of the future you've planned. I just know she wouldn't have left before finishing the scarf she was knitting for me. That nurse I was telling you about – all the victims attended her origami class. I think we should talk to her.'

Suyeon recounted what she knew about Seo Nanju while Violette listened silently. She opened the window and breathed in the crisp air. It was silent as the gears in Violette's brain turned. Suyeon noticed a long scar on her left temple. Had it been any longer, it would have nicked her eye. But that was just the most obvious wound. There were scratches on her face and throat, around her eyes, on her cheeks, earlobes and the nape of her neck. Were they knife scars? No, they looked too short and deep. What weapon could've left those marks? It must've been something with a sharp point but thick… Almost subconsciously, Suyeon combed through the list of weapons she'd come across over the years. Chopsticks, the heel of a shoe, a light bulb, a shampoo bottle, a decorative lamp, a hanger… Wielded with ill intent, the most mundane object could be turned into a lethal weapon. After learning that even a plastic knife meant for a birthday cake could be deadly, Suyeon never ruled out anything. But perhaps the most deadly weapon was the heart. Everything else was merely a tool.

Suyeon couldn't guess what weapon had caused Violette's scars. It wasn't easy for small weapons to leave multiple marks on so many different parts of the body, and besides, they all looked like they'd been made at different times. It would take a while to figure it out. If only she could see them a bit closer up, or feel them.

Time sauntered by, as the sun dipped below the horizon. The clouds thickened, shrouding the moon, rendering the night darker than usual. There was a deep rumble, followed by the tapping of raindrops on the windshield.

Watching the rain fall, Suyeon asked, 'How did you get into this?'

'Had to make a living,' answered Violette.

Although they were safe from the rain, she could feel her skin grow damp. 'Me, Granny Eunshim told me to do it. She said I should become a police officer because I had a soft heart, and it's a police officer's duty to stand with the weak. I didn't have much will to live back then, but she said I could help people like me, people who've been kicked to the ground. Better to become a shield against violence and discrimination than end up like the bastards who hurt me.'

'She must've been very special to you,' said Violette.

Suyeon nodded decisively. Granny Eunshim had made a convincing argument – people who couldn't simply walk away, who couldn't help but look back a couple more times, were born to be police officers and rid this world of injustice. Although Suyeon couldn't afford to have dreams back then, the new prospect had sparked a flame in her. Someone had to lend an ear to those who couldn't speak up, she figured. That was what Suyeon resolved to do. And so she held on, determined to leave a mark in a world that wanted her erased.

'A vampire hunter, huh? Not the world's most common way to make a living,' said Suyeon.

Violette answered after a pause, 'I made a promise.' Her face fell. 'But she didn't hold up her end of the bargain. *One chance*, she promised me. And so I waited until I couldn't any more. I thought we'd meet again soon, but time really flew by. She probably wouldn't recognise me now.'

Suyeon could tell that the person who had worn out Violette's patience was not human. Suyeon wasn't surprised. From the first time she'd met Violette, nothing about her had been ordinary.

'I believe she will. Recognise you, I mean.'

'You think so?'

Suyeon nodded. Violette chuckled faintly. Suyeon suggested again that they should speak to Seo Nanju, but Violette turned her down and stepped out of the car. Suyeon didn't stop her. It looked like Violette had a lot on her mind. Suyeon waited as the night shift began.

Midnight was fast approaching, but Seo Nanju had yet to appear outside, on her break or at the end of her shift. Suyeon tried to call her, but the phone rang on and on until the line went dead. *Is she busy with work still?*

Suyeon's eyes flicked to the time on her watch. Worried that she might have missed Nanju after she'd clocked out, Suyeon turned off the ignition and headed for the sixth floor.

There was only one nurse. Her face etched with a mix of exhaustion and frustration, the nurse informed Suyeon that Nanju had not shown up for work that day, and hadn't answered any calls. Suyeon hurried out of the hospital.

In the driver's seat again, she leafed through the heap of documents on the seat beside her and located the one containing Nanju's address.

***

A green tint lit up the lift.

Suyeon fidgeted as it took its time reaching the twelfth floor. The lift groaned as it scaled the building at a snail's pace. With a jerk, it finally stopped. The door slid open to a long corridor of crammed apartments.

There were no windows, and the neat walls looked like they'd just received a fresh coat of paint. The lights glowed faintly; some of them had gone out. Scanning the numbers written on the doors, Suyeon looked for No. 1210.

Nothing should have happened. Nothing should have gone wrong.

When her feet came to a halt before the door labelled 1210, she felt something sticky beneath her shoes. Fixing her gaze straight ahead, Suyeon took a deep breath. Cautiously, she let her gaze travel downwards. She lifted a foot. A thick, red substance clung to the bottom of her shoe. Suyeon shuffled back. Only then did she see the pool of blood seeping under the door, stretching into the corridor.

Next to her, a woman stepped out of her apartment. Her eyes flicked between Suyeon and the floor before she let out a scream.

VIOLETTE

December 1983

'Don't.'

Violette mumbled, shaking her head. *Should I speak louder? Maybe he can't hear me.*

Her lips quivered as she took another step forward, but it was too late. She'd spoken too softly. *Don't throw him*, was what she'd meant to say. *He'll break if you do*. She should've made that clear. *If only he could turn into a grain of sand or if wings could sprout from his back.*

She would have taken any miracle that could break his fall. But evolution didn't work that way. Humans were horribly weak and broke easier than the ceramic angel hanging on her necklace.

Violette had never noticed the heat of her own breath before. It seared her lips, setting her prayers and the inside of her mouth ablaze. Perhaps her voice had been incinerated. That must be it.

The heavy snow worked fastidiously to bury Maurice in white. Before long it had erased the pool of blood beneath him, and it looked like he was making a snow angel. Violette stood beside him, a fir tree powdered in snow. Raising her eyes, she stared at the chimney. The moon above the horizon was bright and red. *Maybe the sun has accidentally stumbled into the night? Then this must be a dream, and everything that has happened isn't real life, but the opposite. Everything, and every feeling, the opposite.*

Violette stared at the figure standing on the chimney. The man leapt off the roof and landed softly.

As he strolled towards her, he said he had made a mistake. 'I picked a bad one,' he sighed dramatically. 'The blood had been contaminated by wine. There was a sandwich inside the paper bag,' he said with distaste. 'Eating garbage like that can make your blood greasy,' he added.

Violette didn't run. Her glazed eyes drifted back to Maurice as she wondered what the hell her father was doing, lying there like that. She was watching the scene unfold in real time, but couldn't seem to register a thing.

Blanketed in snow, Maurice looked cold. She wanted to bring him home and tuck him into bed. The man held out a hand, but before he could touch her, he was flung to the side. He slammed into a brick wall before landing on the ground with a thud.

Lily, who must have sprinted across the forest, didn't look like a vampire, but a grey wolf. She bared her fangs and raised claws. Her chest heaved as she pinned down her prey with a piercing glare. Not once did she look at Violette. Everything felt so surreal.

Dusting the snow off his shoulders, the man lunged at Lily. Catching him by the jaw, Lily swatted him to the floor. The man chuckled in disbelief. 'Are you *that* angry?' he asked. 'Friends shouldn't be joking around like this. Let's stop wasting energy.' His tone was jovial.

So he's a friend of Lily's. But why wasn't Lily treating him like one? Lily wrapped her fingers around the roots of the man's hair and drove his skull into the wall once more. Violette didn't know *this* Lily.

What was I thinking? Spending all my time with a creature. A predator. What did I expect out of this?

The man wiped the blood from his forehead. Clutched in his hand was the hammer that Maurice used to break the frozen pipes. But before he could bring it down, Lily intercepted the swing and snapped his arm. His anguished shriek was cut short. Grabbing his hair once more, Lily shoved his head into the wall again and again. Violette tore her eyes away from the scene and turned back to Maurice, numbly. Unlike the man who was now drenched in his own blood, Maurice looked clean and serene. She tottered closer to her father. She knelt down and brought his head to her knees.

He was still warm.

But the snow wouldn't tolerate that.

Violette tried to pull him closer, but Maurice's body was as heavy as if it had been dunked in water. *Are there vines tying him down?* It felt like Maurice was anchored to the ground.

Just then, Violette noticed a boy. He'd been standing there from the very beginning – for a long time now. Since before Maurice had shown up, before the man's attack. She had seen him, but hadn't thought about it. Her mind was a mess. How could that be? A stranger, skulking around their house. Violette called out to him. 'Help me,' she pleaded. 'We can take him to the hospital.' Maybe it's not too late to save him. Your friend didn't take all of his blood. He could be better in a few months. *Quick, please.* He's getting colder. Let's go before he freezes completely, before he stops breathing, we have to get him to the hospital.

The boy broke into a laugh, his canines and eyes glinting.

Violette heard a snap. It sounded like a thick branch breaking. The sound of a life ending. Violette didn't turn around. As her eyelids fluttered shut, tears streamed down her face. She heard footsteps approaching. Lily. Violette knew without having to look. Because even if the sun took away every sound in the world, hers were the only footsteps that could pierce through the silence.

When Violette opened her eyes again, the boy was no longer there. *Good*, Violette thought. *He should take Lily with him.*

Did she say that last part out loud? She couldn't recall.

Violette clung to Maurice, who was getting colder by the second. Her chest was tight as she pleaded. Please don't disappear from this world. Please don't become a forgotten word. Stay here with me. Hold onto your temperature, don't freeze. Don't leave. Don't break your promise. Don't leave me alone.

Don't become another grey wolf.

SUYEON

Chantae took in Seo Nanju's apartment with one glimpse and stepped back out into the corridor. Suyeon was there waiting with the nurse's identification card in her hand. Chantae pulled out his phone to look up her details, but Suyeon saved him the trouble.

'Her name's Seo Nanju. Born in 1986, in Nowon-gu. She was a nursing student at a Gyeonggi-do university and started working at Cheolma Hospital three years ago. Before that, she worked at a cosmetic hospital in Nowon-gu. Her birth name was Seo Yeongeun, but she had it legally changed after the Nowon-gu morphine scandal. My guess is that she kept doing the same thing ever since, but off the record: doping up patients in exchange for cash. I would've heard it directly from her today if this hadn't happened.'

Suyeon walked into the apartment and towards Seo Nanju's body, which was covered by a white sheet.

She'd been found dead, leaning against the door, stabbed with a kitchen knife. The weapon had been driven through her abdomen and skewered her organs before being pulled out. Although her organs were severely damaged, the cause of death was determined to be excessive blood loss. By the time the police and paramedics barged in, rigor mortis had already set in, and her body had gone stiff. By the looks of it, she'd been dead for about five to six hours. Suyeon got to the house at twenty-one minutes past midnight, which meant that Seo Nanju had died between five or six o'clock in the evening. Just as the sun was setting.

When Suyeon threw back the white sheet, she was greeted by Seo Nanju's round eyes. Suyeon wriggled her fingers into a latex glove and inspected the nurse's face and neck. Nothing. Her neck, collarbones, arms and wrists were clear. No holes indicating that she'd been sucked dry of blood. Just as Suyeon was about to drop the victim's wrist, her eyes fell upon the bent tips of her fingernails. They were caked in a small ring blood. A sign of resistance.

Next to Seo Nanju's right thigh, a marker indicated the knife's position. At the time of discovery, the knife had been found sitting in her hand with its tip pointing towards her stomach. A clear set up. The chances of a person succeeding in completely pulling out a knife lodged in their body were slim. And apart from cutting their wrists, people rarely chose to end their lives by stabbing themselves with a weapon. In fact, the number of cases was close to zero. The scene was a sorry imitation of something that would never happen. It was screaming to be found out. Upon entering the scene, the entire forensic team knew instantly, deeply, that they weren't looking at a suicide. Yet… it couldn't be a homicide – Seo Nanju's apartment was on the twelfth floor, and footage from the corridor's security camera showed that no one had entered her apartment in the ten hours prior to the incident. Not a single soul. Seo Nanju was the only one who appeared in the footage. The case would likely be chucked out as an unsolved murder or a grotesque suicide. Neither of which felt satisfactory.

But Suyeon knew of a culprit who could explain things. Someone who could enter a twelfth-floor apartment without using the front door – a killer who only emerged after sunset. A draft swept past them. It was only when Suyeon saw the curtains dancing that she noticed the open window. She walked towards it. As soon as she drew the curtains apart, she saw the bloodstained windowsill. Vampire. But why not take their victim's blood instead of committing plain murder?

Chantae came up to her side. In a flat voice, Suyeon asked, 'Sunbae, what if our culprit is not from this world?'

'You mean like a ghost?' Chantae asked absentmindedly. 'I'd rather that honestly.'

'And what if it really is a ghost?'

As Suyeon's voice dipped, Chantae grew sullen, but only for a moment.

'Since when did you make jokes at the crime scene?' he said, giving Suyeon a light bump on the shoulder.

Chantae left her to inspect the evidence found at the scene. *There's just no way,* Suyeon thought. Mentioning the word 'vampire' was out of the question. They would react the same way as she had when Violette had first brought it up. Like the woman had lost her mind.

'This doesn't feel like someone's home,' Chantae remarked. 'There's nothing in the fridge, not even water. How's that possible? There should at least be a chicken drumstick or something somewhere. The bin has been emptied and she barely had any belongings. I'll bet she was planning to leave or was in a hurry to escape. If that's the case, then there's a high chance that whoever she was trying to avoid is the culprit. Let's start by looking into Seo Nanju's relationships, and once we have our guy, we'll know why and how they did it. Of course we'll have to wait for forensics to come back with the print results to see if there *is* in fact a culprit. We're in the middle of contacting the victim's family. If they agree to an autopsy, I'm sure the truth will come to light soon enough. We should head out for now. There's nothing left to see. It's as if a ghost lived here…'

Chantae left the scene first. Just as Suyeon was about to follow, the curtains rustled. Suyeon turned around. There was no wind.

En route to the station, Suyeon sent Violette a text.

> Seo Nanju is dead. Looks like a vampire did it, but stay away from the scene this time. They're treating it as a homicide case. Don't get dragged into it.

Evening came, but no reply.

In the autopsy room, Jiseon explained that the knife had been thrust so deep that its handle was buried in Nanju's flesh and the tip of its blade had almost poked out of her back. Something like that would require the strength of an adult man.

'So it's impossible that the victim did this to herself?' Chantae asked.

'Not entirely, but who would choose such an agonising way to die?' answered Jiseon. 'There *were* signs of a struggle, and the victim ruined her nails in the process of grabbing onto something with all her might, but no other DNA was found. It was her own blood. Lastly, sleeping pills were found in Seo Nanju's stomach, but the amount was small enough that a suicide attempt could be ruled out. She'd probably taken them to help with mild insomnia.'

Meanwhile, the forensics investigator reported that the only prints found on the weapon were Seo Nanju's, but they had also discovered two sets of footprints, which belonged to two different people. It was strange that there were traces of people who had walked around the house with shoes on when no one had been seen entering the apartment. This new revelation only sparked a series of unanswered questions. Frustrated, Chantae paced the room, clearing his throat every now and then before he settled down beside Suyeon. He bent down and re-tied his loose shoelaces.

'Were you looking into the suicides because you thought something like this might eventually happen? Did you suspect the nurse of drugging her patients?' asked Chantae. His folded posture muffled his words.

'Something like that,' Suyeon mumbled, a frown in her voice.

'What made you think that?'

'So many deaths, all from the same hospital. If these old folk were patients in a regular hospital, a case would've been opened right away.'

'Ever heard of congruence, kid? Circumstances that could lead to incidents. We have to consider them. If this had happened in a regular hospital, it would be incongruous, so of course there would be an investigation. But when it comes to these rehab hospitals...' Chantae didn't finish his sentence. He couldn't bring himself to say, 'I'm not surprised.'

'But, of course,' he continued, 'I was wrong and you were right. We're detectives, it's our job to dig into things. Nice work.'

'I had a good teacher.'

'Right, Eungyeong-ie. She was a real piece of work, too, that one... Hang on, isn't this case similar to the one

Eungyeong was pursuing? Where the suspect she was chasing down killed himself? The evidence in the case against him was already pretty damning, right? But on top of that, he had Eungyeong breathing down his neck.' Chantae shook his head. 'He had been schizophrenic to begin with and so he was terrified. Said a bunch of crap about how he'd been forced to do it and hadn't had any ill intent.'

He was lost in the recounting, eyes on the wall. 'When they searched his house, they found a piece of paper with Eungyeong's name, phone number and address written on it. We don't know if he wanted to take revenge or leave behind some sort of message, but his family kicked up a fuss and threatened to sue her. The suit was withdrawn eventually but Eungyeong went on a short break, saying she needed time to rethink her approach. Since then, I try to keep my information private. It's not just me. The people we work with do the same.'

It hadn't been her case, nor was she Eungyeong sunbae's next of kin, so Suyeon was hearing much of this detail for the first time. It didn't surprise her. Eungyeong sunbae was the type of person to hound a suspect rather than sit back and listen to her colleague dish out assumptions.

Chantae cleared his throat.

'A piece of paper with your info was found in Seo Nanju's house. I was informed just now,' he added. 'You mentioned that if you hadn't found Seo Nanju dead, you were going to speak to her… Did she know she was on your radar?'

Suyeon remained quiet. There wasn't anything she could say to release the doubt entangled in his questions.

'No comment, huh?' Chantae asked. Suyeon obliged with a small nod. 'Fine. You should get going soon anyway. Listen, I know you've had your paws on this case since the beginning, but it's not going to be you, now. You're involved in a different way and need to cooperate. Backup's on the way, so tell them everything you know and answer their questions, OK? I'm off to check on the security footage.'

Suyeon nodded again. Chantae left to go back to the office. Suyeon told him that she'd join him soon.

Once the forensics team excused themselves, only Suyeon and Seo Nanju were left in the room. Seo Nanju had had her number. She had been about to reach out first. What would she have said? Those who'd chosen to turn their backs on the world always looked serene and still, happy with the way they'd proven that everything became nothing in the end. But Seo Nanju shouldn't have turned her back yet. She was supposed to stay and answer Suyeon's questions. *Why the fuck are you lying there so comfortably?* Suyeon wanted to shout. She bit back the rage teetering on the tip of her tongue. Steadying her breath, she looked down at Seo Nanju's corpse and began to speak.

'What's the full story? What were you going to tell me? Who killed you? Did you also meet a vampire? Did you really help a vampire? Why did you do it? Why take advantage of people's loneliness?'

Even if the truth came to light and the culprit was put behind bars, a larger fraction of the story would remain untold, for the voices of the dead could never be heard. In this regard, every case in the world should be filed as partly unsolved.

Still no word from Violette. Five hours had passed since Suyeon sent her the message. She fidgeted in her swivel chair, worried that Violette had ignored her and gone digging for clues. Suicides and homicides held very different degrees of gravity. In the case of the latter, every resident in Seo Nanju's building was a suspect, every passer-by on the street became part of the investigation, and every person in the victim's contact list and every one of her colleagues at the hospital would receive a phone call. Given such circumstances, Violette couldn't afford to draw attention to herself. It didn't help that she'd been walking in and out of the hospital pretending to be a detective. Succumbing to anxiety at last, Suyeon dialled Violette's number. But Violette, of course, didn't pick up.

By eight that evening, the backup team still hadn't called. Having spent the whole day keeping an eye on Suyeon, Chantae finally slumped over his desk and drifted off. Suyeon hacked a cough and banged her drawer shut for good measure. Her partner didn't flinch. Satisfied, Suyeon grabbed her gun and left the office.

The rain started as soon as she arrived at Seo Nanju's building. One death alone had turned the building into a haunted house. Suyeon wasn't imagining the desolation and silence. A murder had taken place here. Most of the residents had found somewhere else to stay for the night, and amongst them were those who'd immediately put their apartments up for rent. When Suyeon entered the ground floor lobby, the security guard shot up mid-snore, surprised by the sudden visitor. Recognising Suyeon as one of the detectives, he braced himself for a round of interrogation, but the panic in his eyes dissolved as Suyeon passed by him without a word. Chantae was going to come looking for her when he woke up. He might blow a fuse when he found out that Suyeon had returned to the crime scene without proper permission.

The twelfth floor was eerily quiet. Each time Suyeon lifted her foot, the treacly feeling of blood scraped against her soles, a remnant of the blood that had flowed from Seo Nanju's door. The front door was left open, gaping like a monster's den waiting to welcome Suyeon into its cavernous mouth. Places tainted by death were always cold. Her colleagues would often joke it was because of the ghosts who stayed. That possibility had always made Suyeon's skin crawl, but right now, she wanted nothing more than for Seo Nanju's ghost to show up. She needed to know why Seo Nanju had been looking for her, and if she had indeed been an accomplice. She needed to hear the answers to the questions she'd thrown at Seo Nanju's lifeless body.

Unfortunately, in her entire career, Suyeon had never met a ghost. Dead was dead. The only things that could talk were the traces the dead had left behind. Perhaps that was the curse placed on those who were trapped in this world – that as long as they lived, they were never to see the dead.

The curtains flapped. It quickly occurred to Suyeon that the windows must have been closed earlier, to protect the integrity of the scene. That meant someone had opened them again.

Despite knowing it would be useless, Suyeon dug into her pocket and wrapped her fingers around the grip of her gun. It was an insurance of sorts. If someone nearby heard a gunshot, they'd likely report it. Even if this vampire revealed their presence to Suyeon, they couldn't afford to make their existence known more widely. Otherwise, they'd reveal their full self instead of hiding behind traces of murder.

Passing the bed, Suyeon grasped the ends of the curtains and flung them aside. No one was at the windowsill. Instead, low laughter rumbled behind her.

There he stood, alone in the shadows. The real culprit. His lithe shadow was the first to touch her. As the light slowly revealed his features, Suyeon recalled what Violette had said before.

Gold-flecked irises, a gift of love from God. White, silky skin. Blood-red lips and a finely carved physique. A beauty you'd never forget, even after just one look, and saw even with eyes closed. An entity Suyeon would be able to pick out from a sea of thousands next time.

Drenched in rain from head to toe, the vampire strode up to Suyeon with a smile curdling on his face. The gold in his eyes glistened brazenly, beckoning Suyeon to come closer. He parted his red lips. How beautiful, and how biting.

Violette had described them perfectly. His face was like an iridescent lotus basking in the moonlight. He chuckled as he watched Suyeon's eyes rove from the ridge of his angled nose to the crisp curves of his lips, his long eyelashes and the glowing irises beneath them. He stuck out a hand for Suyeon to shake. Seized by nerves, Suyeon raised her gun and pointed its barrel at him. He looked at the gun, unfazed.

'Ulan de Fayeur. But please, just call me Ulan.'

His laugh was velvety. Almost polite, almost warm.

'I hear you've been looking for me. And that you think I've done something *absolutely terrible*.'

It was Suyeon's turn to speak, but her lips refused to budge. This was different from when she realised that Greta was a vampire. The vampire before her seemed perfectly capable of ending her life right there and then.

'They wanted it, you know. Wanted me.'

His voice and eyes dripped with woe, as if he was yearning for something.

'They were all chosen, but I, in turn, was chosen by them. We gave each other what we desired – the blessing of salvation. It was an exchange. Their blood for a painless death.'

Suyeon couldn't discern a sliver of intent or truth from his words. Was he confessing to his crimes?

'You see, the power to save them is a strength that I simply have. Unlike the gods they pray to, I can't bring myself to look away from their earthly suffering. Their gods have done nothing for them except create a world no different from Hell and leave them there to rot. Despite having all the power in the world, they won't lift a finger to alleviate their pain. So I stepped in. I saved them. They themselves told me this.

'So do not put me in the same box as other gods. For I do not turn my back on sadness and agony.'

'Cut the bullshit.'

Suyeon was relieved her voice came out steady.

Ulan gave an indifferent shrug. 'I don't look for people who don't want my help. Only the lonely plead with me. Those who are alone, but don't want to be. Those who are alive, but not living. People who are sick of their own breath, people who cannot tell apart yesterday from today, trapped in a vessel that is welcome nowhere. Take a good look at me. We live much longer than humans, and have come this far by maintaining the balance between rampant starvation and loneliness. Death is not something to be feared. It is a haven for those who seek to escape this cruel world. It is the perfect salvation.'

Leaning against the windowsill, Ulan studied Suyeon's face. He scoffed lightly but a flash of doubt crossed his face as his brows knitted together. He was not happy. Righting himself, he took a step towards Suyeon.

'How odd. Why aren't you more afraid?'

Suyeon shuffled backward, knowing that she was only a few steps away from being cornered – no, knowing that escape had never been an option in the first place. Water dripped from the leaky tap at a steady tempo. A dry sponge, an almost-emptied bottle of washing-up liquid, disposable spoon and forks lying where plates should be. They all caught Suyeon's eye. Ulan slowly stroked his cheek.

'Now why would a human walk straight towards death even though she fears it? When she knows she'll die? A fascinating contradiction!'

Suyeon herself couldn't believe the way that her feet were inching towards death on their own. But would she have stayed away if she'd known? That the culprit was sure to appear at the crime scene. That she'd come face to face with him. She had, in fact, known this. She'd known since she grabbed her gun that this culprit couldn't be killed by such a useless weapon. Still, she came. Just as that vampire was saying, humans were full of contradictions. Sometimes they leapt straight into death's claws.

Because if they didn't, then they'd be living a life no different from death. Eungyeong sunbae knew she was going to die that day. Her instinct, capable of sensing death even when she herself couldn't, every gene that remembered fear, as well as the many inexplicable phenomena in between, all of these must have inundated her with incessant warnings.

I think a lot about why I was born this way. Why I've got such a big personality, and why I'd rather die than do as I'm told. But I've accepted it now. This is simply who I am. Suyeon-ah, if you're curious about something, you should go for it. This is the only way people like us survive.

Why did those have to be Eungyeong sunbae's last words to her? Suyeon had always resented her for that. Sunbae should've warned her, *Stay out of trouble if you don't want to end up like me.*

But instead, sunbae had taught her that being human means holding fast to those you wish to protect and your unanswered questions even in the face of death. And so, it was now time for Suyeon to satiate her curiosity. Why this hospital? Why kill Granny Eunshim? Why kill Seo Nanju? Her fear began to subside. The creature before her was no different from the countless criminals she'd dealt with. Human or not, it didn't matter. Humanity meant nothing to any of them.

'You killed Seo Nanju?'

Ulan nodded.

'Why?' asked Suyeon.

'Fear got to her head. She wanted to kill me. Brought out a knife, so I tried to calm her down. Alas...'

Ulan shook his head. This was clearly all a joke to him.

'I really had no choice, Detective,' he said.

'What was the relationship between you two?'

'A symbiotic relationship, of course. I killed for her and she worked for me. She pointed out the people who were tired of life.' Ulan smacked his lips regretfully. 'You see, the thing about relationships like this is that they end when there's no more trust. I had no intention of killing her, but she had assumed I would – and here we are.'

Suyeon glowered at him.

'What about the old lady? The last death at the hospital.'

She was the one who'd asked the question, but she couldn't bear to hear the answer. She knew it would be the most trivial reason, and she didn't want to accept that a person's life could end without any dignity or honour. Still, she had to know why Granny Eunshim had died. Even if it meant she would be haunted by it for the rest of her life.

'I was angered by the way she ignored me. But don't resent me. She really did want to die. You saw her suicide note, didn't you? She wrote it herself,' said Ulan flatly.

Suyeon was familiar with this tone, this attitude. The man who'd killed Eungyeong sunbae had been the same. He'd murdered Eungyeong sunbae because he'd been 'angered'. That exact word. She'd seen the taped confession. The man had worn an unbothered expression, as if he was sitting in a class he didn't want to be in. Ulan wandered around the apartment.

'That woman who's always with you… *She's* perfectly capable of stopping me, she's just not doing anything about it. She goes around stalking me, hoping that her lover will show up one day, not caring who lives or dies. It frustrates me, truly. It feels like I'm being *used*. This has happened before, you see. I killed her father in a much worse way than your precious granny. Drained him of blood and threw him off a building. Even then, she didn't stop me.'

Violette's warning flashed in her mind.

Never fall for a vampire's words.

He's only trying to rile you up, Suyeon reminded herself. *Keep your cool. Don't walk into his trap*. Ulan studied Suyeon's expression. Detecting no emotion, his brows furrowed in dismay.

'You're more heartless than I thought.'

'I don't believe a single—'

'She wasn't your real grandmother,' Ulan chuckled.

Two shots rang out. The first was a blank, but the second zipped right through Ulan's shoulder. Frowning, Ulan brought a hand to the wound and rubbed it.

No matter his lies, the person she loved was gone. Nothing was going to change that… nothing…

Suyeon pulled the trigger again. This time, she aimed for his heart. Ulan stumbled backwards from the impact, but that was all. Frowning, he dusted off the side of the chest where the bullet had landed, as if it was just a scratch.

'I can't stand these pesky things. Made for the sole purpose of killing – the devil's work, really.'

Suyeon was unfazed. Keeping her cool, she pulled the trigger again and again. Surely gaining a whole bunch of holes would have an impact on any creature. But her wishful thinking was brought to an end as soon as Ulan snatched her gun away. Without a weapon, Suyeon could only stare down the barrel pointed at her head.

'You really are fearless. I abhor that look. But first, let's put this away, shall we?' Ulan slipped Suyeon's gun into his coat pocket. 'It's *cheating*.'

He glanced at the window.

'I knew the rain would bring the fog, but look at that! You can hardly see a thing. I like nights like this. Good for hiding. Perfect for *killing*.'

Ensnared in his grip, Suyeon was an insect flapping its feeble wings. Ulan dragged her across the room and flung her aside. She crashed into the kitchen shelf before falling onto the floor. One of her ribs hit against a sharp corner and Suyeon felt a shooting pain, but she couldn't make a sound. With every attempt to prop herself up, the searing pain dug deeper into her side. She heard Ulan's approaching footsteps, but she couldn't even sit up, much less run. All she could do was grab onto his ankle with every ounce of strength she had left in her. She held on tight. Because she had to. Because it was the only thing she could do. Because this monster needed to be caught.

Ulan took Suyeon by the chin and lifted her up. His long dark nails cut into her neck and cheeks. Under the pressure of his grip, Suyeon's cheekbones threatened to shatter. She struggled to kick herself free, but Ulan held her right hand down effortlessly and twisted it. A shriek ripped through the room. She bit down on her lip. Drained of all colour, it trembled. Suyeon let her gaze fall. Meanwhile, calm spread over Ulan's face.

'I never thought I would hold a grudge so long either. I believed I could forgive and forget. But once I saw her face, no matter how much it had changed, I knew it was her. How absurd it is that she's already forgotten me. No, surely she remembers. She's just choosing to ignore me. The way she ignored everything last time.'

Suyeon didn't understand a word of Ulan's spiel, but one thing was clear to her: the vampire before her had lived his long life – however many human lifespans that was – foolishly. Suyeon wrestled the words out of her clamped throat.

'Humans… don't hold onto things… for as long as you do. That's how… we keep on living.'

If half a century for a vampire was equivalent to five years for a human being, then perhaps a memory that had faded within a human mind could still be as vivid in a vampire's mind as though it were only yesterday.

Humans are never tethered to their past. They always find an escape. They forget, they bury, they lay to rest, they leave. Then, they welcome a different world.

Ulan wrenched Suyeon's head back. Given the situation, Suyeon couldn't help but wonder if she was too trusting. She'd only just met Violette, yet she was counting on her to save her life. But Suyeon trusted her gut best. The one that had been stirred awake, triggered by the will to survive, the one that told her Violette could be trusted. And it did not disappoint. Through the narrow slit of her half-shut eyes, she discerned a familiar figure. Violette was standing in the entrance, with the door ajar, keeping watch. *Right on cue.* Suyeon smiled weakly in Violette's direction, but as her vision blurred into nothing, she couldn't tell if Violette had smiled back.

Intoxicated by the thought of sinking his teeth into the flesh of his prey, Ulan was oblivious to Violette's presence. But Violette herself must have moved stealthily, considering how Suyeon had taken a while to notice her. She held a knife. Double-edged and razor-sharp. *Looks like something from the Middle Ages*, thought Suyeon absently, noticing the rags wrapped around the dagger's handle.

Violette continued only to watch. Clearly she had no intention of saving Suyeon.

She was waiting. For Ulan to tear Suyeon open. Suyeon was out of options. If she called out to Violette now, Ulan would drop her and make for his new target. And so she followed Violette's lead, though she dreaded it.

When Ulan bit down into the base of her throat, when something sharp tore her flesh, and when a sheet of white flashed before her eyes as she felt her last bit of strength leave her body, she clung on to the wretched monster. So that Violette could drive her knife straight in, for good.

Drained of blood, Suyeon's stomach churned and she broke out into cold sweat. Her vision faded and returned several times, until the white veil no longer lifted. A thunderous clang rang out. A gunshot. But Suyeon couldn't open her eyes.

***

It was still night when she came to.

She didn't know how long she'd been unconscious for, but she realised not much time had passed. She was still sprawled on the parquet floor. It was cold. The instant she parted her lips, a groan escaped. She sensed a presence nearby. She pried her sticky lids open as if tearing flesh apart. *What is that? A monster splitting itself in two?*

Her vision refused to come into focus. Mustering up her last bit of strength, she narrowed her eyes. When she tried to move her arm, only her pinky twitched. Suyeon could feel her soul slinking out of her now. Still, there remained a steady thump. The sound of her labouring heart pumping blood. The finger within her sight was pale, and her throbbing shoulder was the only indication that she was still alive. It seemed the fog had taken it upon itself to enter the room, inviting darkness to follow. Suyeon looked up at the hazy figure once more. *It's two people.*

Violette drove the knife lodged in Ulan's abdomen even deeper. Their faces were close enough for their breath to touch. Ulan's bloodied hands were wrapped around Violette's, and they shivered tensely. Suyeon strained to keep her eyes open.

As crimson blood dribbled out of him, Ulan spoke. His speech was a jumble of languages, making it difficult for Suyeon to understand. Among it all he seemed to be saying that he hadn't done anything. *You have no right to resent me, I've done you no wrong.*

Using her full weight, Violette shoved her weapon further in, deep enough for its tip to emerge from Ulan's back. The vampire writhed. He let out a feral cry. But it was as if Violette heard nothing.

'There are three circumstances when a victim can be saved,' Violette spoke, stone-cold and composed. 'When their murderer doesn't kill them, when their murder is prevented, and when their last chance of surviving doesn't slip away.'

With a twist of Violette's knife, Ulan's howl pierced the night sky. His thick nails clawed into her arms, impaling her leather jacket and flesh, but Violette made no sound, gripping her weapon tighter.

'You knew that monster would come. Wasn't that why you were at our house that day? You wanted to watch me die. Well, in that case, when that bastard went after an innocent man instead, you should've stopped him. When that person was on the ground fighting for his last breath, you should've *saved* him. When I screamed, begging for help, you should've helped me. Must I spell everything out for you? Tell you how I saw you laughing? Would that explain why you're here?'

Is that her blood running down her hands? Violette looked on the verge of collapse.

'Why? Why didn't you do anything? Did it bring you joy to see my father die? To see the girl I love leave me?'

Ulan couldn't answer. His grip on Violette's arms loosened. His hands flopped to his sides where they remained completely still.

He was dead. The heartless murderer had died by Violette's knife.

You won, Suyeon wanted to say, but she was too weak to offer her partner a smile. The building spun as nausea swept over her. Releasing the knife, Violette climbed off the vampire's body, but unable to hold herself up, she slumped to the floor. Suyeon held out her hand, but she couldn't reach Violette's. All she felt was the warm slickness of blood. Her eyes traced the red flow. She desperately wished that it would lead to Ulan, but her gaze eventually landed on Violette's abdomen.

Thick fog. Recumbent bodies. Blackened blood. The night was in disarray, yet it stood in absolute silence. It was as if the fog had swallowed the noise, and nothing had happened at all. Suyeon recalled the nightmarish scenes, she remembered the immutable cold. She wanted to hold onto Violette before her body turned frigid like Ulan's, but her own body would not cooperate. *Why am I always a step behind?*

'Violette,' she called.

But Violette didn't look at her.

The steady rise and fall of her chest told Suyeon she was still alive. But as if she'd lost the will to live, Violette's eyes were absently fixed on the ceiling. Suyeon despised that look. She'd seen it before – on Granny Eunshim, Nanju, and Eungyeong sunbae. *Why do the eyes of the deceased hold nothing but the ravenous air of death?*

Suyeon wanted to shout. To tell Violette to stay with her. To get someone to call an ambulance. To ask them to stop the ceaseless bleeding. To tell Violette, 'Don't die like you've been waiting for this moment.'

But in the end, the tips of Violette's fingers stilled.

The fog started to lift, unveiling a reddish moon. Suyeon wiped the film of blood from her eyes. She saw a woman climbing in through the window.

Who is that? Is she human? The woman approached Violette. Suyeon could tell she was of Ulan's kind. Yet she was different.

The woman knelt down beside Violette. Her hair was long and black. She had pale skin and dark red lips, and wore blue shoes with yellow socks…

What a strange woman, thought Suyeon, as if from a distance.

Suyeon kept her eyes on the pair right up until she passed out. The woman caressed Violette's hair, tangled with blood. Bending closer, she looked Violette in the eyes, and wrapped her fingers around the pendant at her throat as she said something. Nothing Suyeon could understand. Taking the woman's hands in hers, Violette pulled off her necklace. She handed it to the woman as she spoke.

But Suyeon couldn't make it out.

The woman who had introduced herself as a detective had a scar running along her right arm. A mark like that could be caused by dragging something sharp, a knife for instance, across the skin. The wound must've gone untreated for a while, judging by the way that the scar looked old, yet remained visible. There were other scuffs on her arms, but Suyeon's eyes were transfixed on the biggest scar. *Knife*. Lying on her hospital bed, Suyeon thought about the knife she had seen. The one that had been driven straight into a heart. The woman cleared her throat, wresting Suyeon out of her reverie. Suyeon looked at her and returned to the conversation.

'I can come back later if you're not feeling well. You should get some rest anyway,' said the detective.

Suyeon shook her head, assuring the woman that she was fine.

Much to her surprise, when Suyeon had opened her eyes again, she'd found herself on a bed in a private ward, and not smashed against the concrete in front of a crummy building. She was greeted by Chantae, who told her that she'd been asleep for two days. While she was unconscious, she'd been heaved onto an operating table, and slept through several nightmares so terrible that her sheets had to be changed four times. Chantae's lips twitched, as if they were itching to ask questions, but the woman detective had walked into the room before he could speak. She introduced herself as a detective working in the criminal investigation department in West Incheon, and said that from now on, she'd be taking over the case that Suyeon had been so faithfully pursuing. The 'Cheolma Rehabilitation Hospital Morphine Addiction and Suicide' case, in her words.

Suyeon stared down at her own arm, wrapped up and in a sling. Did she break an arm? She tapped on the cast, but underneath the thick layer of bandage, she felt nothing. The woman dragged a chair over and sat down beside Suyeon's bed. Taking out a voice recorder, she pressed the start button and placed the device on the drawer. It was protocol to get permission before recording a conversation, but knowing that Suyeon would agree, the detective skipped the formalities and went straight to her point.

'You have a duty to recount the entire incident without leaving out any details. Do you agree?' asked the detective. Suyeon nodded. 'First, I'll go over the information we've received, I'd appreciate it if you could confirm the details or correct any misinformation.'

‘OK,’ Suyeon croaked. She could use a sip of water, but thinking it might be awkward to ask, she only wetted her lips. The detective opened the file in her hand. She took out a piece of paper covered in writing, and began to read out every word clearly.

‘From 14 March to 25 April, six suicides took place in Cheolma Rehabilitation Hospital. It says here that it was on 11 April that you began to suspect that this might be part of a group suicide, after the fourth suicide occurred.’

When the detective gave Suyeon a look seeking confirmation, Suyeon nodded. The detective returned to the paper, scanning past some trivial sentences before reading out the next section.

‘You didn’t think that the victims committed suicide due to depression or because of the other suicides that were happening around them, but that they had been influenced in some other way. That was why you looked into the nurse working on the sixth-floor ward, Seo Nanju, and discovered that she had a history of administering morphine injections in exchange for money. With that, you had reason to believe that the patients were suffering from hallucinations, which could’ve led to their suicide, but…’ The detective trailed off as she rummaged through the file. She handed a photograph to Suyeon. ‘Your suspect was found dead.’

Suyeon glanced down at the picture of Seo Nanju’s dead body. The gruesome image didn’t stir any feeling in her. When Suyeon noticed that the detective was studying her face, she suddenly realised the detective's interrogative tone. This woman wasn't just seeking to sort out details. She was suspicious about why Suyeon had taken it upon herself to investigate the case, and was looking to uncover the truth behind Seo Nanju's death. In other words, she was writing Suyeon's name onto her list of suspects.

'You were found alone in Seo Nanju's apartment by the returning forensic team in the morning.'

Alone.

Suyeon chewed over the word.

'The doctor told me about the condition in which you arrived at the hospital. There are two things I'm curious about. One, *why* did you go back to Seo Nanju's house that night? It seems you failed to inform your colleagues of your visit. Of course, I'm sure you'd gone to carry out your own investigation. Was there any other reason?'

Suyeon nodded, signalling that she understood the detective's suspicion.

The detective continued, 'Two, your condition. Your right arm and ribs were fractured, and you'd lost a lot of blood. If help had arrived a bit later, you might not have lived to see another day.'

The detective paused. She regarded Suyeon earnestly. Though her eyes were stern, the look she gave read like a plea: *please, say it so I don't have to.* It occurred to Suyeon then that the detective knew something. She recalled the night she sought out Greta, looking for confirmation. Had she worn the same look?

The detective sucked in a breath. 'You'd lost a lot of blood but had no open wounds… and the floor where you had collapsed was spotless. It's quite hard for me to wrap my head around that.'

What sort of reaction was the detective expecting? Perhaps the right one would be to gasp and ask, 'What do you mean?' or to act surprised, but Suyeon remained quiet. Because no matter how ridiculous the truth may have sounded, it was still the truth.

'And,' the detective continued, 'besides yours, someone else's blood was found at the scene.' She handed Suyeon another photograph. Bloodstains on the floor. They belonged to someone else. Suyeon hadn't bled like that.

'Gunshots were reportedly heard. There was blood at the scene that wasn't yours, but all that was found at the scene was your gun. The only prints found at the scene were yours, and the only person found at the scene was you, Detective. Around that time, security footage shows a woman heading towards the apartment, but there's no footage of her leaving the apartment. It's like she simply vanished. What's more, that woman had paid Seo Nanju a visit several days before her murder. Since she didn't appear on camera on the day of Seo Nanju's murder, we only found out later, but as it turns out, the two of you have been seen together on multiple occasions. A staff member at the hospital even testified that she was working with you. As your partner.'

The detective's eyes were on fire. Still, Suyeon made no response. Instead, her thoughts circled around the fact that Violette had known Seo Nanju.

Seeing that Suyeon wasn't going to give her a proper reaction, the detective's stiff shoulders slackened as she let out a despondent chuckle. Sighing in resignation, or perhaps relief, she gathered her documents and stood up.

'I'll let you get some rest. I'll be back tomorrow, so maybe think about it…'

'I do think about it.'

The detective looked at Suyeon warily as she pushed the chair back to its original position.

'I think about everything. I can help with the investigation,' said Suyeon.

She had no problem with sharing the experience of working this case. After all, as a detective, it was her duty to do so. But Suyeon was worried about sharing 'everything'.

If she told the detective everything, would she believe her? Suyeon's best guess was no, she wouldn't.

'You don't have to believe everything I say. You can just listen.'

The detective nodded immediately, assuming she'd been given an easy task. And so, Suyeon went back to three weeks ago, 11 April, the day of the fourth suicide, when the first seed of doubt took root.

***

When the detective left at dawn, the rain tapped against the window as if it had been scheduled. Lying on her side, Suyeon stared at the window in a daze. She thought back on the conversation earlier.

The detective had looked perplexed. Suyeon didn't blame her; she herself was still wrestling with disbelief. At the very least, Suyeon was thankful that instead of scoffing and leaving her seat, the detective had met her with an open mind. She agreed that except for the extraordinary bits, Suyeon's testimony matched the sequence of events and provided a concrete explanation.

The hospital was dark and quiet. When Suyeon turned her head, she saw the silhouette of the officer guarding her door. *What if I told him everything?* she wondered. If he didn't believe her, too, then would she be more willing to accept that she'd imagined everything? Suyeon raised her right arm. The cast weighed it down. She winced at the memory of the pain that had surged through her hand. An unfamiliar ache throbbed in her shoulder. Suyeon sat up. She raised her right hand and ran her fingers along her neck. Slowly, peeking out from the cast, her fingertips traced the curve of her neck, coming to a stop just above her shoulder. There they were. Two holes.

Violette would have got a kick out of this. To see Suyeon, who had known so little, become one of the few lucky ones who'd survived a vampire.

Where is she anyway? Suyeon strained to recall the face of the woman who'd stroked Violette's hair and said hello. Surely Violette was still alive? She must be.

***

Suyeon was discharged after two weeks. She'd been interviewed a few more times, but since they were dealing with a case without a corpse, there was no murderer to pin down. When faced with repeating herself to a new young cop, she'd declined to speak to him, and nobody mentioned vampires to her.

The investigation dragged on, leaving behind only a trail of doubts. While she was bedridden, Suyeon often looked out the window to see if Violette would come to visit her. But the only person who came was Chantae. He dangled his car keys in front of Suyeon and helped carry her things out of the hospital.

On the drive home, Chantae encouraged her to get some sleep, but Suyeon couldn't. She rolled down the windows to feel the warmth of the new season. The sky was blotted with dark clouds, but the wind was welcoming. While Suyeon admired the little bits of green sprouting from the trees, Chantae informed her that Cheolma had closed its doors for good. After a pause, Suyeon asked.

'Where did all the patients go?'

'I suppose their families came to get them or they were moved to better hospitals,' replied Chantae.

'I see. That's good to hear.'

The breeze warmed her cheeks.

There goes another season, Suyeon thought. The clouds were growing pregnant with rain. For a while, they drove on in silence.

'That detective told me about the conversation she had with you. She said to keep it between ourselves since it has nothing to do with the case.'

The world went on quietly. The war Suyeon worried about hadn't yet begun. People carried on as usual, oblivious to the smell of blood.

'Shock can mess with our memories sometimes,' said Chantae as he pulled up to a red light.

Suyeon didn't blame him. She was relieved. Fact or fiction, nothing was going to change. Life would go on the same, with someone else leaving her side once again. *But that is why life always comes to an end, because our hearts can only withstand so many farewells. Enduring that pain for eternity would mean we're living in Hell.*

'You'll get through this, kid. You always have. We're just living in a world that is wider and darker than everyone else's. But what can we do? It comes with the job. So take it easy, alright?'

Staring out of the window, Suyeon spotted a familiar face in a crowd. There she was, breathing, laughing, living amongst everyone – perfectly fine. The heavy clouds relented at last. In the middle of umbrellas going up one by one, Greta stood there. Carefree. Rain-soaked. Spotting Suyeon, she waved.

As Chantae said, nothing would change. But in a world that was wider and darker, perhaps the scent of their loneliness was much stronger.

'They're right beside us,' Suyeon said, her voice detached. 'So be careful. The only way we can protect ourselves is by making sure no one is left alone.'

Because in every corner untouched by sight, and deprived of light, they were out there, breathing in the scent of lonely blood.

AUTHOR'S NOTE

How strange, yet lovely, that we're meeting through *The Midnight Shift*.

I still believe that there are creatures in this world that we may never meet.

I wonder if you think so too?

It's with this belief that I've written this novel – for the elusive creatures of this world, for the happiness of every being on Earth.

Seon-Ran

A NOTE ON THE AUTHOR

A lover of sci-fi always dreaming of the universe and waiting for aliens, **Cheon Seon-Ran** made her debut with *Broken Bridge* in 2019. She was awarded the Grand Prize in the 4th Korea Sci-Fi Literature Awards for her novel *A Thousand Blues*. She's continued writing novels since.

A NOTE ON THE TRANSLATOR

Gene Png is a literary translator and illustrator based in Seoul. She was awarded the Grand Prize in Poetry at the 53rd *The Korea Times* Modern Korean Literature Translation Awards.